Also by Adam Rubin

Tales from the Multiverse: Volume Two

THE HUMAN KABOOM

ADAM RUBIN

— *illustrated by* —

DANIEL SALMIERI   DANIEL GRAY-BARNETT

GRACEY ZHANG   MARTA ALTÉS

RODOLFO MONTALVO   ADAM DE SOUZA

putnam

G. P. Putnam's Sons

G. P. Putnam's Sons

An imprint of Penguin Random House LLC, New York

First published in the United States of America by G. P. Putnam's Sons,
an imprint of Penguin Random House LLC, 2023

Copyright © 2023 by Adam Rubin

G. P. Putnam's Sons is a registered trademark of Penguin Random House LLC.
The Penguin colophon is a registered trademark of Penguin Books Limited.

Visit us online at penguinrandomhouse.com.

Library of Congress Cataloging-in-Publication Data
Names: Rubin, Adam, 1983– author. | Gray-Barnett, Daniel, illustrator. |
Montalvo, Rodolfo, illustrator. | Zhang, Gracey, illustrator. | Souza, Adam de, illustrator. |
Altés, Marta, illustrator. | Salmieri, Daniel, 1983– illustrator.
Title: The human kaboom / Adam Rubin, Daniel Gray-Barnett, Rodolfo Montalvo,
Gracey Zhang, Adam de Souza, Marta Altés, Daniel Salmieri.
Description: New York: G. P. Putnam's Sons, 2023. | Series: Tales from the multiverse; volume 2 |
Summary: "A collection of six stories, each one featuring an explosion of some sort"
—Provided by publisher.
Identifiers: LCCN 2022006926 (print) | LCCN 2022006927 (ebook) |
ISBN 9780593462393 (hardcover) | ISBN 9780593462416 (epub)
Subjects: CYAC: Explosions—Fiction. | Humorous stories. | Short stories. |
LCGFT: Short stories. | Humorous fiction.
Classification: LCC PZ7.R83116 Hu 2023 (print) | LCC PZ7.R83116 (ebook) | DDC [E]—dc23
LC record available at https://lccn.loc.gov/2022006926
LC ebook record available at https://lccn.loc.gov/2022006927

Printed in the United States of America

ISBN 9780593462393

1st Printing

LSCH

Design by Cindy De la Cruz
Geometric background image courtesy of Shutterstock
Text set in Skolar Latin, Emblema, and Nobel

For my high school English teacher Mr. Reid.
Thank you for encouraging me to share my imagination on paper instead of just whispering it to Dina at the back of the class.
Thank you for staying in touch and becoming a supportive friend.
Thank you for understanding that I'll never feel comfortable calling you Tim.

Information plus time equals knowledge.
Knowledge plus time equals wisdom.

—Juan Herrera, Jerez, Spain

INSPIRATION IS EVERYWHERE

●-●————————————●-●

Hello, friendo. It's me, Adam Rubin. I wrote this book, as well as some others you might have read. (But if not, that's okay. Just play along for the rest of the introduction.)

Over the past few years, I've had the great pleasure of meeting a bunch of you in person. We got to high-five and pose for pictures and share some laughs at the bookstore. You asked excellent questions, which I was happy to answer: My favorite color is blue, I was born in 1983, and yes, I do have all twenty of my original fingers and toes.

The most popular questions—from first graders to middle school students to gray-haired librarians—were all related to the theme of inspiration. Where the heck do I get the ideas for all my stories?

The answer is in giant type at the top of the previous page: *Inspiration is everywhere.*

Maybe you think I'm exaggerating. "This place stinks," you say as you glance around. "There's no inspiration here."

Well, I say, "Poppycock!" Which is a very fun word to say: *poppycock.*

There are an infinite number of stupendous ideas floating right in front of your face, just waiting to be discovered. They might be invisible at the moment, but we can change that . . .

Look, here's a silly little doodle I made in five seconds.

Nothing to it, right? Just a few squiggly lines. Can this drawing really be the inspiration for your next great story? You bet your butt it can.

All you have to do is fuzz your eyes and open your mind. Some people call it daydreaming. (My math teacher used to tell me to quit it, but it's actually a highly valuable skill.)

When you give your brain permission to play, your imagination starts to run wild. The squiggly lines offer a million different possible interpretations: the hot sun on a summer day, a dancing octopus, a blaring horn, a stinky wheel of cheese, a glowing crystal ball, a squashed spider, a crown, a throwing star, a tunnel, a shimmering magic ring, a bubble popping, a volcano seen from above, a cannonball that crashed into a parking lot, a very hairy belly button, a radioactive grapefruit, an inter-dimensional portal . . . I could go on.

The point is, every single thing in the universe—no matter how small or random or boring it might seem at first—can transform into the spark of a thrilling idea.

Still don't believe me? Flip to any page in this book and plop your finger down without looking. Now read the words you're pointing to. What if that was a clue that led to the revelation of an ancient mystery? What if those were your great-grandfather's dying words? What if you met someone with that phrase tattooed on their face?

You can't help but think about those words a bit differently now, right? It works kind of backward, but if you decide to be *interested* in something, no matter what it is, that thing becomes more *interesting*. It might even become fascinating and, eventually, inspirational.

Instead of flipping through a book, you could go to a museum, walk through the woods, or visit any city in the world. That's why I keep saying *inspiration is everywhere.* You just have to learn how to recognize it.

The problem is that most folks think inspiration feels like a lightning bolt. They think inspiration goes *SHAZAM!* Your hair stands on end, your teeth chatter, and maybe even a little pee comes out. But the truth is, the feeling of inspiration is more like a single raindrop. It's often so subtle, you'll miss it if you're not paying careful attention.

However, if you *are* paying attention, you'll start to see ideas almost everywhere you look, and you'll have to write it all down so you don't forget!

Me? I like to carry a pocket-size notebook and pen wherever I go. I highly recommend you give it a try. Anytime you see something or hear something or think of something interesting, make a note to remember it for later.

But keep in mind, you're not trying to generate some big inspirational breakthrough; you're just collecting a bunch of mildly fascinating fragments of notions that tickle your brain. If anyone else were to read through your notebook, it might seem more like a collection of nonsensical scribbles than a collection of great ideas. But that's okay. That's the whole point, actually . . .

I know how hard it can be to start writing without a "big" idea that motivates you to get going, so allow me to lend you a lightning bolt.

SHAZAM! Here's the title for your next great story: "The Human Kaboom."

Yes, that also happens to be the title of all six stories in this book. But each of those stories is totally different (aside from the six secret wormholes that connect them).

And *your* story, even though it begins with the same three words, will end up being even *more* different from mine because your unique imagination will take the initial inspiration in unexpected directions I never could have dreamed of!

Of course, you need a lot more than one idea to tell a whole story. You've got to come up with a hero and a plot and dialogue and a whole slew of other colorful details.

Well, anytime you need another idea to build out your story, just flip through the collection in your notebook. And here's the most astonishing part: All of those random words and phrases you wrote down will suddenly take on new meaning. They become names of characters and descriptions of settings. They give you specifics to use for priceless treasures, hilarious shenanigans, and nefarious plans that will make your story feel special.

Through some mysterious subconscious alchemy, your wide-ranging idea collection becomes a powerful source of highly personal inspiration. I promise, if you spend a few weeks jotting down all your brain tickles, the next time you want to write a story, you won't feel intimidated at all. In fact, you'll be thrilled to get started.

"But I can't wait that long," you say as you pull at your hair. "I want to start writing already!"

Calm down. You can't rush. Creativity is the process of taking things in, digesting them, and changing them into something new. Kind of like a burp—if you try too hard to force it, you can make yourself puke by mistake.

Luckily, the process of exploration is one of the great joys in life. If you like, you can get started immediately. As I've already mentioned, *inspiration is everywhere*, which means it's wherever you are *right now*. Look around you! It's on the ceiling. It's under the couch. It's in the shapes of the clouds and in the songs of the birds. It's in the picture frames on the wall and in every single book on your shelf.

Hopefully, you'll find a few ideas you can use in this book too . . . It might be something I wrote in one of the stories or, even better, something I didn't—something hiding between the lines on the page that no one can see but you.

Because that's the big secret: If you go around expecting to discover something amazing, you will. A thousand tiny epiphanies will reveal themselves. Inspiration is not a brief flash of lightning; it's a constant glow of enthusiastic appreciation.

When you're surrounded by inspiration, it feels like you're levitating. It's the greatest feeling in the world. And now that you know what you're looking for, you'll start to find it *everywhere*.

CONTENTS

I.

THE HUMAN KABOOM

(the one with the gigantic space prank)

illustrated by

DANIEL SALMIERI

Trudy and Jam pressed their faces to the windows of the space elevator to get a better look at the gigantic naked man floating in near-Earth orbit.

"Look! You can see his—"

"Trudy Chartreuse!" Ms. Kilroy clapped her hands sharply. A long-suffering middle school teacher, she had zero patience for hijinks, especially on field trips. Double especially on field trips to space.

Ms. Kilroy's eighth-grade class had won a cereal box contest for an all-expenses-paid visit to Corpus Gigantus, the largest amusement park in the solar system. The "park" was, more specifically, a humongous working replica of the human body that had been launched into the exosphere for educational purposes. It was filled with thought-provoking scientific exhibitions, and the rides and attractions were highly informative. However, even the most diligent students were often distracted from the biology lessons by the chance to use a hover pack, which is what all the visitors used to fly around the park.

As the space elevator ascended, the city below shrank away until the whole state was visible through the windows in the floor. Meanwhile, a "full moon" filled the view through the windows in the ceiling. The students tittered as they strained against their seat belts to shield their eyes.

Ms. Kilroy glared at Trudy for riling up the other kids. Trudy shrugged her broad shoulders as if the accusation were preposterous. Her tight braids were pulled up into a mountain of pink string, purple beads, and black hair. It bobbed on top of her head as she turned to Jam, who, in Trudy's estimation, always knew the right thing to say.

Jaime Flacco was short and skinny. His first name was pronounced HIGH-may, which was excruciatingly close to *heinie*, and that was what the other kids had insisted on calling him for years until Trudy had rechristened him Jam in the middle of sixth grade.

"We're just trying to learn anatomy, Ms. K." Jam smiled and clasped his hands like a choirboy. His thick glasses slid down his nose and nearly fell from his face. He pushed them into place with the back of his wrist for the seventeenth time that day.

Trudy nodded and smiled so wide her molars showed.

Ms. Kilroy sucked her teeth and sent her dangly earrings swinging. She had a shaved head and a no-nonsense attitude. She had been a teacher in the city for most of her life. And at that point, she'd had almost every kind of student pass through her classroom: teacher's pets, smart alecks, goody-two-shoes, mean girls, nice girls, bullies, jokers, dweebs, nerds, jocks, punks, goof-offs, show-offs, prodigies, lamebrains, loudmouths, wallflowers, duds, dudes, dorks—the list goes on. But in her many years of teaching, Janet Kilroy had never met a pair of mischief-makers as clever, versatile, and downright entertaining as Jam and Trudy. She'd had to select a new descriptor for this troublesome twosome. She called them *weisenheimers*.

Jam and Trudy hit it off at lunch on the very first day of middle school. They made each other laugh. They liked the same games and bands. Jam let Trudy copy his homework, and Trudy threatened anyone who gave Jam a hard time. After two years of classes together, they'd become an inseparable team and had shown impressive dedication and creativity in honing their skills as agents of gentle chaos.

One time, they hid a live frog in their art teacher's iced tea. Another time, they reprogrammed the clocks to get extra recess. Trudy always carried a pocketful of googly eyes to stick onto posters and bring inanimate objects to life. Jam always carried a marker to add funny doodles to signs and advertisements. He was often too shy to speak up in public, but Trudy would say or do anything to get a laugh. Some of the jokes she thought of herself; others were whispered to her by Jam.

Ms. Kilroy had desperately wanted to exclude the disruptive duo from the field trip. She had always dreamed of visiting Corpus Gigantus someday, and the last thing she wanted was for a couple of weisenheimers to ruin her trip. But the principal had insisted Jam and Trudy go along. Mostly because he didn't want to have to look after them for the day, but also because Trudy was the one who had sent in the winning contest entry form, and Jam the one who had answered all the trivia questions correctly.

The space elevator picked up speed as it ascended past the atmosphere.

"Gluteus maximus!" declared Trudy. "Isn't that right, Jam?"

"Yes," said Jam. "That is the anatomically correct term used by doctors and nurses, so it couldn't *technically* be considered offensive by *anyone*."

Ms. Kilroy begrudgingly agreed, but the other eighteen students failed miserably to suppress their giggles as the humongous heinie grew closer and closer.

None of them had any idea of the terrible danger that lurked in the shadowy crevices of Corpus Gigantus.

A FIELD TRIP to the biggest body in the solar system was an opportunity to pull the biggest prank in the solar system.

At least, that's how Trudy saw things. Jam had needed some convincing.

"We'll be heroes!" mused Trudy, draped backward over the edge of Jam's bed. They hung out at his house most days after school, playing video games and backgammon or watching funny videos. "Everyone will say, 'Oh, that's Trudy and Jam. They pulled the biggest prank of all time!'"

Jam did not look up from his homework. He would never admit it to Trudy, but he was bursting with excitement to explore the giant body in person. Biology was one of his favorite subjects. He had watched countless videos about Corpus Gigantus, explored the attractions in VR, and even written an essay about it for extra credit when he was in fifth grade. He could explain the intricacies of the endocrine system and discuss the difference between the nervous system and the vascular system. He even knew all the words to "Big Body Boogie," the official park theme song.

Jam never mentioned any of this to Trudy, of course. He didn't want her to think he was a nerd.

"I'm excited for the hover packs," Jam said. His glasses accidentally slipped from his face onto his notebook.

"I've always wanted to wear a hover pack." Trudy waved her hand through the air like it was flying back and forth. "Maybe we could do a prank with the hover packs." She sat up and looked at Jam with her eyebrows raised.

Jam retrieved his glasses. "Hmm . . ." He knew he would have to come up with something good to impress Trudy, and it would be hard to top their recent hijinks at the museum.

The whole grade had slept over, their sleeping bags sprawled across the floor between the exhibits. Trudy and Jam had pretended to be asleep, and then in the middle of the night, they'd crept around like ninjas, markers in hand, writing on the faces of their classmates—*chump* on a forehead, *boobs* on a cheek, *turd* on a nose.

Sneaking around in the dark and making mischief was a recipe for giggle fits, and since they knew that even the smallest peep could wake their dozing victims, they had to hold in their hysterics as best they could. Which was risky, because it had to come out somewhere, and silent convulsions of glee are a very easy way to accidentally wet your pants.

By the time they were finished, tears of laughter soaked Jam's and Trudy's faces. Which was better than the alternative.

They were even smart enough to graffiti themselves with dirty words before slipping back into their sleeping bags, so that in the morning, all suspicion was directed at the kids with no writing on their faces. No one seemed to notice how easily the ink washed from Trudy's and Jam's skin. For everyone else, they had used permanent markers.

It took hours of brainstorming and research, but

eventually, Jam and Trudy came up with a prank idea worthy of Corpus Gigantus.

"We could get in so much trouble for this!" Trudy shimmied with glee as she examined the plan she'd sketched out in crayon. "Do you really think it will work?"

"I honestly don't know," said Jam, a touch of fear in his voice.

"If it does, we'll be legends." Trudy smiled and put her arm around his shoulder.

Suddenly, Jam wasn't so worried about getting in trouble.

THE HARDEST PART had been resisting the overwhelming urge to do anything funny during the weeks before the field trip. Ms. Kilroy had warned them. Even a minor offense would get them left behind.

They had been on their best behavior.

Trudy got so bored she started raising her hand and answering questions correctly just to pass the time. Jam didn't make a single snide remark under his breath.

Ms. Kilroy had a sneaking suspicion that Trudy and Jam were up to no good. And as per usual, Ms. Kilroy was right. Regardless, she reveled in the relative peace of her classroom.

There was no note-passing when she turned around to write on the board, no armpit farts when she bent over to retrieve a dropped pencil, not even a single peep from the weisenheimers at the back of the class when she labeled a diagram of the human reproductive system. (That level of restraint had taken extraordinary effort from Trudy.)

But when the space elevator finally arrived at the docking station on Corpus Gigantus, it was too late for threats. Even the normally quiet kids in class essentially lost their minds with excitement. They threw off their seat belts and rushed to the doors of the elevator before they were open. The outburst of gleeful anticipation was deafening.

"Quiet down, children. This is supposed to be educational!" said Ms. Kilroy sternly. Though even she couldn't help smiling when the elevator doors cracked open to reveal a circular preparation room outfitted with twenty-one sets of translucent safety suits, matching helmets, and, most importantly, hover packs.

The kids all ran, screaming, to claim a locker and get dressed.

"Slow down!" warned Ms. Kilroy. "Be careful!"

Jam was too distracted by the panoramic view to rush. The elevator docking station was pierced through the enormous flapping earlobe of Corpus Gigantus. The official entrance to the park was above them, through the ear canal, which led directly into the head. Off to the side, Jam could see rocket-powered auto-bots trimming the hair on the gigantic scalp, like goats munching grass on a mountainside. Earth was visible below, and Jam could see swirling cloud formations floating around the planet.

"Wow," marveled Trudy.

"Yeah," said Jam.

"I expect you all to be on your best behavior today," Ms. Kilroy announced as the class was busy getting dressed.

"Yes, Ms. Kilroy," droned the students in unison.

"I'm looking at you, Mr. Flacco and Ms. Chartreuse."

"Yes, Ms. Kilroy," droned Trudy and Jam.

"Why have you brought so much water, Jaime?" asked Ms. Kilroy.

Jam had multiple bottles clipped to his belt and shoved in the pockets of his cargo shorts.

"In case I get thirsty," he answered without skipping a beat.

"You're going to drink two gallons of water in a single day?"

Jam looked at Trudy. "I brought enough to share."

"Can I have some?" asked a perfectly nice kid named Lester Best.

"Uh," Jam hesitated. "Sure." He handed a bottle to Lester, and Ms. Kilroy went off to put on her equipment.

Lester unscrewed his helmet, lifted it from the neck of his safety suit, and took a big swig from the water bottle. But before he could swallow, Lester's eyes went crossed and he spit out the whole mouthful, spraying liquid all over the inside of his helmet.

"Gah!" Lester gagged. "This water tastes like soap!"

"Shhh!" threatened Trudy, shaking her fist.

As soon as the elevator doors closed behind them, everyone in the preparation room began to float. Gravity was very mild in the park, and moving around took some getting used to. Jam and Trudy bonked into each other as they tumbled toward the ceiling.

"Stop messing around, you two!" shouted Ms. Kilroy, upside down, kicking her feet through the air in a feeble attempt to right herself.

Jam quickly figured out how to use the boots of his safety suit to cling to any surface. The soles of the shoes were sticky, which made walking in low gravity much easier. Some of the other students floated chaotically, gently bouncing off the ceiling and spinning in dizzying circles.

Suddenly, an orange light filled the room, and everyone's hover pack switched on. The light turned yellow, and autopilot activated on the packs, repositioning each student comfortably onto a seat in front of a locker. The light turned green, and a door opened to reveal a glowing white bacterium. It looked like a giant sausage covered in hair, with a thin, ropelike tail. The creature wiggled through the air into the preparation room and started speaking.

"Good morning, Ms. Kilroy's class! Congratulations on winning the Super Sugar O's Sweepstakes, and welcome to

Corpus Gigantus, the biggest amusement park in the solar system, rated five stars on Tripadvisor, and internationally renowned for 'fun in the flesh'!" The bacterium sparkled with light to accentuate her excitement. "I am Microbe 421C, but you can call me Cece. I will be your guide through this astronomical anatomical amusement, which is sure to astound and amaze."

Trudy rolled her eyes, but Jam was mesmerized by the enormous talking bacterium.

"We will be exploring the human body via hover pack today. As you are all under eighteen, your propulsion systems are set to auto."

The students groaned.

"Merely a safety precaution!" said Cece brightly. "Ms. Kilroy, I will adjust yours to manual in a minute so you can control your own movement when necessary."

Ms. Kilroy smiled nervously.

"Everything you see today is a perfect replica of the inner workings of your own bodies, blown up to ten thousand times the normal size! In fact, there are billions of bacteria, just like me, squiggling through your guts at this very moment!"

"Ew, gross!" groaned Trudy. The kids all squirmed with disgust.

Cece leaned over to Ms. Kilroy and whispered, "Gets 'em every time." She turned back to the group. "Yes, it IS gross. From the Latin *grossus*, meaning 'LARGE'!" Cece laughed and slapped Ms. Kilroy's back with her flagellum. "Wordplay!"

Jam couldn't help but chuckle. Trudy harrumphed and crossed her arms.

"Off we go!" Cece swam out the door, and the hover packs glowed blue, propelling the students into two neat rows behind her.

Ms. Kilroy had some trouble controlling her hover pack at first. She accidentally flew into a different group of students that was passing overhead with a different microbe tour guide.

On the weekend, many of the visitors to the park were families or tourists on vacation. (There was a luxury hotel in the left foot of Corpus Gigantus.) But on a Tuesday morning, almost everyone there was on a field trip with their school.

As Ms. Kilroy struggled to wrangle her hover pack controls and rejoin her class, she wound up accidentally cartwheeling, head over heels, in the opposite direction. Cece darted over and wrapped her flagellum around the teacher's ankle to help her along.

Trudy huffed and fidgeted as her own hover pack carried her along in a much too orderly fashion.

"What a waste," she said to Jam, who was busy examining the regulator panel of the hover pack on the student in front of him. "Killjoy gets manual control, and she doesn't even know how to use it." Trudy stretched her arm back and awkwardly groped the side of her pack, searching for a switch to release her from autopilot.

"Be patient," cautioned Jam. "Wait till we get to the heart."

"We are now entering the ear canal," Cece whispered through speakers installed in the helmets of the students floating behind her. "Be very quiet. These organs are quite sensitive!"

The ear canal was like the entrance to a cave that led to a vast underground cavern. The lights from the preparation area no longer illuminated the passageway ahead of them, so Cece began to glow brighter to guide the way.

"We are now passing the malleus, incus, and stapes," said Cece. "Also known as the hammer, anvil, and stirrup. These tiny bones allow the body to hear."

Trudy made a fart noise with her mouth. The rest of the students burst out laughing.

"Trudy!" barked Ms. Kilroy.

"Shhh," said Cece gently. The class quieted down. "Do you hear that?"

A low thumping grew louder and louder. Jam could actually feel the sound, like when a car with tricked-out speakers passes by, blasting a song with amped-up bass.

BUM BUM, BUM BUM.

"That is the pulse!" whispered Cece with excitement. "We are about to enter the jugular vein, which will bring us to the center of the circulatory system, the literal heart of this whole operation!"

The guide's enthusiasm was beginning to annoy Trudy. She looked over at Jam to see him pulling out a screwdriver he'd slipped into one of his gloves.

"As we enter the bloodstream, you will be surrounded by red blood cells, busy little beavers that transport oxygen throughout the body. Don't be afraid—they are harmless, and they will help us on our way. So just relax and go with the flow. Ready? Ms. Kilroy, why don't you go first?"

"Oh." Ms. Kilroy hesitated. "I really think I should wait to make sure all the children—"

Cece gave Ms. Kilroy a gentle shove.

"YAHHHHHHH!" the teacher screamed as she plunged

into the current of the bloodstream, which whisked her away like white-water rapids.

"Who's next?"

One by one, the kids jumped into the bloodstream and whooshed away on a river of humming little red doughnuts.

"Wheeeee!"

"Geronimo!"

"Banzai!"

Trudy and Jam were at the back of the line. While Cece was busy helping the other kids, Jam leaned over and used the screwdriver to flip the governor switch that was obscured by a "tamperproof" cover on the back of Trudy's pack. The hover pack control stick lit up, and so did Trudy's eyes.

"Now do me." Jam turned his pack to Trudy. "It's the white toggle under the blue light."

Trudy flipped the switch and withdrew her hand only an instant before Cece turned around.

"Last one in is a rotten egg cell!" the microbe joked.

Jam tried to appear innocent, but even the single-celled tour guide could tell there was something strange about his smile.

"Do you have to use the bathroom, young man?" she asked. "I can see you are VERY well hydrated."

"No," replied Jam, his collection of water bottles sloshing suspiciously. "I'm fine. Let's go, Trudy." He grabbed her hand, and they both jumped into the bloodstream.

SPLOOSH!

The little red doughnuts were warm, 98.6 degrees Fahrenheit to be precise. It felt like tumbling through a ball pit mixed with a warm bath.

Cece's voice came on through the speakers in their helmets. "Relax and let the current take you," she sang. "All veins lead to the heart, and that's our next stop on the tour!"

The students whooshed through the bloodstream, giggling.

"Who needs hover packs when you have AEROBIC RESPIRATION, amiright?" Cece said, then chuckled at her own joke. "When we come to the intersection of the jugular vein and the subclavian vein, I will direct you into the superior vena cava. Be sure to bear left, Ms. Kilroy."

"That's when we go right," Jam whispered to Trudy.

Trudy winked.

As they traveled, the pounding pulse got louder and louder. The blood cells rushed along in spurts to match the deep, rumbling whoosh.

BUM BUM, BUM BUM.

One by one, the group was circulated into a large crimson chamber. A neon sign overhead showed glowing white letters: LEFT.

"Welcome to the left ventricle!" Cece corralled the group and reactivated the automated guidance on their hover packs. "We are now in the heart."

The walls of the chamber contracted and expanded in a hypnotic rhythm. A swirling current of little red doughnuts danced about in a sweeping spiral, then rushed out of a flap in the ceiling that opened and shut in time with the beating of the pulse. The kids oohed and aahed.

Ms. Kilroy was awestruck. She floated over to the side of the ventricle and placed a hand on the pulsating wall. She placed her other hand on her own heart, which was racing. She was so distracted by the majesty of the human body that she didn't notice when her two most mischievous students snuck off.

JAM AND TRUDY blasted through the body at max velocity, racing away from the rest of their class, who were busy marveling at the hypnotic process of oxygenation in the heart—when the blood changes color from maroon to cherry red.

"This is waaaay better!" shouted Trudy as she barrel-rolled through the bloodstream behind Jam. They were much more skilled at controlling their hover packs than Ms. Kilroy. They'd had plenty of practice from playing *Turbo Quest VR*.

Jam stopped short, and Trudy looped around to join him.

"I think we might have missed the turn." He looked back where they had come from. "We'll have to fight against the current. It's way stronger in the arteries."

"Whatever you say, Dr. Science." Trudy accelerated her hover pack full blast, dodging squishy red doughnuts as she swam upstream.

They made their way from the chest, up the neck, down the jaw, and into the mouth, where they found a storage area under the tongue. A blast of hot, stale breath gusted from the trachea and overpowered the air filtration on their safety suits.

"Ugh, it stinks like a spoiled sardine sandwich in here!" Trudy tried to hold her nose, but her hand bonked off the glass of her helmet.

"Yeah, this place needs a good cleaning," said Jam. "That's what they use this stuff for."

Industrial-size boxes of baking soda, huge tubes of fluoride, and coil upon coil of hoses were stacked behind teeth as tall as twenty-story buildings. Trudy examined the labels on a rack of pressurized canisters that looked like giant scuba tanks.

"H_2O_2—this is it!"

"Nice!" said Jam. He patted his various water bottles and canteens. "Now we've got everything we need."

Jam hugged the tank with his skinny arms and tried to pick it up, but it was too heavy for him to manage on his own. Trudy gave him a hand.

"We are gonna be famous for this." She smacked the side of the canister and grabbed ahold of one end. "Let's go."

The two kids reentered the bloodstream, carrying the big tank of hydrogen peroxide between them.

"Hey," Trudy said. "What do you call it when you fart and sneeze at the same time?"

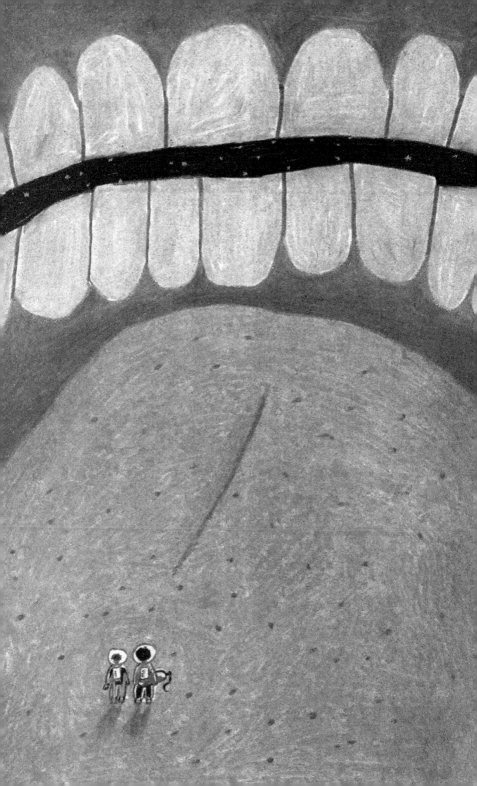

"A snart," said Jam without hesitation. He reconsidered. "Or maybe an ah-choot. Like 'toot.'"

Trudy laughed. "What do you call it when you laugh and burp at the same time?"

Jam thought for a moment. "A giggle belch?"

"A chuckle hork." Trudy giggled and belched loudly.

Jam laughed so hard he dropped the canister. They both fell into gut-busting giggles. Trudy hooted so hard that snot shot out her nose. This only made them both laugh harder, of course. Not to mention the fact that she couldn't wipe her face without taking off her helmet, so she had to try and shake the mucus off. Pretty soon they were both laughing so hard their stomach muscles hurt.

Eventually, they calmed down enough to pick up the canister and keep moving.

"Where are we now anyway?" Trudy asked.

"The brachial artery." Jam pointed. "This will take us down the upper arm to the radial artery in the lower arm, and there we should be able to reach the epidermis of the palm through a sweat gland."

Trudy made a sarcastic, overly impressed face.

"I mean, I don't know . . ." Jam shrugged. "I think we go this way."

"Why do you do that?" Trudy scowled.

"Do what?"

"Pretend not to be smart. Do you think I'm dumb enough to buy it? I'm not as stupid as I look, you know."

"You don't look stupid," blurted Jam.

"No?" Trudy raised an eyebrow.

"No, you look . . ." Jam blushed. "You're actually super smart! If you just paid a little more attention . . ."

"What are you—Mr. Life Advice now?" asked Trudy. "You sound like my dad."

"Never mind. Forget it."

Their smiles faded, and they flew through the artery in awkward silence.

"Hey," offered Jam. "What do you call it when you scream and pee at the same time?"

Trudy ignored him and blasted ahead at full speed.

KAVOOSH!

WHILE MS. KILROY and the other kids were spellbound by the breathtaking magic of the alveoli in the lungs, Trudy and Jam were struggling to squeeze a stolen canister of hydrogen peroxide up through a sweat gland below the right palm of Corpus Gigantus.

"You're stepping on my foot!" complained Trudy.

"Sorry!" said Jam.

"I can do it myself." Trudy knelt to get her shoulder underneath, then stood to shove the canister halfway through the gland above her head.

"Hang on," warned Jam. "We need the secret ingredient."

Trudy understood. "Right." She left the canister stuck in place and began to unzip her safety suit. "Turn around."

Jam obeyed.

Trudy checked to make sure Jam wasn't looking, and then she pulled down her sweatpants. Six bags of active yeast were strapped to her legs. She removed the smuggled ingredients from their hiding place and set them by her feet. Then she pulled up her pants, rezipped her safety suit, and breathed a sigh of relief.

"Okay," she said to Jam, who turned back around.

They wriggled through the sweat gland and out onto the surface of the skin with their supplies. When they looked around, they could see glowing stars in every direction. Some white, some yellow, some red. Big, small, twinkling, dim—more stars than they'd ever seen in their lives.

"Wow," marveled Trudy.

"Whoa," murmured Jam.

They were so distracted by the majesty of space, they didn't notice that the bags of yeast and the canister of hydrogen peroxide were floating away from the surface of the hand. The sticky pads on the bottom of their boots kept them safely grounded to the surface of Corpus Gigantus, but unfortunately, their supplies weren't wearing boots, and by the time they noticed the objects drifting off into outer space, it was almost too late.

"Oh no!" Trudy snatched all six bags of yeast before they were out of reach, and managed to wrap her legs around the canister of hydrogen peroxide. But that didn't leave her with any limbs left to control her hover pack. So she started to float away from the giant hand as well.

"Trudy!" Jam activated his hover pack and grabbed

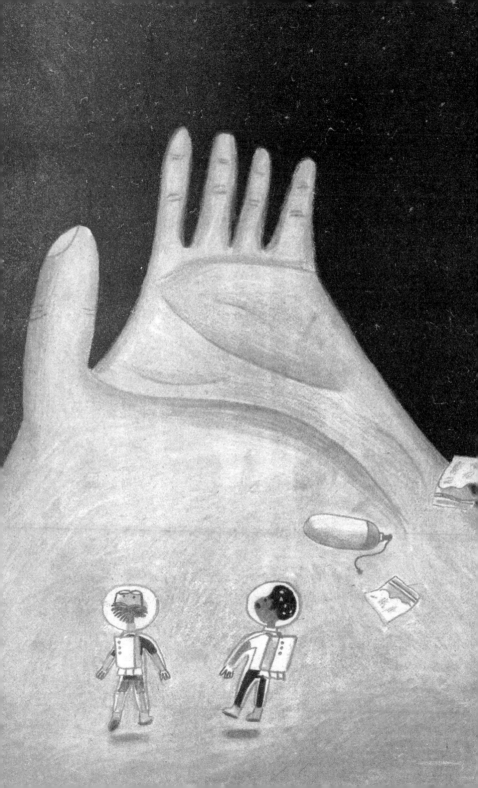

Trudy's suit. He towed her back to the palm, where they landed with a soft thud.

"That was close!" gasped Jam.

Once Trudy realized they were safe, she pushed him away. "Get off me!" she said. Then she grinned. "We've got work to do."

The enormous fingers of the giant hand loomed overhead like towering stone pillars. The lines in the palm were as deep as trenches, so Trudy and Jam used one as a path to reach the center.

Jam removed the bottles from his belt and pockets. They were all full of water mixed with liquid soap. He handed one to Trudy.

"This is gonna be awesome." She bit her lip and began to unscrew the cap.

"Wait!" Jam stopped her. "Once this stuff mixes, it's gonna explode. We've gotta be ready to run."

"Okay, okay. What's the plan, Jam?"

He puffed up his chest a bit and went to adjust his glasses, but his hand bonked against his helmet. Trudy snorted. Jam threw his head back to encourage his spectacles to slide back into place. It worked.

"I'll lay down a puddle of soapy water," he said. "The surface tension will keep it from floating away. You sprinkle the yeast over that."

"Got it."

"The hydrogen peroxide will start the reaction, so that comes last."

They mixed the ingredients in the middle of the palm and then backed away with the canister. Each one found a sweat gland and wriggled inside. With only their heads poking out, they looked like curious gophers in the middle of a grassy field.

"Ready?" Trudy opened the nozzle on the canister and rolled it toward the puddle of chemicals.

"Duck!" shouted Jam. And they did.

FWOOOOOOOOOOOOOOOOOOOF!

CROUCHING BELOW THE surface of the skin, they heard a monstrous foamy explosion followed by a gargantuan gurgle and a furious fizz. They waited for the noise to subside and then poked their heads above the surface to see what had happened.

The entire palm was covered in a lake of elephant toothpaste. Jam looked over at Trudy. A dollop of white foam sat atop her helmet. She looked like an ice cream sundae.

"We did it!" She pumped her fists in the air and danced in a circle. "You're a genius."

Jam beamed. "Phase one: load foam—complete."

Trudy balled up a handful of foam and hurled it at her friend.

WHAP!

The white fluff splattered across Jam's helmet, and the smile faded from his face. "Of course you realize"—he clenched his teeth—"this means war!"

Trudy and Jam decided to have a little fun. Well, a lot of fun, really. The most fun either of them had ever had in their entire lives. An epic hover-pack-fueled foam fight on the palm of a giant hand floating in space. They hurled wads of elephant toothpaste, like snowballs, across the massive palm, and hid between the giant fingers to ambush one another.

WHAP! WHAP! KAVOOSH!

The two pals were having such a knee-slapping good time that they almost forgot they were blatantly violating at least twenty-seven park regulations.

An alarm blared in their helmets, and flashing red lights illuminated the tips of the giant fingers.

"Jangus!" squealed Jam. "They caught us!"

Trudy squeezed her eyes shut and wished she could plug her ears with her fingers. She frantically searched for an escape route.

"Come on!" Trudy grabbed Jam by the hand, and they ducked below the foam to hide.

"This is a security alert!" said a voice with a Russian accent. "All guests, please proceed to the left cheek." Jam and Trudy looked at each other. "This is not a drill."

"What the heck?" Trudy stood and looked around as Jam stayed crouched, still hiding. "There's nobody here."

Jam climbed to his feet and wiped the foam from his helmet. The red lights were still flashing, but they were alone.

"What's going on?" he wondered.

"WHAT'S GOING ON?" demanded Ms. Kilroy. Cece had switched the teacher's hover pack to autopilot, and the whole class was zooming through the body at top speed.

"I'm not sure." Cece sounded worried. "I've never seen anything like this. It is not standard security protocol."

Ms. Kilroy frowned.

"But I'm sure everything will be fine," Cece said, trying to convince herself. "It's probably just a drill."

"They just said it wasn't a drill!" shouted Ms. Kilroy.

"Ms. Kilroy, I'm hungry," complained a tall kid with braces.

"You should have thought of that before the emergency procedure," she scolded.

The class arrived at the head, along with hundreds of other visitors, and they were all led out of the ear and onto the cheek to await further instructions.

The Russian-accented voice came over the speakers once again. "Please direct your attention to the emergency exits."

The crowd turned to face the space elevators and watched with horror as their only escape route exploded in flames and fell away, stranding them all aboard Corpus Gigantus.

The voice on the other side of the microphone began to laugh with malevolent glee.

"DIMITRI!" A GOOGLY-EYED Russian fellow burst into the control room, panting.

The tall, slender man holding the microphone stopped laughing. "Vat is it?"

The other fellow sputtered for a bit, trying to catch his breath. "Ve . . . should have . . . brought hover packs . . . I am sveating through my oonderpants."

Dimitri pressed his palm to his face. He had imagined his moment of glory a bit differently—surrounded by an elite crew of professional hijackers, maybe wearing matching windbreakers. But he'd had to take what he could get in order to accomplish his lifelong goal, and few were sympathetic to his cause outside the small Russian village where he lived.

So there he was, working with a sweaty schlemiel and

a bunch of his elderly neighbors, who had never hijacked anything before in their lives, let alone the most famous amusement park in the solar system.

"Your underpants are soggy. Is that vat you came rushing in here to tell me?"

"No!" The googly-eyed fellow snapped to attention and saluted Dimitri. "Ve have gathered all the wisitors on the face, and the bombs are being put in place . . . Hey, that rhymes!"

Dimitri tried to ignore the last comment and let a tiny smile curl his lips. "Very good." He had been planning this mission for years, ever since Corpus Gigantus was first constructed.

The giant human body was locked in synchronous orbit with Earth, which meant it hovered over the same location at all times. The company that had constructed Corpus Gigantus had done extensive research to determine the optimal positioning for the enormous human-shaped bio-structure, calculating a location that would have the most minimal impact on the fewest number of people. That location was directly above a remote village in Russia called Ishkabibble. Dimitri just happened to live in Ishkabibble, and ever since he was a young boy, whenever he glanced up at the sky, he was greeted by a tremendous tush.

Most of the residents of Ishkabibble were too busy milking yaks or harvesting grain to care about the butt cheeks that were visible above them on a clear day, but Dimitri had taken it personally. To him, it was an outrage.

But after years of effort—handing out flyers to recruit volunteers, stitching together old cosmonaut suits, running crypto scams to buy a decommissioned space shuttle, security systems research, tactical planning, even baking cookies and making punch for the weekly meetings—all his preparation had paid off. He was standing aboard the notorious Corpus Gigantus and was about to blow the whole thing to smithereens.

Well, not the whole thing. Not the head.

Dimitri thought that was a nice dramatic touch. Leave the head for them to remember him by. Plus, he didn't have any interest in hurting the hundreds of schoolchildren who were currently on board. That would make him a villain, and Dimitri did not want to be a villain. He wanted to be a revolutionary.

He stroked the small remote detonator he held in his hands. "Soon, ve vill take back the skies."

TRUDY AND JAM were hovering through the bloodstream in the arm when they spotted a strange figure ahead of them.

"Quick, hide!" said Jam. They ducked into a smaller vein and out of sight.

Peeking around the corner, they saw a burly bearded

man in an old-fashioned space suit dragging a cart full of spiky black bowling balls. He stopped to take a look around before unloading them.

"Crap!" Trudy pulled Jam back around the corner. Their hearts were pounding. Trudy tried to put a finger to her lips, but her hand bonked off her helmet.

She poked her head out once again and saw the man jamming one of the spiky bowling balls into the wall of the vein. He pressed a button, and a red light on the ball started blinking.

"They're bombs!" whispered Trudy with hardly a sound.

"Bombs?!" replied Jam a little too loudly. He tried to cover his mouth with his hand, and his fingers bonked off his helmet.

Trudy pulled her head into her shoulders and froze. Jam was so worked up his glasses were fogging under his helmet. Trudy eventually gathered the courage to take another look.

"Don't. Move," she mouthed, making no sound at all.

Silently, she crept to the edge of the wall.

The next noise she made was extremely loud. So loud, in fact, that it almost made the bearded man who grabbed her release his hands from her arms to cover his ears.

"AIEEEEEEEEEE!" shrieked Trudy with a volume that surprised even herself. She tried to break free, but the bearded man was much bigger and soon had Trudy's arms pinned behind her.

"*Calm down*," he said. But he said it in Russian, which Trudy did not understand. She kept screaming and kicking as hard as she could. The Russian man struggled to control her. *"If you don't shut up, I will shut you up myself."*

Though Trudy did not know exactly what he was saying, she got the gist when he reached into his belt and pulled out a laser blade.

Trudy shut up.

"Hey!" Jam puffed out his chest and tried to look as intimidating as possible. The effect was about as threatening as a growling puppy. "Put. Her. Down." He pointed at the ground dramatically.

The Russian laughed. *"Fine,"* he grunted in his native tongue. *"Stay here and get blown up with the rest of the body."*

He tossed Trudy on top of Jam, and they landed in a heap. Jam's glasses fell from his face and rattled around inside his helmet. He couldn't see. But Trudy could, and when she looked down the tunnel in search of an escape route, she saw a dozen blinking bombs embedded in the walls of the vein.

The Russian removed their hover packs and examined them with admiration. *"These will come in handy for me."*

"Give those back!" demanded Trudy, but she doubted the man could understand her. Even if he could, she was sure he wouldn't listen.

"Babushka, vodka, Sputnik, stroganoff!" Jam shouted every Russian word he could think of. Strung together, they made no sense at all. The rough translation was something like, "Grandma, alcohol, satellite, creamed beef!" This did nothing to help convince the angry Russian to give them back their hover packs.

However, it was such silly and unexpected nonsense that it did make the burly bearded man laugh. Hard. So hard that he didn't notice the pack of snarling white puffballs approaching him from behind.

By the time he stopped laughing, the pack had him surrounded. The puffballs growled and bared their teeth like ferocious wolves. Before the Russian could figure out what was happening, it was too late.

"THIS IS COMPLETELY unacceptable," grumbled Ms. Kilroy. "How are we supposed to get back to Earth now that the elevators have exploded? This seems like a very inefficient security measure."

"It's not a security measure!" Cece waved her flagellum frantically. "Corpus Gigantus has been hijacked!"

Ms. Kilroy stopped to recalculate. "That would explain the maniacal laughter . . ."

"We've got to do something!" Cece darted back and forth, trying to get a better look around.

Hundreds of visitors, dozens of park staffers, and a handful of their captors were corralled by the hijackers into a tight cluster on the left cheek of Corpus Gigantus. Teachers were shouting, kids were crying, and tour guides were pleading for calm.

The hijackers wielded laser blades and stun shields. They wore bulky patched-up cosmonaut suits from the 1990s.

"Quiet down!" complained an old Russian woman who had been a florist back in Ishkabibble. As a girl, she used to savor every sunny day, but after twenty years of fuzzy buttocks glaring down at her whenever she tended her garden, she had been disgruntled enough to join up with Dimitri and his cockamamie plan.

The other hijackers were also Ishkabibble residents. One was the mail carrier; another was the butcher. Two of them sold used automobiles, and one was an amateur astronomer. Aside from the stun shields and laser blades, none of them looked particularly intimidating. They seemed kind of tired, and they kept arguing with each other in Russian.

"What do you suppose they want?" asked Ms. Kilroy.

"Whatever it is, they're not gonna get it." Cece looked around anxiously. "It's only a matter of time until the white blood cells show up."

"The white blood cells?"

"Corpus security. They're like trained attack dogs that ravage any threat to the health of the body." Cece shivered. "I'm scared of them myself. I can only imagine what they'll do to these invasive organisms."

TRUDY HAD WATCHED in horror as the snarling white puffballs ripped the bearded Russian limb from limb. By the time Jam got his glasses back on, the man was in pieces and the vicious attack became a feeding frenzy.

While the hungry puffballs were busy devouring the last remains of the hijacker—bones, clothes, and all—Jam and Trudy retrieved their hover packs and snuck them back on as fast as they could.

KAVOOSH!

They blasted away in hopes of escape, but a thick cluster of puffballs appeared out of nowhere to block their path.

"Quick! This way!" said Jam.

They turned around but stopped short when they

realized they were trapped from both sides. They hovered back to back, trying desperately to calm the growling beasts that were slowly closing in on them.

"Good puffballs . . ." cooed Trudy. "Nice puffballs . . ." She sounded like she was trying to tame a rabid dog. This gave Jam an idea.

He leaned over and yanked one of the blinking black bombs from the wall. Waving it over his head, he called to the pack of puffballs, who suddenly stopped snarling and snapped to attention.

"Who wants the ball? Do you want the ball? Do you want the ball?" He heaved the bomb as far as he could over the pack of puffs. Then he grabbed Trudy's hand, and they hovered full speed in the opposite direction.

Before they could get very far, a thick cluster of puffballs blocked their path once again. They started barking aggressively, and Jam was sure he would be devoured in a matter of seconds—until one of them dropped the blinking ball at his feet and they all went silent, waiting expectantly.

"They want to play fetch," Trudy gasped.

Jam stopped trembling. "They want to play fetch!" He picked up the bomb. "Okay, you want to play fetch?" The puffballs started vibrating with excitement. "Go fetch all of these!" Jam pointed to the other bombs lining the walls of the vein.

The white blood cells dashed off to retrieve the bombs.

"Wait!" shouted Jam. The puffballs paused. "Don't . . . don't bring them back here."

"Yeah," added Trudy. "Don't bring them back here!" She paused too. "Where do they bring them?"

Jam gritted his teeth.

"What's the plan, Jam?" pleaded Trudy.

Then it hit him all at once, and he smiled so wide his glasses fell off his face again.

"SET THE TRIPOD down there," instructed Dimitri. He had over-powdered his cheeks with makeup to hide his acne on camera, and his hair was slicked back so tight he couldn't touch his top lip to his bottom one.

"*Da, Dimitri.*" The googly-eyed Russian with the sweaty oonderpants checked the shot through the viewfinder and gave a thumbs-up. "Ve are ready to livestream venever you are."

Dimitri reviewed his note cards, then looked out over the crowd gathered on the cheek below. It was quite a view from the tip of the nose. He had selected a very dramatic location to deliver his manifesto. He patted the detonator in his pocket. His lifelong dream of blowing Corpus Gigantus to bits was only minutes away.

"Take back the skies!" shouted Dimitri as he pumped his fist in the air. He reconsidered. "Take back the skies." He pounded his chest twice with his fist, then pointed up with one finger. "Take back the sky? Maybe it should be singular." He took out a pencil and scribbled something on the card.

"Vat about this?" The sweaty cameraman clapped his hands twice, put his hands on his hips, galloped in a circle, then jumped into a starfish position with both hands pointing upward. "Take back the skies!"

Dimitri's mouth hung open as he searched for some sort of response. Fortunately, a voice crackled over the walkie-talkie, saving him from the awkward moment.

"*Status check*," requested the voice in Russian.

"*Chest is clear.*"

"*Left leg is clear.*"

"*Right leg is clear.*"

"*Left arm is clear.*"

Dimitri waited intently before grabbing the walkie-talkie from the cameraman. "Right arm? Report."

Silence.

"Alexi?"

No response.

Dimitri's eyes narrowed. "Someone go check on Alexi. Now! Ve are about to start the livestream!"

"*Da.*"

"*Da.*"

"*Da.*"

"*Da.*"

"Damn," spat Dimitri. He shoved the walkie-talkie into the other man's chest.

From the nose, he could see over the entire body of Corpus Gigantus. He strained his eyes and squinted at the right arm. There was some sort of white foam covering the palm of the hand.

"Sixty seconds, ve go live," said the googly-eyed Russian.

Dimitri returned his attention to his note cards. "Ve vill not stand for this egregious breach of peachy cheeks . . . Trembling mounds of fuzzy buttocks in the clouds . . . Think of the children!"

He cleared his throat. "Red leather, yellow leather. Red leather, yellow leather," he said, overenunciating every syllable. It was a vocal warm-up he had once learned in an online acting class. He bounced on his toes and boxed an imaginary opponent, psyching himself up for the culmination of all his painstaking planning and hard work. He took a deep breath and turned to face the camera. "Let's do this."

"Three, two, one . . ."

JAM AND TRUDY carefully crept through the nasal canal, slipped out the right nostril, and snuck through the forest of the mustache to join the crowd of hostages on the cheek. The white blood cells were roving through the behemoth body, retrieving the bombs as Jam had instructed. That was phase two of his new five-part plan to thwart the hijackers and save the day. Phase one: load foam. Phase two: extract explosives.

"Do you really think this is gonna work?" Trudy wrapped her arms around a giant mustache hair and tugged. It was as tall and as strong as a palm tree.

"*The bigger the headache, the bigger the pill,*" quoted Jam.

"What the heck is that supposed to mean?"

"It means an impossible problem requires an equally impossible solution," admitted Jam. He stood on his toes to try and get a look over the crowd gathered on the giant face. Everyone was bunched together, looking worried. Their hover packs had been confiscated, and many had been separated from their groups.

"There are too many people," complained Trudy. "What are the odds we'll spot someone we know?" And just as she finished asking her question, Trudy locked eyes with someone she knew quite well: Ms. Kilroy.

"Trudy!" said Ms. Kilroy under her breath. "Jam!" Her face twisted with confusion. Why were those two weisenheimers all the way on the other side of the crowd? When had they snuck away? How did they still have their hover packs? She immediately feared for their safety. And maybe more so, she worried they would find a way to make the situation even worse. She beckoned menacingly with a single curled finger, but Trudy ducked below the crowd and vanished from her sight.

"Killjoy spotted us!" whispered Trudy to Jam.

"Shoot!" Jam quickly dropped to all fours to hide.

"What are you guys doing?" whispered a redheaded kid with a bow tie. He shifted from side to side, glancing at the nearby Russian holding a stun shield. "Do you know if there's a bathroom around here?"

"Shhh!" hissed Trudy.

"What did I do?" protested the redhead.

"We're trying to stop them from blowing this place to smithereens," explained Jam.

"Cool!" marveled the redheaded kid. He crossed his legs tightly. "Can I help?"

"Fine." Trudy rolled her eyes.

"What's everyone looking at?" Jam asked.

"The leader is up there," said the kid. "He's making some sort of speech, but no one can hear it."

"All right," said Jam, recalculating. "We're running out of time. Trudy, you handle phase three, and we'll move to phase four: stash in stache."

"Right, wait. Which one is phase three again?"

"Taunt and tickle."

"Oh yeah." Trudy smiled and rubbed her hands together with devious glee.

"Meanwhile," said Jam, "we've got to get everyone to gather in the mustache, without raising suspicion."

"Okay," said the redhead, "I'll go this way." He dropped to all fours. "Gather in the mustache. Pass it on!" he whispered, crawling through the crowd as fast as he could.

WHILE JAM AND the redhead tried to stay as inconspicuous as possible, Trudy did just the opposite. She activated her hover pack and shot straight up to the tip of the nose.

Ms. Kilroy shut her eyes and tried to pretend it was someone else's student flying overhead.

Dimitri was staring intently into the blinking red light of the camera, trying to look heroic. His speech was going even better than he had rehearsed it. His view count was in the millions. It was being shared live by news outlets in thirteen countries. He was so swept up in delivering his dramatic manifesto that he didn't notice the commotion below as his comrades discovered that one of the hostages still had a functioning hover pack.

Oblivious to their shouted warnings, he continued. "There are those who call this abomination Corpus Gigantus, but I call it Crapus You Can't-us."

In his notes, it said (*pause for laughter*), but feeling he was on a roll, he carried on.

"Soon, this monstrosity will be but a memory. The skies will be clear, untainted by greed once again. This is my vow, as sure as my name is—"

"Chumpface McButtmuncher!"

Dimitri squeaked and stopped talking. A young girl, her helmet stuffed with braided hair, was flying her hover pack behind him in full view of the camera. Despite the detailed note cards he held in his hand, Dimitri was speechless.

Trudy took off one of her boots and flung it at his head. "I'm talking to you, you dog-breath turd burglar!"

The boot bounced off Dimitri's helmet and knocked him out of his stupor.

"Get out of here!" He pointed at Trudy, inadvertently

spoiling the choreography for his big ending. His face flushed, and he shouted at the cameraman, "Get her!"

The cameraman turned too quickly and tumbled down the bridge of the nose, until he came to a stop between the eyebrows.

Trudy laughed hysterically. She hovered to the camera and kicked it over.

"Hey!" said Dimitri. Then he shouted some colorful Russian words at Trudy. He leapt up, trying to grab ahold of her, but Trudy danced through the air and out of the way.

"Nice try, you scum-sucking orthopedic duck fart!" She circled around him, bobbing and weaving just close enough to encourage him to swipe at her. "You can't catch me!"

Below, the hostages had gathered in the mustache, and whispers of rebellion rippled through the crowd.

The hijackers with the stun shields were too busy watching their leader being taunted by a foulmouthed child to notice that their captives had all moved into a dense cluster amidst the stalklike whiskers on the upper lip. They stood in a wide circle, their mouths agape, gazing at the outrageous scene unfolding above them.

"Come back here!" growled Dimitri.

"Oh! You almost got me that time!" teased Trudy.

She spun him around in circles, back and forth across the tip of the nose. His feet shuffled to and fro, to and fro.

"It's a highly sensitive patch of skin," Jam had told Trudy when he first explained the plan. "Very ticklish."

The giant nostrils of Corpus Gigantus flared outward, and the whole face twitched, knocking the crowd from their feet. It felt like an earthquake.

Corpus Gigantus rarely moved at all, but external stimuli could trigger involuntary reactions in the biological structure, and just like anyone, if something tickled the tip of its nose, it was bound to scratch the itch.

And so, the tremendous right arm of the body began to move.

First, it bent at the elbow, the forearm rising taller than a skyscraper. Then the hand, covered in foam, began to approach the face.

Dimitri saw it coming. It was impossible not to.

Trudy flew out of the way with plenty of time to spare, but the Russian was trapped at the top of Snout Mountain with no escape. The shadow of the arm crept over him until he was cloaked in total darkness, and even though the humongous hand moved slowly, it was so gobsmackingly huge that the final foamy impact could have crushed a Volkswagen.

FOOOOMMF!

The hand smacked the face, and foam blasted out from under the palm, raining down on the crowd gathered in the tangles of the mustache, where they were protected. When the hand moved away, there was a lump of foam on the tip of the nose where Dimitri had been standing.

The crowd cheered. But they were quickly hushed by the dozen hijackers who surrounded them with stun shields. One touch from the sizzling electrified force fields would feel like trying to swallow a lightning bolt.

"Quiet!" demanded the largest of the hijackers.

One of the men who had planted the bombs grabbed Trudy in a bear hug from behind. She wasn't the only one with a working hover pack.

"Let go of me!" she screamed.

"Bring her here!" The elderly Russian florist stepped forward. "And block off the nostrils so they can't escape."

Jam's teeth chattered as he watched Trudy struggle. But so far, everything was still going according to plan.

"It's time someone taught you proper manners." The old lady hijacker tried to slap Trudy across the face, but her hand bonked off Trudy's helmet.

"Wow," mused Trudy. "It's like you fell out of the stupid tree and hit all the branches on the way down."

Hijackers with stolen hover packs flew into position to block both escape routes up the nose. Trudy winked at Jam. It was time for phase five: nostril jostling.

The Russians brandished their stun shields to discourage any hostages from trying to flee through the nasal passages. But as they floated amidst the nose hairs, standing guard, the vibrations from their hover packs created a considerable nasal irritation.

Corpus Gigantus inhaled sharply, and the hovering

hijackers were violently vacuumed into the nostril cavities, bouncing between boulder-size boogers. A stupendous sniffling noise startled the bear-hugging hijacker enough for Trudy to wriggle free. She ran off to hide in the safety of the mustache with Jam.

"AAAAAAAHHHHH . . ." The gargantuan mouth of Corpus Gigantus opened wide, with a rumble so loud it shook Dimitri back to consciousness.

His helmet was cracked, his speech was ruined, and he was buried in a mound of foam. Bruised and bleeding, he was lucky to be alive. He realized he had missed his opportunity to gain prestige, but he still had a chance to make his point.

He reached into his pocket and found the remote detonator.

"AAAAAAAHHHHH . . ."

Jam and Trudy couldn't be sure if the wily white blood cells had followed their instructions and found all the bombs. But if they had, there wouldn't be any explosives left distributed in the body. They would all have been collected and gathered together in the anus.

"Hang on!" shouted Jam.

"Here it comes!" warned Trudy. Their fellow hostages hugged mustache hairs and held on for dear life.

"Take back the sky!" croaked Dimitri, and he pressed the button on the detonator.

The timing was impeccable.

Corpus Gigantus sneezed hard, knocking the unsuspecting hijackers off the face and into space.

At the exact same moment, a blazing fire exploded out from between the cheeks of Corpus Gigantus's behind.

It was the largest snart in the history of the universe.

Though when Trudy told the story, she called it an ah-choot.

Ms. KILROY DID a lot of yelling when she found out what had happened. But after she was done yelling, she was too relieved to be mad. She gave Trudy and Jam a hug.

The story was picked up by every news outlet around the world. Before the rescue transport had landed back on Earth, reporters were climbing over one another to score an interview with the two young heroes who had thwarted the hijackers and saved the day.

Of course, there were calls for Corpus Gigantus to upgrade its security systems, but in the meantime, everyone was just glad that none of the visitors had gotten hurt.

Super Sugar O's put a photo of Trudy and Jam on the front of the box as a way to say thank you, and the pair went on the late-night programs to make jokes with the hosts. But after a while, their lives returned to normal, more or less.

None of the kids made fun of Jam anymore, and Trudy had discovered a newfound love for anatomy. She even hinted that she might like to become a doctor someday. Possibly a proctologist.

This pleased Ms. Kilroy very much. In fact, she was a little sad to see Trudy and Jam go off to high school. She hated to admit it, but she thought she might get bored without the hijinks of her two most entertaining students.

On the last day of class, Jam gave Ms. Kilroy a signed Super Sugar O's box with him and Trudy on the front. It said, *Us weisenheimers couldn't have done it without you.*

Trudy simply gave her teacher a warm goodbye hug. She also stuck a sign to her back. It said, *I secretly love boogers.*

And as Trudy walked out of the classroom, snickering with Jam, she had absolutely no idea that Ms. Kilroy had stuck a sign on her back too. It said, *I secretly love learning.*

II

THE HUMAN KABOOM

(the one with the New York detective)

illustrated by

GRACEY ZHANG

B ack in the 1970s, the Grand Ballyhoo Hotel was, without question, the schmanciest hotel in all of New York City. Guests included kings and queens and world-famous movie stars, all of whom considered the luxurious accommodations of the seven-star hotel to be even more comfortable than their own palaces and mansions.

The lobby alone was three stories tall, with lush plants cascading down the walls, Italian marble floors, and an ornate fountain that served as home for a pair of elegant white swans. Tuxedo-clad musicians played classical music in one corner of the entrance hall while fashion models and sultans played backgammon in another.

A squadron of porters in crisp red uniforms dedicated their full attention to the comfort of every guest. No detail

was overlooked. Each room was perfumed with cedar oil, each table decorated with fresh flowers, each bed draped with crisp silk sheets and festooned with pillows so fluffy they nearly floated above the mattress.

The porters at the Grand Ballyhoo Hotel were a highly impressive group of impeccably trained, clean-cut young men.

Except for one.

Nutley Bumstead was, unfortunately, a schlub. The same uniform that made the other porters look distinguished made Nutley look like one of those trained monkeys that dance to accordion music. He was gangly and poorly groomed. He was easily distracted and astonishingly forgetful. However, he was also hardworking, fiercely loyal, and, most importantly, the nephew of the owner of the hotel.

To maintain the sterling reputation of the Grand Ballyhoo (and avoid general awkwardness), Nutley was given "special" assignments and mostly kept behind the scenes. Somehow, he still managed to bungle things up from time to time.

One unseasonably warm September evening, Nutley found himself in the unusual position of making room service deliveries. He was dispatched to the fifth floor of the hotel with a pyramid of champagne glasses balanced precariously upon a silver tray. Whereas the other porters could manage such a tray at a trot with one hand, Nutley held on for dear life with both, tiptoeing along at a painfully slow pace, trying his best not to spill. The happy hour drinks were gifts for the guests, sent by the executive director of hotel management himself, a sophisticated Frenchman named Monsieur Florimond François Et Voilà.

Et Voilà had given Nutley specific instructions. He was to begin his deliveries with the Emerald Suite, regardless of what it said on the sign on the door.

"Please, do not disturb . . . or else." Nutley read the typewritten note out loud. He began to sweat, struggling to determine how to knock without letting go of his tray with either hand. In a sudden burst of inspiration, Nutley turned sideways and struck the door twice with his head—hard. He grinned, briefly impressed with his own ingenuity. But the impact to his noggin left him dizzy.

Nutley staggered backward, stumbled forward, and fell. The silver tray flew into the air, and the delicate tower of glasses shattered to the ground.

Upon greeting the floor with his face, Nutley noticed a mysterious goo seeping out from under the door to the Emerald Suite. He prodded the goo with his finger, sniffed it cautiously, and touched it to his tongue. The flavor was somewhere between rust and boogers.

TWENTY MINUTES LATER, the executive director of hotel management went up to investigate why his least-favorite employee had not yet returned from what should have been a very simple errand. Et Voilà stepped out of the elevator to find Nutley slumped on the floor, slurping champagne from shards of broken glass and rubbing his ankle.

"*Zut alors!*" swore Et Voilà under his breath in French. "Anozer fine mess you've made."

"It wasn't me!" protested the porter.

"Shhh!"

Et Voilà strove to maintain the illusion of perfection in his hotel at all times. He glanced down the hall—no guests in sight. In a blink, he had plucked a small brush from his coat pocket, tidied the glass from the carpet, and piled it onto the tray. He helped Nutley to his feet and shooed him away with the mess.

The Frenchman smoothed his lapel and smiled with satisfaction. An unpleasant scene had been avoided. But there was still the matter of the Emerald Suite.

Et Voilà pressed his ear to the door. He didn't hear the familiar clickety-clack of a typewriter inside. He knocked quietly, trying to be discreet. There was no response, so he knocked a little louder. And then louder still. By that point, he couldn't help but notice that the hall carpet below the door was damp with something other than champagne. The mysterious goo clung to the bottom of his shoe.

"Professor Garfunkel?" called Et Voilà. He tried the knob. The door was locked. Concerned for the safety of his elderly guest, he checked again to make sure no one was coming and then expertly forced the door open with a single strike of his shoulder.

The scene on display inside that room was so grotesque, so gruesome, so utterly grisly, it caused the famously unflappable Frenchman to squeal like a piglet in a vise. He clapped his hand over his mouth to muffle the sound of his own distress, then covered his nose with a monogrammed handkerchief to stifle the stench.

Et Voilà stepped inside to survey the room, snatched a silver key from a table in the entryway, then darted back out and slammed the broken door behind him. He gasped for a breath of fresh air.

Curious neighbors had poked their heads into the hall after hearing the high-pitched scream. Et Voilà tried to assure his guests that everything was all right. If they returned to their rooms, he added, they would soon be delivered a complimentary glass of champagne, to apologize for the disturbance.

When the coast was clear, Et Voilà sprinted down the hall to call the police.

THE FIRST POLICEMAN to arrive was a rookie who happened to be on patrol nearby. Et Voilà wished to deal with the matter as swiftly as possible, so he quickly whisked the young officer up to the Emerald Suite and opened the door. But nothing in the police academy had prepared the man for what he saw inside that room. He gasped, let out a tiny squeak, and puked on his own boots.

Further authorities were called to the scene.

The detectives were stumped. The sergeant was baffled. The captain had never seen anything like it in his thirty-five years on the force. They blocked off the room with bright-yellow CAUTION tape as Et Voilà desperately scurried up and down the hall, ushering inquisitive onlookers back to their rooms.

The last thing he wanted was for the brutal spectacle to be made public. The Grand Ballyhoo had a reputation to maintain, after all. So when he saw the flash of a camera go off, he panicked.

Et Voilà chased after the photographer, threw a goo-covered shoe at the man's head, and pleaded with the police to seize the incriminating evidence. But it was no use.

The next morning, an unforgettable image of a graphic murder scene was printed on the front page of the most popular newspaper in town, the *Gotham Gazette*:

A human skeleton sat cross-legged in a chair at the center of a luxurious hotel suite. All the tables in the room were covered with arcane artifacts, scientific equipment, and anatomical diagrams. Everywhere, there were books: stuffed onto shelves, piled on tables, stacked in towers that nearly scraped the ceiling. On the desk sat a well-loved typewriter; on the floor, a wristwatch, a key, and a walking stick shaped like a snake. And then, of course, there was the aforementioned goo.

Every surface in the room was dripping with what

appeared to be semi-liquefied body parts. A nose lay on the couch, an ear on the carpet, a tooth on the table. It seemed as if the victim had burst apart like a water balloon, flinging skin and spraying guts in all directions—a corporeal explosion that left nothing behind but a skeleton, bone-dry and smiling.

The humongous headline above the photo put it much more succinctly: HUMAN KABOOM!

LATER THAT DAY, a mustachioed potato of a man named Conworth Pennypincher III sat in his insurance office, staring at the front page of the *Gotham Gazette* and trying to remember why the murder victim's name sounded so familiar.

You'd never know it from his threadbare suit or his crooked haircut, but Pennypincher was a wealthy man. He was also incredibly tightfisted. He agonized over every single cent he spent. This made him a formidable businessman (and a dreadful dining companion).

Thirty years of miserly negotiating had transformed his family's rinky-dink insurance agency into the most profitable firm in the city. Despite its success, Pennypincher refused to renovate the place, which was still tucked away in a crumbling downtown tower with low ceilings and dim lighting.

His private office was furnished with filing cabinets he'd recovered for free from a half-burnt building, a folding chair he'd found in an alley, and a dilapidated desk that had once belonged to his grandfather. He used every pencil down to the nub, bought all his clothes secondhand, and insisted his underpaid employees bring their own toilet paper from home.

To his credit, Pennypincher was very good at his job. He delighted in crafting insurance contracts. Thousands of customers paid monthly to ensure that, in case of accident, injury, or death, the agency would provide a payout. Pennypincher, of course, arranged all the contracts so that the payments he distributed were only a small fraction of the payments he received. His profits were astronomical.

But even still, he would have to pay out from time to time. And every single check he wrote to someone in great need upset him so deeply it made his nose bleed.

Pennypincher was still perusing the paper when the ting-a-ling of a delivery bell distracted him. A message had arrived via a pressurized tube.

The transparent tube that led to his office was just one branch of an air-powered communication system that sprawled below the ground and behind the walls of buildings throughout New York City. The intricate network of pneumatic tubes was kept top secret, and fewer than a hundred people were granted access to use it.

When Pennypincher retrieved the delivery canister from the tube and read the message inside, he tore his copy of the *Gotham Gazette* to shreds. Then he shoved the scraps of newspaper up his nostrils to prevent his one good shirt from getting stained with blood.

There was only one person who could assist him in such a tricky situation.

He wrote out a note on the back of an old memo (he always reused paper to save on costs), folded the page, shoved it into a canister, and dropped the canister into the slot of the pneumatic delivery system. He shut the door of the receptacle and pressed the appropriate buttons on the control panel to set the location for delivery.

Then he pulled an old-fashioned scissor switch, which unleashed a burst of compressed air. The canister blasted up through the tube in the ceiling and vanished from sight.

PENNYPINCHER'S MESSAGE WHIZZED through the system of secret tubes, hidden from view of the residents of the city. It swooshed below sidewalks and whooshed behind walls. The canister traveled at top speed past Union Square, around the Chrysler Building, up Fifth Avenue, and under the East River, until it reached its final destination: a humble one-bedroom apartment in Queens.

Ting-a-ling!

EDNA CHANG DID not need to check the message in the receptacle to know who it was from. There was only one person who sent communications to her apartment via pneumatic tube.

"Abraham Lincoln!"

She scolded the TV. A clueless contestant on her favorite game show, *Quizam!*, had failed to come up with the correct answer.

Edna was a retired high school social studies teacher with no family and few friends. Her late-in-life second career as an insurance claims investigator had happened by accident. A rotund, mustachioed man in a threadbare suit had offered her the job after overhearing her haggle ferociously for three cents at a fruit stand downtown. At first, she thought the man might live under a bridge, but Pennypincher quickly provided his credentials and she decided to pursue the opportunity, since it was more exciting than bingo night at the Y.

"Lake Titicaca!" She threw a ball of yarn at the screen as a different contestant guessed incorrectly.

Deep down, Edna had always dreamed of being a detective, though she didn't quite look the part. She was seventy-three years old and not even five feet tall. However, she possessed a very special talent that made her a sort of undercover supersleuth. Edna had a photographic memory. It was an ability she'd had since childhood, a source of much amusement for her parents and much frustration for her exasperated teachers.

Over the years, Edna had developed additional techniques to enhance her recall to the point that she rarely, if ever, forgot anything. Phone numbers, addresses, dates, names—if she saw or heard a piece of information even once, she remembered it forever.

Edna Chang was a literal know-it-all, which made for awkward social interactions. Having a conversation with her was a bit like having a conversation with an encyclopedia, informative but not much fun. Eventually, the novelty would wear off and friends would fade away. She never married.

"The bubonic plague!"

Edna finished her cup of tea and hit the clicker to turn off the television. She loved hot tea, and the older she got, the hotter she liked it. Her hands felt empty without a cup or a mug, and her fingers got cold, so before she got dressed, she set another kettle on the stove to boil. By the time the kettle started singing, she had tended to her plants, donned her coat, and was ready to head downtown. The ripping-hot water went straight into an insulated thermos with a generous pinch of black tea leaves, and out the door she went.

EDNA'S BLACK LEATHER slippers padded through the gilded revolving doors and into the once-glorious lobby of the Pierrepont Tower. She approached the shabby security desk, but her short stature prevented the guard from seeing her. Not that he was paying close attention. He was staring intently at the crossword puzzle in that morning's *Gotham Gazette*, deep in thought, and chewing his pencil.

"Did you get forty-five across yet?" Edna inquired.

Startled, the guard dropped his pencil and looked up. Finding no one, he stood to peer over the desk.

"*Haver of extreme tides in New Brunswick.*" Edna pointed to the crossword. "Bay of Fundy."

"Oh." The guard grimaced. "I hadn't gotten that one yet. Thanks."

"I'm here to see Pennypincher." Edna nodded at the elevator bank beyond the security barrier.

"One moment, please." The guard consulted the appointment book.

"Edna Chang. That's Chang, rhymes with 'pang'—twenty-six down: four-letter word for 'sharp feeling of guilt.'"

"Right. Didn't get that one yet either, but thanks again." The guard shoved the newspaper into a drawer. "I don't

see any appointments listed for Mr. Pennypincher, Mrs. Chang."

"*Ms.* Chang. 'MS,' as in 'abbreviation for state used to count seconds'—fifteen across."

The guard scrunched his brow.

"You must be new. The last guard was named Joe—tall man, thick sideburns, scar on his left cheek. Before Joe was Damon—Puerto Rican fellow, wife Sofia, children Nano, Abner, and Pia."

"Well, I've been working here for three weeks," the guard replied, "and if there ain't no appointment in the book, I can't let you through."

Edna closed her eyes and rubbed the bridge of her nose between her thumb and forefinger, trying hard not to lose her temper. "Young man," she said with as much sweetness as she could muster, "I suggest you let a harmless old woman go about her business. I'd hate to have to speak with your supervisor, Deandra Reynolds. Or her supervisor, Colin Robinson. Or we could go straight to Norm Peterson, head of building security.

"I assure you Mr. Pennypincher is expecting me," she went on. "And besides, the longer I stand here waiting, the less of your precious crossword challenge remains for you to enjoy. Twelve across: 'kaput.' Fourteen down: 'whippoorwill.' Thirty-two down: 'Istanbul . . .'"

The guard wasn't sure whether to scream or applaud. Eventually, he settled on a sort of exasperated grunt, then lifted the rope barrier for Edna.

"And what is your name, by the way?" she asked as she passed through.

"Pancho Rodriguez."

"Pancho Rodriguez." Edna winked. "I won't forget it."

THE HAGGARD EMPLOYEES of the Pennypincher Insurance Agency heard the elevator ding and turned their attention toward the entrance. A silhouette appeared in the mottled glass window of the front door. Well, part of a silhouette. Just the top of a tiny head.

"It's her!"

The secretaries, functionaries, actuaries, and clerks all dove under their desks or fled the room.

"Who's coming?" said the new guy, still sitting at his desk.

"Shhh!" warned a woman hiding in the coat closet.

Edna turned the knob and opened the door. Papers fluttered like tumbleweeds in a ghost town. She grinned and strutted past the rows of desks toward Pennypincher's private office at the back of the agency.

"Hi!" chirped the new guy. "Would you like a cookie? Fresh from the bakery this morning." He stood and offered a box tied with red-and-white string.

Edna examined the cookies, examined his face, and crinkled her nose. "I'd love to, but I try not to eat anything that's been touched by a man who doesn't wash his hands after going to the bathroom."

The new guy's eyes went wide.

Edna explained as she walked away. "There's powdered sugar on your fingers and also on the zipper of your pants. Which is open, by the way."

The new guy looked as if he were about to cry. Gentle giggles rippled throughout the office, though all of his coworkers were still hidden from sight.

Edna called over her shoulder before entering Pennypincher's office. "Also, the report on your desk? The math is wrong. You forgot to carry the one."

"Ms. Chang!" Pennypincher waved her in. The agitated insurance agent had just finished a cigar and was already fumbling to light another. He purchased only the very cheapest option available, a brand called Don Flato, which he'd discovered in the vending machine of a gas station bathroom. The smell was like burnt hair, and the taste was even worse.

Edna coughed and waved a cloud of blue smoke from her eyes as she closed the door behind her.

"Apologies for the stench." Pennypincher gulped at the burning tobacco log and nearly choked on the noxious fumes. "As you know, I smoke when I'm agitated."

Even though she only worked part-time, Edna was Mr. Pennypincher's favorite employee. The money she had saved the company over the years had paid her meager salary many times over. Her official title was senior claims investigator, and her job was to protect the company from scams and deception. Edna enjoyed the work so much—uncovering lies, unraveling falsehoods, and generally proving other people wrong—she would have done the job for free.

"What do you know?" she asked from the doorway. She did not approach the desk, did not sit, did not make small talk.

"The policyholder's name was Melvin Everett Garfunkel, a wealthy eccentric who maintained residence in the Grand Ballyhoo Hotel for the past twenty years. They're saying he was murdered." Pennypincher waved his hand over the desk, and scraps of torn newsprint fluttered to the ground. "I assume you've seen the paper."

"I read it on the way over." She sipped from her thermos. "And finished the crossword downstairs."

"Well, take a look at this." He passed a document to Edna, who studied it through a magnifying glass she pulled from her satchel. "Five years ago, Garfunkel took out a policy for one million dollars to be paid out in the event of his murder. I accepted because the policy was so specific. Old age, illness, accident wouldn't pay a penny. Only murder. He seemed like an innocent fellow. A retired English professor! I was sure it was a safe bet. But now . . ." He made an exploding sound and gestured with his hands. "Murder."

"Suspicious," said Edna.

"Agreed," Pennypincher replied. "And that's not all. The

policy doesn't pay out to a relative, nor a charity, nor an academic institution."

"Who is the beneficiary?"

"Miroslav Pakak."

"Ah, yes, Micky the Greek." Edna remembered reading about him. "Spent three years in prison for blowing up a falafel factory. Wanted for charges of arson, racketeering, tax evasion, and jaywalking. Known associate of Hans Ferrari and Guthrie Canard. Notoriously snappy dresser and reportedly allergic to stone fruit."

"What, you don't remember his birthday?"

"March ninth, 1943," said Edna. "It was a Tuesday."

"You never cease to amaze me, Ms. Chang." Pennypincher sucked hard on the Don Flato resting between his lips and leaned back in his chair. "My contact in the police department sent over this dossier. It's not much to go on, but they've agreed to let you examine the crime scene before removing the body. You'll need to get over to the Grand Ballyhoo right away. The hotel manager will be expecting you."

Edna gathered the papers and pushed the empty folder across the desk back toward Pennypincher. "I assume you'll want to reuse this."

"You know me too well." An ember at the tip of Pennypincher's cigar glowed bright red and dropped into his lap. A wisp of smoke rose from his pants. The hot ash burned through several layers of polyester before coming to rest on a highly delicate patch of skin.

Pennypincher yelped, fell backward out of his chair,

and frantically smacked at his crotch while launching into another coughing fit.

Edna tucked the relevant documents into her satchel. "I'll see myself out."

ON HER WAY to the subway station, Edna stopped by a bodega—a kind of all-purpose New York corner store that sells everything from batteries to bagels. She had visited this particular bodega many times. Edna poured the remnants of her thermos into the gutter and went inside.

Wasif was reading a book behind the counter, as always.

"Hello, sweetie! How are you?" cooed Edna. "You are so handsome. Yes, you are!" She reached over to pet the flame-orange cat who greeted her with enthusiastic chirps.

"I guess Clem missed you." Wasif's silver mustache shimmied as he smiled. He saved his page with a losing lottery ticket and put his book down.

"I missed him too. But he never comes to Queens to visit *me*."

Wasif crossed his arms. A light-blue shirt perfectly complemented his deep-brown skin. "You never invited him."

"Ah, well, it's nice to see him anyway." Edna handed the empty thermos to Wasif. "Fill it up to the top this time, if you don't mind."

"You have never paid me a single penny, and yet somehow I am constantly at your service," Wasif mused.

Steam danced from the spout as he poured boiling water into the thermos.

"The last time I checked, water was free." Edna picked up the book from the counter and flipped through the pages. *Nefarious Nightmares in Newark* by Stalker Cane. "You and your fictions—why not learn about the real world?" she scoffed. "Besides, you've read this one already."

Wasif smirked. The woman noticed everything.

"I like the wild stories! The real world is not nearly as interesting!" He stopped pouring. "Though the news today does sound like something out of a mystery novel . . . Might that explosive murder have anything to do with your visit this fine day?"

"The man is smarter than he looks," Edna said to the cat.

Clem meowed.

Wasif handed her back the thermos, filled to the brim. "Careful! It is very hot."

Edna sprinkled a pinch of tea into the water. "Unless the laws of physics are different in this ramshackle emporium, it's one hundred degrees Celsius—just the way I like it."

She snapped on the cap and gave Clem one last scratch under the chin before leaving. Wasif watched the steam rise from the insulated thermos and clenched his teeth as Edna took a sip.

"Your lips must be fireproof," he said.

"Wouldn't you like to know . . ." she replied.

Edna winked at Wasif and left the store.

EDNA DESCENDED THE stairs into the crowded subway station. She fished around in her satchel for a token and dropped it into the turnstile. *Ka-chonk!* The bars nearly reached her chest as they turned. She could easily have ducked under them, but she always paid the fare. Many of the other passengers did not.

Two teenagers bounded over the turnstile with the grace of gazelles. Two sparkly ladies in high heels crammed together to pass through on one token. A bald man in a trench coat got stuck as he tried to squeeze past the metal bars.

"Lose some weight, pops!" the teenagers taunted.

The sparkly ladies laughed.

Edna waited on the platform for the A train to arrive. A throng of colorful characters buzzed and bobbed. Some were clad in expensive linen suits, others in skintight leather. They had gathered from lands near and far to live on a tiny, noisy island just off the coast of the United States. Some of them were not American, but all of them were New Yorkers.

The train arrived with a deafening squeal and a shower of sparks. The outside was covered in a vibrant mishmash of graffiti, and the inside was stuffed with humans of every conceivable shape and size.

The doors opened, and Edna burrowed into the train

car. A young accountant stood and offered her his seat—one of the few benefits of having wrinkly skin and white hair.

Edna sat and removed the Pennypincher files from her bag—crime scene photos, witness statements, hotel blueprints, even the victim's tax records and medical history. A photo slipped to the floor, and a man with an Afro retrieved it for her.

"Far-out!" he said when he lowered his sunglasses to examine the image. It was a photo from the crime scene at the Grand Ballyhoo, the same one that had run on the front page of the newspaper. *"Tear the roof off the sucker!"* The guy laughed and returned the photo.

Edna smiled politely and went back to examining her documents.

"Isn't it awful?" a pouty girl with hair down to her knees said as she clung to a strap on the ceiling. "I saw it in the paper. What an awful, awful way to go."

"It's a conspiracy!" muttered a walleyed man in a fedora, waving a stubby finger through the air. "Nixon and the Russians are working together to put explosives in toothpaste. Any one of you could blow at any moment!"

A rabbi rolled his eyes. "It was an act of God. No trace of explosives was found at the scene. How else do you explain it?"

The train was abuzz with gossip.

"Aliens!"

"Mole people!"

"Communists!"

Edna couldn't help but chuckle.

"The most obvious explanation is not murder," announced a bookish woman in high heels, "but rather, a little-known scientific phenomenon known as spontaneous human combustion."

"That happened to my uncle!" a construction worker chimed in. "Right after Thanksgiving dinner." He made a loud armpit fart. "Smelled awful!"

Everyone laughed.

A mariachi band squeezed onto the train and struck up a tune with full enthusiasm. Edna decided to get off one stop early and walk the rest of the way.

Too much sensory stimulus could be overwhelming for her. The dozens of strangers on the train would likely soon forget about the elderly Asian woman, but Edna would remember every single one of them—what they said, how they said it, what they wore, even how they smelled.

She wriggled through the crowd onto the platform and sighed a breath of relief when the train pulled away and she found herself alone.

EDNA STROLLED THROUGH Central Park on her way uptown. She studied the architectural schematics of the hotel while sipping her scalding hot tea.

Most investigators keep notebooks to jot down facts related to their cases: names, times, addresses, etc. Edna didn't even carry a pen. She didn't need one.

Some people's brains are wired a bit differently, and it's easier for them to recall things that other folks might forget. But Edna had also trained to enhance her natural ability, and she'd developed a special technique that made her memory impeccable.

The technique she used was quite simple, in theory. She would convert information into visual images, then organize those images with connections she could use later on to retrieve the relevant facts or figures.

Some memory experts use the familiar layout of a house to create connections—a memory palace, they call it. But Edna's apartments in the city had always been minuscule. So instead, she used her body to organize her memories. Specifically, the postures and movements of modern dance.

One of the secrets to an effective memory technique is creating outrageous images. Each memory expert uses their own personal code to translate facts and figures into visual symbols. The stranger something is, the easier it is to remember. And so, as unsuspecting pedestrians filed past, the tiny woman strolling down the sidewalk was not just reading papers and drinking scalding hot tea, she was also concocting an utterly ridiculous dance sequence in her mind:

Edna juggled a robin's egg, a beehive, and a bottle of orange juice as she waved her hands over her head and kicked her right leg out to the side—this locked in the victim's height (six foot six), weight (180 pounds), and age (eighty-four). Edna jumped over a blue tree, ducked under a purple fork, and dove into a green cloud—this captured the date, time, and location of the incident. A silverback gorilla sat on her bent left knee, windmill strumming a guitar strung with snakes—this represented the personal possessions recovered at the scene.

An increasingly ludicrous scenario unfolded in Edna's mind, combining flamboyant dance moves with outlandish confabulations until every detail of every page of every document was recorded and stored in her mental depository.

When she was done, she dropped the papers in a trash can across the street from the Grand Ballyhoo Hotel.

EDNA WHISTLED AS she admired the building. It was a gorgeous feat of architecture—twenty-six stories adorned with ornate stone decorations. She circled the block to check all the entrances against the blueprints she had memorized, then headed for the front door.

She was greeted by two courteous porters as she entered the hotel. On one side of the palatial lobby, she spotted a gaggle of reporters aggressively shouting questions at a man in a white dinner jacket. It was the executive director of hotel management, Florimond François Et Voilà. Despite his welcoming demeanor and hospitable tone, Edna could tell he was fretting over the negative attention the sensational murder mystery had brought to his upscale establishment.

"No furzer inquiries, please. I beseech you! Ze fifz floor is closed until furzer notice. All guests have been conveniently relocated and zeir rooms upgraded considerably. Just one more example of ze unparalleled hospitality we offer at ze Grand Ballyhoo Hotel. Now, please, you must leave ze lobby as we are preparing for a private event zis evening." He waved away the journalists, and as the porters lured the last one out with a handful of tiny shampoo bottles, he sighed a breath of relief.

"*Excusez-moi, Monsieur Et Voilà.*" Edna caught the man's attention in his native French.

"*Oui?*" He spun around looking for the speaker but glanced right over Edna's head.

"I'm here from the Pennypincher Insurance Agency."

"Ah, yes." Et Voilà looked down at the diminutive detective and smoothed his lapel. "But of course, madame." He bowed. "Please follow me to ze library, where we might enjoy a bit more privacy."

Et Voilà slid shut the double doors of the library and motioned for Edna to have a seat on the chesterfield by the window. The walls were lined with towering shelves of color-coordinated books. A ladder with wheels provided access to the topmost volumes.

"Can I offer you anyzing to drink, Madame . . ."

"Chang. And, yes. I would love some hot water. Boiling hot, if it's not too much trouble."

Et Voilà picked up an old-fashioned telephone and gave the order. He unbuttoned his jacket and sat down on the edge of the sofa opposite Edna.

"Tell me about Melvin Everett Garfunkel," she said. "He's been staying with you for almost twenty years. Is that correct?"

"*Oui.* Professor Garfunkel has been with us nearly as long as I have been working here at ze Grand Ballyhoo."

"Is it common for a guest to stay that long?"

"Common? No. But a resident of ze Grand Ballyhoo enjoys a certain level of luxury zat is not offered anywhere else. Gourmet dining, fresh-cut flowers, housekeeping, laundry, complimentary champagne happy hour, twenty-four-hour room service . . ."

"And did Professor Garfunkel often indulge in these luxuries?"

Et Voilà pursed his lips. "No. Not often."

"He must have been well known around the hotel, having lived here for so many years."

"Well, no. Not particularly."

"How come?"

"Professor Garfunkel was a very private person. He preferred to be left alone and generally avoided ze company of others. I myself spoke to him on only a small handful of occasions."

"Isn't that a bit odd?"

"Madame Chang, comfort is of ze utmost importance in ze business of hospitality. For some, it is Turkish bath towels. For others, it is a tiny chocolate-covered cherry on ze pillow. For ze professor, it was ze strictest privacy that made ze Grand Ballyhoo such a happy home."

"But he must have become familiar to some of the staff whom he saw on a daily basis."

Et Voilà laughed without making a sound. "*Au contraire, madame.* Not at all. He seldom left his room, and when he did—"

"He used the secret passage that leads to the service exit?" Edna relished watching the Frenchman's face flash with surprise. He leaned in closer.

"Madame Chang, I hope I can enjoy your confidence in ze same way zat Professor Garfunkel enjoyed mine."

"But of course."

"Some of our more . . . *cautious* guests may request access to ze private stairwell if zey wish to avoid being seen as zey come and go. Movie stars, politicians—ze Grand Ballyhoo has a well-earned reputation for discretion. Discretion is of ze utmost importance in ze business of hospitality."

"I see." Edna's tone betrayed her skepticism.

"Zere is nothing illegal or untoward here, madame. It is quite common practice in ze finest of hotels. Of course, what people do in ze privacy of zeir own rooms is none of my concern."

"Unless they happen to explode."

He crossed his legs. "Yes, but zat is most unusual. Is it not?"

"Who else had access to the room?"

"Zere are only two keys zat can open ze door to ze Emerald Suite. They cannot be duplicated. Professor Garfunkel insisted that a special lock be installed."

"And who had access to these keys?"

"Ze professor had one, of course. It was found among his personal possessions when zey discovered ze . . . ze . . ." He made an exploding motion with his hands. "*Zut alors!* What a fiasco."

"And the other key?"

Et Voilà folded his hands in his lap. "It is stored in my personal office for safekeeping. In the basement of the hotel. In a small lockbox, to which only I know the combination. If you like, I can retrieve it for you to examine."

"That won't be necessary." Edna noticed a sudden abundance of detail in his answer—a common sign that someone is nervous, or lying.

There was a polite knock before the door of the library

slid open. A handsome porter carried in a tray and placed a tea set on the table in front of Edna.

"Even a recluse like Professor Garfunkel needs groceries, laundry, medicine," she said. "Did he run these errands himself?"

Et Voilà gestured to the young man in the crisp red uniform. "Our dedicated staff is available seven days a week to assist with any deliveries or housekeeping requests."

"Did you often fetch items for the professor, young man?"

The porter opened his mouth, glanced at Et Voilà, and said nothing.

"I'll take that as a no," Edna surmised. "But then who did?"

Et Voilà exhaled deeply and nodded to the porter, who made a shallow bow and sped off to fetch Nutley.

NUTLEY BUMSTEAD SAT on the couch next to Edna, sweating profusely and squeezing his hat in his hands.

"There's no reason to be nervous, Mr. Bumstead."

"Ha! No one ever calls me Mr. Bumstead." Nutley shook his head. "Nutley, Nutter Butter, Nutso, Jughead, Buster . . . Boss calls me *Bouffon*." He beamed proudly. "It's French." Et Voilà cleared his throat, and Nutley's enthusiasm faded. "I mean . . ." Nutley floundered, frantically searching the room for a clue of what to say next and finding none.

In the silence, Edna looked to Et Voilà for explanation.

"Nutley is one of our most important staff members," said Et Voilà as he patted Nutley's knee. The porter smiled.

"Ze late professor sent him on errands from time to time because he knew he could be trusted." Nutley bit his lip. "Isn't zat right, Nutley?"

The porter nodded violently. Edna's eyes narrowed.

"Monsieur!" The handsome porter burst into the library with a worried look on his face.

"Not now, Jacques," scolded Et Voilà.

"But, monsieur, there is a *situation* with the prime minister."

They heard shouting in the lobby, followed by a loud crash.

Et Voilà leapt to his feet but hesitated to leave Nutley alone with Edna. There was more shouting in the distance. "I am terribly sorry, Madame Chang. Might we reconvene at anozer time?"

"No trouble at all," said Edna. "Meanwhile, Nutter Butter here can show me to the Emerald Suite. I'd like to examine the crime scene, and time is of the essence."

Et Voilà pursed his lips again. "But of course," he grumbled. "Jacques will accompany you as well."

"That won't be necessary," said Edna. She patted Nutley's knee. "We can manage, just the two of us."

Another crash from the lobby drew Jacques out the door.

Florimond François Et Voilà had no choice but to relent. "Very well. I will join you on ze fifz floor as soon as possible. Nutley, please escort Madame Chang to ze Emerald Suite. Zere is a police officer waiting for you."

Nutley gulped.

Et Voilà clicked his heels, bowed, and left the room.

NUTLEY LED EDNA to the elevators while biting his tongue. Literally. From across the lobby, Et Voilà managed to catch his eye and made an aggressive shushing motion.

Edna turned too late to see it.

The arrow on the indicator above the elevator ticked slowly down from sixteen.

"This may take a while," grumbled Edna. "Maybe we should take the secret staircase instead?"

"You know about that?" Nutley whispered.

Edna nodded slowly. "I know about all sorts of things."

Nutley took the bait. "Oh yeah?"

"Yeah," said Edna coolly. "Like the fact that you read every issue of *Super Dude* the day it comes out."

"How did you know *that*?" Nutley wondered.

"The comic book sticking out of your back pocket. It's brand-new. I saw it advertised in the window of a shop on the way here."

"You are an excellent detective!" Nutley realized too late that he'd shouted. He looked up to find Et Voilà scowling at him from the other side of the room. "Sorry." Nutley tried to remember the instructions his boss had given him. "Discretion is of the uppermost importance in the business of . . . hospitals?"

"Something like that." Edna sipped her tea.

The elevator doors finally opened and some well-dressed

guests stepped out into the lobby. Nutley bowed at them awkwardly.

Edna locked eyes with Et Voilà as the red-faced prime minister ranted and raved. She waved politely. The elevator doors closed, with her and the dim-witted porter alone inside.

"I imagine you were very busy with errands for an elderly guest who rarely left his room."

Nutley snorted. "You wouldn't believe me if I told you."

"I don't know, I've heard some pretty strange stories in my line of work."

"Oh yeah? Well, what about—" Nutley stopped abruptly. "No, wait. I'm not blabbing. I'm keeping my mouth shut. Showing you to the suite, and that's it. I don't want to get in trouble."

"Trouble? Why would you get in trouble?"

"Forget it," muttered Nutley.

"Sometimes I wish I could," Edna sighed. "It's probably not that interesting anyway."

Nutley pouted.

"I bet what you saw was pretty boring, actually."

Nutley couldn't help himself. "Oh yeah? How about ostrich eggs, chain saws, barbed wire, vats of acid, a fetal pig in a jar, shrunken heads, almanacs of poison—"

Nutley realized he was counting on his fingers. He stopped midsentence and covered his mouth with his hand.

Edna's mind sprang into action, cataloging each detail with a flurry of fantastic images. The ostrich egg splattered against the chain saw, which flipped over a barbed

wire fence and splashed
into a vat of acid, where
it spanked the fetal
pig, which smooched a
shrunken head, which
got smooshed—*splat*—
between the pages of a
giant almanac of poison.

Edna blinked, and
the sequence was com-
mitted to memory.

"I have to admit,
that does sound pretty
strange," she said. "But you
weren't supposed to tell me
any of that, were you?"

Nutley shook his head vigorously,
his hand still covering his mouth.

"Well, don't worry. I won't tell your boss."

"Phew!" Nutley huffed with relief.

"If you answer just a few more questions . . ." Edna
pressed the emergency stop button, and the elevator gears
ground to a halt. She turned on the boy like a tiger corner-
ing a mouse. "When was the last time you saw Garfunkel
alive?"

Nutley backed into the corner of the elevator. "I—I—I
hadn't seen him for a couple of weeks. I can't remember.
I think he was sick. He was getting all skinny and pale.

Started donating boxes of stuff to charity. People do that when they die, right? I figured maybe he was dying. Not murdered dying—sick dying! I didn't know he would be murdered. I swear! And the saddest part is when I talked to him yesterday, he sounded like he was feeling much better."

"Wait. You saw Garfunkel yesterday?"

Nutley shook his head. "No, I couldn't look. I don't want to see any more dead bodies. I couldn't even look at the photo in the paper this morning. I feel terrible. I know I screwed up. I just forgot. I'm so sorry!"

Every answer Nutley gave filled Edna with more questions. When did he last see Garfunkel? What other dead bodies had he seen? What *exactly* did he screw up? Edna massaged her forehead, trying to keep her thoughts straight.

"What did you forget?" She decided that was as good a place to start as any.

"The key!" blurted Nutley. He buried his face in his hands. "My boss is gonna kill me. I'm no good at keeping discretions."

"That's why they had to break down the door. You locked the extra key in the room by mistake." Edna was putting the pieces together. "But what were you doing in there?"

"The room was too hot. Strange weather for September, right? Good for baseball, though. I heard the heat helps Seaver with his changeup."

"Focus!" Edna shook Nutley by the collar. "What were you doing in the room?"

"The professor bought a big, fancy ceiling fan. Artsy-fartsy frou-frou dealie. Must have been super expensive.

Even showed up in a refrigerated truck—extra cold, get it? 'Cause a fan is supposed to keep you cool." Nutley tapped his temple, feeling clever.

Edna was dumbstruck. Nutley continued.

"Garfunkel went to stay with a friend who had air-conditioning or something. Left a note for me to install the fan and turn it on for him, and a number I should call when I was done. So I did like he asked." His lip began to tremble. "I didn't mean to forget the key!" he moaned. "You don't think it's my fault, do you? Boss says I could get in big trouble if I don't keep my mouth shut . . . I'm so sorry!"

Nutley slid down the wall and started sobbing.

Edna patted the boy's head. If the room was empty when he arrived, Garfunkel must have died sometime after Nutley left. But if the forgetful porter had left the extra key behind, Garfunkel would have been the only one who could open the door. Could a murderer have snuck in through the window? Had the old man unwittingly welcomed a visitor with nefarious intent? Edna would have to examine the crime scene to find out.

Plus, she was very curious to see the big, fancy fan. It didn't appear in any of the police photos.

DING!

When the elevator doors opened, Edna saw that a room at the end of the hall was blocked off with police tape. A young officer dozed in a chair beside it.

"That must be the Emerald Suite," said Edna.

Nutley remained seated on the floor of the elevator. "Please don't make me go in there," he said. "I don't want to talk to the cops. I don't want to see Professor Garfunkel splattered all over the floor. It's not right to leave him like that."

"Okay, okay," Edna assured the quivering porter. "You can wait here. And don't worry—as soon as the investigation is finished, we'll get it all cleaned up and give his bones a proper burial."

Nutley looked confused.

"You mean, the skeleton?" he asked. "That's not the professor."

"What?" Edna was distracted by a strange hissing noise coming from inside the Emerald Suite. It was loud enough to wake the officer from his nap. "Shhh!" she said as she approached the door. She paused briefly to read the typewritten note taped to the door. Then she closed her eyes and listened intently.

The next sound she heard knocked her from her feet.

KABOOM!

A fiery explosion ripped through the hallway and flung Edna backward onto the carpet. She tumbled head over heels but somehow managed to hang on to her thermos. When the initial shock wore off, Edna coughed and wiped the dust from her eyes.

The door had been blown off its hinges, and through the smoke, she saw a shadowy figure pass the window inside the room. She shouted, but the ringing in her ears made it sound like a whisper.

Edna struggled to her feet and stumbled forward to investigate. The carpet was on fire, and stacks of books were ablaze. Edna recognized the odor of dynamite. Someone was trying to destroy the crime scene.

The skeleton had been blown to bits, but the floor was still wet with goo. Edna wheeled around looking for clues, trying not to lose her footing and slip. Typewritten pages fluttered through the air. She hurried to the open window, skating through the goo, and stuck out her head.

A crowd was gathering on the sidewalk below, gawking at the blazing fire and the smoke billowing out of the fancy hotel.

Edna looked up and saw someone climbing the fire escape. Without thinking, she clambered out the window and went after them.

She scrambled onto the metal steps. The culprit spotted her and started running up the stairs. Edna chased after them as quickly as her little legs could carry her. She was out of breath after climbing twenty-two flights to reach the hotel rooftop. There she spotted a man in a three-piece suit, doubled over, gasping for air with his hands on his knees.

"Stop!" shouted Edna, panting.

The man yelled something nasty in a foreign language and staggered to the edge of the roof. He hesitated, then clumsily tumbled over the side of the building.

Edna darted after him to see where he'd gone.

He landed with a crunch on some rickety scaffolding ten

feet below. He groaned. Edna shimmied down delicately
and landed a few feet away from him.

When he struggled to his feet and pulled out a knife,
Edna froze.

"Back off, Grandma," he snarled, breathing heavily as he slashed the gleaming switchblade through the air.

"You're Micky the Greek." She recognized his face from the mug shot in the case file.

"Why does everyone still call me that?" moaned Micky the Greek. "I'm Croatian. I've told them a thousand times!"

"Why did you do it? Why did you kill Garfunkel?"

"I didn't!" growled the gangster. "But I'll be damned if anyone stands between me and that insurance money."

"How did you know him?"

"I didn't! I never met the guy. No idea who he was, but I got a paper right here that says I've got a million smacker-oonis coming to me." He waved a typewritten letter, then waved his knife. "Unless some snooping detective tries to screw it up."

Something about the letter looked oddly familiar to Edna. "You didn't even know the man?" she asked.

"Listen, lady, someone tries to give me free money, I don't ask questions." He lowered his gaze. "You, on the other hand . . . you ask too many."

Micky the Greek stalked toward Edna and tightened his grip on the knife.

Edna stepped back and bumped against the railing of the scaffolding. The platform teetered high above the street. She was trapped with nowhere to run. She squeezed her thermos and looked around frantically.

"You've had a long life, lady. It's gotta end sometime, right?"

As the gangster loomed over her, Edna pried the lid off her thermos. When he lunged forward, she tossed a mugful of scalding hot tea into his face.

"Ahhh!" screamed Micky the Greek. "My face! My beautiful face!"

He staggered backward, clutching his scorched skin. Edna stepped forward and kicked him between the legs as hard as she could. His screaming ascended two octaves.

"Aieeeeee!"

Micky the Greek did an accidental backflip over the rail of the scaffolding, landed on a rough-hewn staircase, and smacked his head against the floorboards. He bounced down twenty-six flights of stairs before landing in a dumpster in the alley below. (When he regained consciousness two days later, even he couldn't remember which country he was from.)

Edna pulled out her magnifying glass and retrieved the letter dropped by Micky the Greek as he tumbled down the steps. It was just a brief note, listing only the basic information about the insurance policy. No date and no signature. It could have been written by anyone.

EDNA TOOK A cab back downtown. She stepped gingerly out of the car, then winced as she pushed open the door to the bodega. She was covered in dust and bleeding from her ear.

"Good lord, woman," exclaimed Wasif. "What have you gotten yourself into this time?"

"Quit your pity party and fill me up."

Edna shuffled forward and collapsed into a shelf of cereal boxes. Her empty thermos clattered across the tile floor. Clem meowed and licked her hand.

Wasif rushed to the phone to call an ambulance, and Edna let out a long sigh.

"It doesn't make any sense," she muttered. "Ostrich eggs, barbed wire, chain saws . . ."

"Shhh . . ." Wasif knelt beside her and pressed a wet towel to her forehead. "Save your strength. You're wounded."

Edna began to slur her words. "Poison, acid, shrunken heads . . ."

"We can talk about the books later. For now, rest."

Edna shivered and opened one eye. "What books?"

"The Stalker Cane alphabet mysteries. I've got them all."

"A fetal pig?"

"That was *The Barbarous Butcher of Bensonhurst*. One of my favorites."

"What?"

"The murder weapon was a stillborn piglet. Stalker Cane always comes up with the most ghoulish and diabolical modus operandi. That's what makes him such a great mystery writer."

Edna was losing consciousness. An ambulance siren blared in the distance.

"Mystery writer . . ."

"You're welcome to borrow them anytime," he said.

But Edna never heard Wasif's kind offer.

WHEN EDNA REGAINED consciousness, she found herself in a hospital bed. Her left arm was in a sling.

"Look who's awake." The doctor checked her chart and smiled. "What do you remember?"

"Everything," replied Edna.

"Well, you're lucky to be alive." The doctor set down the chart and stood at the edge of the bed. "Tell me, what was a woman your age doing in a knife fight?"

"You should see the other guy." Edna tried to move her arm and groaned.

"Easy, Ms. Chang. You've lost a lot of blood and fractured your clavicle. It will take some time to heal."

"There goes my dream of pitching for the Mets."

The doctor wheeled a skeleton over from the corner to

explain. "As you can see, the clavicle supports the entire weight of the arm, so you'll have to keep it in a sling for at least four months. We've stitched up the wound and—"

"Wait. What is that?" Edna tried to sit up, and groaned again.

"What is what?" The doctor looked at the skeleton, confused.

Edna tried to recall the details from the crime scene photos. Her memory was fuzzy from the pain medication. Elephants, talking trees, and a sardine sandwich danced through her mind as she tried to recover the memory she was searching for. Eventually, from the depths of her brain, the image of the smiling skeleton snapped into focus.

"The bones! They're different from the ones in the photo. The shoulders are too wide. The hips are too narrow."

"Ah." The doctor nodded. "You're very observant, Ms. Chang. This is a *male* skeleton, but despite the slight differences, you can still see how—"

"Get me a telephone."

"Ms. Chang, I'm afraid—"

"Get me a telephone NOW!"

IT WAS RARE that Pennypincher was happy about paying anyone, but the fee Edna charged was a small fraction of what he would have had to cough up if the Garfunkel policy had been fulfilled.

"The police concurred with your assessment. The skeleton in the Grand Ballyhoo was definitely female—couldn't have been our guy." He offered her a cigar from the box on his desk. She declined.

"And forensics confirmed that the letter sent to Micky the Greek was written on the same typewriter as the note Garfunkel left on the door of his room—every capital letter 'P' was deformed in the same way. Even the lead detective was impressed you noticed that. It's more than enough to void the policy. Excellent work, Ms. Chang."

"Thank you," said Edna.

Pennypincher struggled to light a match. "Of course, all anyone wants to talk about is the fact that Garfunkel was secretly some famous author. Stacker . . . ? Striker . . . ?"

"Stalker Cane."

"That's it." Pennypincher searched his desk for a lighter. "Reporters have been calling all day: Why did he fake his own death? How did he do it? Where is he now?"

"All good questions," said Edna.

"What do I care?" Pennypincher leaned back in his chair. "You know how those creative types are . . . As long as I don't have to pay, I'm happy!"

Edna smiled and took a sip from her thermos. Her other arm was still in a sling.

"I'm terribly sorry about your injury, by the way. But I hope you don't assume I'll be covering your medical bills. That was not part of our agreement. Also, I apologize for making you stand, but the chairs were needed elsewhere in the office."

A long silence was broken by the delivery bell.

Ting-a-ling!

A canister landed in the pneumatic tube. Pennypincher retrieved it, took out an envelope, and handed it to Edna. She removed the check inside, and a small trickle of blood dripped from Pennypincher's left nostril.

"If you're not going to keep the envelope . . ."

"Of course," said Edna, handing it over.

"WELL, IF IT isn't the famous detective!" teased Wasif, waving the morning's paper at Edna as she entered his store. Despite the sling, she was in good spirits.

The front-page headline read SUPER SLEUTH EXPOSES STALKER CANE MURDER SCAM, and the photo below showed Edna unsuccessfully trying to hide her face from the camera.

She scrutinized the paper briefly. "I look old."

"You look great!" protested Wasif.

Edna blushed.

Clem emerged from a nap on a shelf and started snaking his way between Edna's legs. She stooped gingerly to rub his head.

"I can't believe Professor Garfunkel was secretly Stalker Cane!" Wasif smacked the paper. "I should have figured it out for myself. The whole scene was as gruesome as one of his books. A real-life murder mystery! Do you think he's still out there somewhere?"

"I don't think so." Edna smirked.

"You'd think the cops would've noticed the skeleton was female." Wasif shook his head.

"Well, she was an unusually tall female," Edna mused. "Plus, they were probably distracted by the grotesque spectacle."

"So you met with Stalker Cane's publisher?"

"A lovely woman. In thirty years, she'd never met

Stalker Cane in person. Had no idea who was writing all those stories."

"And you got to see the manuscript for the final book?"

"I did."

"Well, what's it about?" Wasif was giddy with anticipation.

"Why don't you read it yourself?" Edna reached into her satchel and pulled out a typewritten manuscript. "They let me keep a copy." She dropped it on the counter with a smile.

"Booyah!" Wasif clapped his hands. *Zodiac Zappers at Zabar's.* He read the title out loud. "Oooh, I can't wait. Thank you!"

Wasif flipped through the pages and noticed the letter "P's" were all filled in with ink where the hole in the middle should be. He shook his head with admiration. "I still can't believe you figured it out. A blotchy letter 'P'? Most people would not have remembered that."

"I remember everything," muttered Edna to herself.

Clem began to purr.

"Stalker Cane foiled by a speck of gunk on the 'P' key and the sharpest detective in all of New York City." Wasif was beaming.

"Technically, I'm a claims investigator, not a detective." She winked. "And I never would have figured it out if it wasn't for you."

Now it was Wasif's turn to blush. "Oh, all I did was read too many stories. You're the one with the mega-memory."

"No, it's true! I couldn't have made the connection if you hadn't insisted on droning on about your beloved mysteries."

Wasif tried to hide his smile. "Well, you could have mentioned my name to the newspaper reporter."

"All I said was 'No comment'! They made that other stuff up. I never implied that Garfunkel faked his own death or ran off to Acapulco."

"So you did read the article."

Edna shrugged.

"There are just so many questions left unanswered," Wasif said. "Why would Garfunkel pay a gangster to stage a murder? Why would he go through so much trouble to keep his identity a secret from his fans? And, most importantly, how does a human being explode inside a locked room without anybody hearing anything?" He stroked his silver mustache. "I guess we'll never know the whole story."

"Hmm," said Edna.

"You know more than you say, woman?"

Edna shook her empty thermos, and Wasif took it from her hand.

"Well . . ." She waited for a customer to pay, then looked over her shoulder to make sure they were alone. "Do you really want to know?"

Steam filled the air as Wasif opened the tap. "Of course!" he huffed.

A twinkle of excitement lit Edna's eyes. "You can't tell *anyone*."

Now Wasif was excited too. "Who would I tell?"

Edna locked the door and flipped the OPEN sign to CLOSED.

"Everyone thinks that Garfunkel was Stalker Cane, but I never said that."

Wasif scrunched his nose with confusion. "But clearly this book was written on his typewriter..."

Edna sprinkled a pinch of tea into her thermos and gestured at the manuscript. "Take a look at the dedication page."

Wasif flipped the pages open, and Edna handed him her magnifying glass.

"For MEG, my dearest fan, and our ongoing pursuit of an impenetrable mystery."

Edna raised her eyebrows. An invitation to Wasif to try and figure it out for himself.

"Meg... Megan? Margaret?"

Edna shook her head. A customer outside banged on the glass.

"Come back later!" shouted Wasif. "Meg... Meg... M... E... G... Melvin Everett Garfunkel!" said Wasif with delight. "But why would he dedicate the book to himself?"

"Because," Edna explained, "*he* wasn't the writer. *She* was."

"She? She who?"

"Stalker Cane. It's obviously a made-up name, but it's a very specific kind—an anagram. Unscramble the letters and you get Karen Castle."

"How on earth did you decipher that?"

"I didn't." Edna sipped her tea. "At first. But I kept

thinking about something the porter from the hotel told me. He said he didn't want to see any more dead bodies."

"Do lots of people die in hotels?"

"More than you might expect," Edna noted. "Certainly more than the manager of the hotel would like the public to know about. I tracked Nutley down at the comic book shop and squeezed the whole story out of him. Turns out he found a corpse in the Royal Penthouse Suite only a week before the Garfunkel incident.

"He went in to prepare the room and found a deceased woman tucked into the bed. No one knew who she was or how she got in there, but Nutley said she died with a smile on her face."

"Creepy."

"I did some digging down at the morgue and found out the woman had dedicated her body to science. She was a rare specimen. Over six and a half feet tall. Her bones were preserved for medical study and then delivered to the Emerald Suite at the Grand Ballyhoo as instructed in her will. Nutley put the skeleton in the room himself, having no idea it was the same person he'd found upstairs a week earlier. It didn't seem out of the ordinary, considering the other oddities he'd delivered to that room in the past."

"So that's where the skeleton came from! But how is Karen Castle connected to Garfunkel?"

Edna pulled an old photograph from her satchel. "They took a writing class together in college."

Wasif gasped. A dapper young man smiled at the camera, his arm around a shy-looking young woman. They both happened to be extraordinarily tall, and exactly the same height. "This photo must be fifty years old."

"It's the most recent one I could find. To say that Karen Castle was camera-shy would be an understatement."

"What do you mean?"

"She had extreme agoraphobia—was afraid of people, crowds, public places . . . It got worse with age, to the point that she could hardly bear to leave her hotel room."

"Wait . . ."

"That's right. Garfunkel was probably the only person who had laid eyes on her for years. He kept her comfortable, did her shopping, ordered her research materials, and went to the stores to get the latest books. He kept her existence a total secret so that she could focus on her writing."

Wasif smacked his forehead. "I don't believe it!" He marveled at his shelf full of Stalker Cane novels.

"It would have all gone according to plan if Nutley hadn't forgotten the key in the room."

"What do you mean?" asked Wasif.

"They were counting on Micky the Greek to destroy the crime scene with one of his infamous explosions."

"Aha! I was wondering why that criminal was involved."

"But the hotel manager spoiled the plan when he broke in to retrieve the missing key," Edna explained. "He was probably trying to protect the hotel's reputation more than his least-favorite porter. But regardless, if he had been more forthcoming from the start, it could have saved me a lot of running around."

"I bet he's none too pleased that his fancy-pants hotel is now mobbed with Stalker Cane fans." Wasif chuckled. "But . . . what happened to Garfunkel if he didn't flee to Acapulco?"

Edna sipped her tea casually. "Well, that's the part that's really gruesome."

"Go on," said Wasif, his eyes wide.

"The blood and the guts they found sprayed all over the place?"

"Yeah, they found a nose and fingers too."

"*That* was Garfunkel."

Wasif cringed. "What?"

"The old man died first. They must have known it was coming. Maybe he was ill. Regardless, for the plan to work, Castle had to move Garfunkel's body. She couldn't go outside or talk to anyone because of her phobia. So what could she do?"

"She could get the dim-witted porter to dispose of it."

"Right, but even Nutley would've called the police if he knew it was a corpse . . . And this is where you've got to admire the woman's morbid imagination—she uses corrosive acid to melt down the body, then she packs it into three small boxes and tells the porter they're books for donation."

"She spoke to him?"

"She cracked the door open and handed him an address for delivery. He saw Garfunkel's watch on her wrist, his rings on her fingers, and he was convinced. Thought the poor guy was just losing weight from his illness."

"Where did he take the 'books'?"

"A loft in SoHo. Some avant-garde sculptor from Germany. She thought the whole thing was an art project. Molded the 'materials' into a very specific shape as per the request of a generous benefactor."

"A sculpture?"

"It arrived just a few days after the skeleton. Nutley put it in the room, then called the number on the note to tell 'Garfunkel' it was ready."

"But he really called Micky the Greek, didn't he? When he thought he was talking to Garfunkel."

"Yes, and that was the gangster's signal to go blow up the Emerald Suite, confuse the evidence, and collect the insurance money."

"But Nutley bungled it up," said Wasif.

"Exactly. He installed the fan but forgot the key, which led to the discovery of the human remains before Micky the Greek had a chance to set off the explosion."

"I guess they underestimated him." Wasif reconsidered. "Or maybe they overestimated him."

"The most amazing part is that Garfunkel and Castle must have been planning this for years," said Edna.

"How do you know?"

"Because the dedication has been the same in the past three books."

A lightbulb went on in Wasif's head. "To my dearest *fan*. Oh my word. The ceiling fan! That was the sculpture! That was Garfunkel?!" He shuddered.

"That's why it arrived in a refrigerated truck. The poor kid installed it and left it spinning after he left—slowly melting and splattering all over the room."

"Grisly," marveled Wasif. "Better than any of the books . . . Who else knows?"

"Just you, me, and the cat," said Edna. "This brilliant woman gave the world so many mysteries—shouldn't we let her keep one for herself?"

Wasif nodded and closed the manuscript.

"I'll tell you what," he said. "I'm so impressed, the water is on the house."

III.

THE HUMAN KABOOM
(the one with the stupid rock monsters)

illustrated by
RODOLFO MONTALVO

*K*ABOOM!

When the flaming meteor collided with Earth, the whole planet shook for a week. Entire cities crumbled to the ground. Tsunamis devastated the coasts. Ash and smoke choked the plains. But when the dust settled and the fires were extinguished, people thought the worst was over.

No one expected the rock monsters.

Before the meteor crash, people would joke about how a boulder looked like a head or a foot, or how the side of a hill looked like a giant creature, curled up and sleeping.

After the meteor crash, those same people were horrified to realize they'd been right all along. The cosmic impact awoke a race of ancient beings from hundreds of millions of years of subterranean slumber.

Entire mountain ranges yawned to life, blinked their eyes, and immediately began to destroy everything in sight.

Well, not exactly *immediately*.

Time passed differently for the rock monsters. The smallest ones lumbered about like tranquilized elephants (and were roughly the same size), while the largest ones (some so big they pierced the clouds) seemed to move in super-slow motion. Despite their lack of speed, their size and strength and vast numbers resulted in global chaos.

They smashed skyscrapers, busted bridges, and flattened forests. The rock monsters were impervious to bullets and fire. Sure, the military managed to blow up a few of them with missiles, but even still, people around the world were forced to flee for their lives, and civilization on Earth was changed forever.

Governments disbanded, leaders went into hiding, and armies turned on each other. Internet outages caused mass confusion and widespread panic.

But in the midst of the pandemonium, it was discovered that the rock monsters couldn't swim. In fact, they sank like . . . well, like stones.

It was a glimmer of hope in very dark times. So all the human beings who had survived the initial onslaught tried to escape to the sea.

Which is how Victoria, Isa, and Miguel Dewsberry found themselves charging toward the harbor, loaded with random survival supplies, unsure if they'd ever be able to go home again.

GARGANTUAN ROCK MONSTERS curled themselves into balls and rolled down streets, crushing trucks and pulverizing squishy humans by the dozen. People were shouting, car horns were blaring, and the three Dewsberry kids ran after their father as fast as they could, trying not to lose him in the crowd.

When they reached the harbor, they frantically searched the docks for a boat in working condition. Eventually, they found a little dinghy that no one had claimed. As their dad yanked the starter cord to get the engine going, Victoria, Isa, and Miguel climbed aboard.

Victoria was a high school water polo star, tall and muscular, with a pug nose and short hair. She had her mother's speckled green eyes and wide nose. She wore two backpacks stuffed with clothing and supplies she had prepared for the trip. Her younger sister, Isa, was wide-eyed, artistic, and observant. She had a heavy duffel slung over her shoulder and held a large box in her hands. Inside was a solar-powered water filtration system.

Their little brother, Miguel, was the youngest of the family. He had his father's freckles and big ears. Miguel still threw tantrums (despite the fact he was old enough to cross the monkey bars), and as they climbed into the boat, he was wailing. He'd abandoned his bags in a fit before reaching the harbor, and the only thing he'd brought with him was his baby blanket, which he carried everywhere.

"Please, calm down," pleaded their exhausted father.

But Miguel refused and continued bawling.

Victoria was used to her little brother's outbursts, but she had never seen her dad so upset. When the outboard motor finally roared to life, he did a celebration dance. But when a rock monster in the distance swatted a helicopter from the sky, his smile faded.

While Isa tried to soothe Miguel, their father took Victoria aside, gave her a hug, and tucked a blaster into her backpack. "Be careful," he whispered to his eldest daughter. "And take care of your brother and sister." It was only then that Victoria realized he was not coming with them.

"Where are you going, Daddy?" asked Isa. Somehow, she already knew.

"I'm going to find your mother," he said.

The last time they'd seen their mother, she was caring for patients at the hospital, and earlier that day, the whole medical building had been decimated by a boulder attack.

Miguel started wailing even louder. Their dad hugged them all one last time, then climbed out of the dinghy onto the dock.

"But where should we go?" asked Victoria, trying not to cry.

"Away," said her father, tears dripping down his cheeks. "Far away from here. As far away as possible."

"But I don't know how to drive a boat!"

"The handle controls the rudder to steer, the throttle

controls the speed," he explained as quickly as he could. "You can do this! Remember: Together you're stronger."

A barrage of stones rained down from above and smashed one of the other boats that was trying to escape.

"Go!" their father shouted, rushing to untie the rope that held the dinghy to the dock.

The waves from the hail of stones nearly tipped them into the water, but Victoria wrestled with the rudder until the front of the boat pointed away from the harbor, toward the open sea. She twisted the knob to full throttle, and the dinghy zoomed off at top speed.

They didn't get very far.

THE BOTTOM OF the boat scraped against some floating wreckage in the bay and started taking on water. Victoria managed to steer the boat to a tiny, deserted island less than a mile from shore. They disembarked in the shallows and pulled the dinghy up onto the beach.

They sat in the sand, watching the rock monsters annihilate their hometown. Towers crumbled to the ground. Bridges collapsed into the bay. The destructive rampage lasted throughout the night. Victoria, Isa, and Miguel watched it all without sleeping a wink.

When the sun rose the next morning, the shore was cloaked in an eerie silence. The rock monsters had retreated, and it finally dawned on the Dewsberry kids that they were on their own, with no parents or anyone else around to help.

Exhausted, they huddled together against the damaged boat and cried themselves to sleep.

VICTORIA WOKE A few hours later and found Miguel dozing in Isa's lap. Without waking her siblings, she crept off to take a look around. She climbed the hill that faced the beach. At the top, there was a small clearing surrounded by coconut trees. The island wasn't much bigger than a city block. The north side had steep cliffs, battered by violent tides, but the south side had a gentle slope and a peaceful, sheltered cove. The wreckage of ships and other smoking debris littered the harbor to the east, and a vast expanse of open water filled the horizon to the west.

Birds flocked overhead, and Victoria found herself wishing she had wings too.

Back on the beach, Miguel woke with a fright and clutched at his blankie. "Where's Vicky?"

"Shhh." Isa rubbed his head without opening her eyes.

"Vicky!" Miguel scrambled to his feet and cupped his hands to the sides of his mouth. "VICKY!"

"Don't call me Vicky!" shouted Victoria from the top of the hill.

Miguel whirled to spot his sister and started running toward the sound of her voice. "I'm coming!"

"Stay there, Gordo!"

"I'm coming. Hold on!"

"Stay there, I said!"

By the time Miguel reached the top of the hill, he was sweaty and covered in sand, his face streaked with tears.

"Don't sneak off like that!" He stamped his foot.

"I didn't sneak off," Victoria explained. "I'm doing reconnaissance."

"Re-conna-wha?"

"I'm looking around. I'm investigating." Victoria patted his head. "We might be here a while."

Isa climbed the hillside carrying a smooth black slab in her hand. "My meme stone stopped working."

Victoria pulled her own device from her backpack. It was also dead. "I think there might be network connectivity problems." She frowned at the flaming satellites that streaked across the sky.

Miguel eyed a large rock suspiciously and backed away from it. "Is it safe here?"

"I think so," said Victoria. She suddenly remembered the blaster in her backpack.

I hope so, she thought to herself.

Miguel kicked at a pile of pebbles. "How come only some of the rocks came to life?"

Isa raised the device in her hand to search for the answer to her brother's question (it was a good one). For as long as she could remember, she would receive an instant response to any query she might have had. But staring at the blank

face of the meme stone reminded her that things were different now. It also reminded her of something she had learned in science class years ago.

"There are three different kinds of rock . . ." she recalled. "Some are made from seashells and stuff . . . Some are made from volcanoes . . . And some are super old. Like, from before there were even seashells on Earth." She squeezed her eyes shut as she struggled to retrieve the details from her memory. "Ignoramus . . . Ignatius Reilly . . . IGNEOUS!"

Isa felt proud of herself for remembering the correct name, but this information did nothing to calm Miguel's frazzled nerves.

"Look." Isa picked up a pebble and smiled, to reassure her little brother. "I'm pretty sure all the ones that are gonna come alive already did. Don't worry."

Miguel took the pebble and tossed it aside. "What about Mom and Dad?" He felt himself starting to cry again.

"It's okay, Gordo," Isa said. "They've got each other. Mom is probably just trying to help as many people as she can. Dad will find her. They'll figure it out." She looked pleadingly at her older sister. "Right?"

Victoria stared out at the sea and said nothing.

THEY SEARCHED THE boat for anything useful and hauled their belongings up from the beach to the clearing at the top of the hill near the cove. Their hastily gathered supplies were limited: a Bic lighter, the solar-powered water filter, an emergency first-aid kit, a box of nutrient flake food rations, and a tackle box full of fishing supplies. Victoria and Isa had packed plenty of clothes. Miguel had only what he wore on his back.

As for communication, their meme stones were useless and the boat had no radio. They had no flares. They had no phone. They had no way to call for help, and no one knew where they were.

Or so they thought.

"LAAAAAAAAAND!"

The ground trembled, and the Dewsberry kids fell silent. The bellowing sounded like thunder, so loud they could feel the vibrations rattle up through the ground and into their bones.

"OOOFFFFFFFFFF!"

Miguel crouched down, expecting an earthquake. Victoria clutched her backpack with the blaster inside.

"ROOOOOOOOOCK!" The last word trumpeted forth with such power that coconuts fell from the trees.

"Stay here," Victoria whispered. She snuck down to the beach to investigate. When she broke through the under-brush and spilled onto the sand, she discovered the source of the ear-splitting noise.

Three rock monsters stood at the edge of the mainland facing the island. One was enormous, the size of an apartment building, and roughly rhinoceros-shaped, with four legs, a thick torso, and a giant horn. The middle one was the size of a house and almost human-shaped. It had two arms and two legs but no head—its face was in its chest. The smallest was just a boulder with a mouth and three eyes. It was looking straight at Victoria.

"LAND OF ROCK!" thundered the boulder monster.
Victoria quickly ducked behind a tree.

"TOO LATE, MEAT BAG! CHUNK SEE YOU!"

"LLLAAAAAAAAA . . ." the biggest rock monster began
to roar very, very slowly.

Chunk turned. "QUIET, CLIFF!"

"...AAANNNDDD..."

"CRAG ALREADY SAY THAT!"

"...OOOOOOFFFFFFFFFFFF..." Cliff droned on so loud the sound made waves across the bay.

Chunk rolled its eyes. "NOW WE WAIT."

"... RRROOOOOOOOOOOOOOCCCKKKK!" Cliff stopped bellowing and cracked a smile that took a full minute to spread across its face.

The enormous monster spoke and moved so slowly that Victoria's fear almost gave way to impatience.

"What's going on?" whispered Miguel as he stumbled onto the beach. Isa followed close behind.

"I told you to stay put!" hissed Victoria. "Hide!"

The kids peeked out from behind the tree as the terrifyingly slow monsters glared at them from across the water.

"ROCK! SMASH! MEAT!" The smallest monster bounced up and down, pulverizing the ground below.

The biggest monster's smile faded and turned angry. It stomped its feet and began to stampede toward the water, in excruciatingly slow motion.

"CLIFF, STOP!" warned Chunk. "CRAG, STOP CLIFF!"

Crag, the middle monster, tried to grab ahold of the enormous monster as it galloped into the sea, but Crag succeeded only in tripping and toppling over.

"CLIFF, NO! ROCK SINK!" Chunk rolled toward the water but retreated with fear as a wave crashed in. "AHHH! WATER BAD!"

"What's wrong with them?" asked Miguel.

"I think they're a little slow," said Isa. She watched as Cliff crashed into the sea and sank to the bottom of the bay.

"BLUBLUBLUB . . ." The slow-witted giant was trapped under the water by its own immensity.

"POOR CLIFF," sighed Chunk.

Crag was still reeling from the fall, slowly flailing its arms and legs like a hippo stuck in a vat of molasses.

"They're stupid!" marveled Miguel. His fear evaporated, and he stepped out from behind the tree. "Hey, stupid!" he shouted.

"Miguel, shhh!" hissed Victoria to no avail.

"Come and get me, rocks for brains!"

Crag grew angry and began to march toward the water's edge.

"CRAG! NO!" cautioned Chunk. "REMEMBER WHAT HAPPENED TO CLIFF?"

Crag thought for a few moments in silence.

"CLIFF SINK INTO SEA!" Chunk reminded him.

Crag finally remembered and nodded, ever so slowly.

Miguel turned to his sisters and shrugged.

Isa stepped out from behind the tree as well. "I think the bigger they are, the slower they are," she said.

"MORE MEAT!" Chunk stomped up and down with rage.

"You can't get us! Nanny nanny poo poo!" Miguel shook his butt at the rock monsters and stuck out his tongue.

"BLUBLUBLUB!" rumbled Cliff from deep beneath the waves.

"CRAG!" commanded Chunk. "THROW ROCK! SMASH MEAT!"

Crag swept its hand over the sand and picked up a large stone. The monster reared back, lifted its leg, and then lurched forward to hurl the stone across the bay.

The children's eyes went wide as the stone flew through the air toward the island.

They ran.

SPLOOSH!

The stone landed well short of the beach and crashed into the salty water.

"COBBLESTONES!" spat Chunk.

"Ha!" Miguel darted back out onto the beach. "You can't reach us!" He patted his behind and taunted the giant rocks.

"Stop that." Victoria shoved him to the sand and peered across the water to try to get a better look at the monsters. "You'll just make them angrier."

"Who cares? Those dum-dums are so dense they sink. They're too stupid to be scary."

Isa was amazed at how long it took Crag to realize it had missed. "They really are slow," she said.

"COBBLESTOOOOOOOOOONES!" muttered Crag.

"Let's go," announced Victoria. "They seem to be the only two left. Maybe they'll forget we're here. We have more important things to worry about right now, anyway."

"Like what?" asked Miguel.

"Like food." Victoria's stomach grumbled.

Victoria shimmied up a tree and knocked down some coconuts. But it wasn't so easy to get them out of their thick, heavy shells. Isa kept checking her meme stone for guidance. She knew it wasn't working but found it hard to break the habit. Eventually, she stashed it away in her backpack, and her pocket felt weirdly empty without the device inside.

They tried to crack open the tough green coconut husks by smashing them repeatedly against a jagged rock. It was very tiring work. Eventually, Victoria realized it was easier to keep the coconut still and drop the heaviest rock possible on top of it. This saved a ton of energy and made the job much quicker.

Once they had smashed and peeled off the green husk, they needed to reach the fruit inside the hairy brown shell. Isa found some scissors in the tackle box and poked through the bowling ball holes in the coconut so they could easily sip the liquid inside.

Miguel refused to drink the nutritious coconut water ("It tastes like feet!") or eat the sweet white flesh of the fruit ("Soggy Styrofoam!").

"Coconuts are gross," he insisted. He ripped open a packet of desiccated nutrient flakes, but unfortunately, the whole box was pumpkin-spice-flavored.

Instead, he collected a hatful of bright-red berries that

were growing on a bush nearby. They appeared to be sweet and delicious, but five minutes after eating them, Miguel was doubled over with painful cramps.

"Eat some coconut," suggested Victoria. "It might help calm your stomach."

Miguel groaned.

Isa rummaged through the first-aid kit. "Here, take these." She opened a packet of tummy tablets and handed the pills to her brother.

"I can't swallow pills," he protested.

"Just try," commanded Victoria. "Only babies can't swallow pills."

Miguel eyed the pink tablets in his hand. They seemed to grow bigger by the second. He popped them into his mouth and took a swig of water. He tried his best, but it felt like trying to swallow Ping-Pong balls. He choked, sputtered, and sprayed a bit of liquid from his nose.

"Tilt your head back," suggested Victoria.

He did, and a strong cough sent the two pills rocketing skyward.

Isa and Victoria fell about laughing.

"I wish I could've gotten that on video!" squealed Isa.

Victoria finally caught her breath and wiped the tears from her eyes. "You know those are chewable, right?"

THE SISTERS COLLECTED seawater and set up the solar filter in a nice sunny spot on the beach while Miguel recovered from his experiment with the poisonous berries. When the cramps had passed, he decided to examine the fishing equipment they had found in the boat. There was a long red pole and a box full of hooks, line, weights, and assorted colorful lures designed to look like things fish eat: shrimp, worms, flies, and other kinds of bugs.

Miguel had never been fishing before, but he had seen someone go fishing in a content clip once, and it didn't seem all that hard. He knew he had to bait the hook, and he knew he had to wait. Bait and wait. That was the sum of his knowledge on fishing. The rest he would have to discover by trial and error.

Normally, Miguel did not have the patience to learn how to do something he wasn't already good at, but he was highly motivated to experiment after eating two bags of dusty pumpkin-spice nutrient flakes. He'd added water to create a porridge-like substance, but the consistency did nothing to improve the flavor.

Miguel joined his sisters in the cove on the south side of the island. The water was crystal clear. He could see dancing bunches of seaweed, and the occasional curious crab scuttled by his feet. Crabs seemed way too close to bugs for Miguel to consider eating. Though Victoria was already busy thinking of ways to catch one for dinner.

After waiting for almost an hour, Miguel hadn't spotted a single fish in the cove. He picked up the fishing gear and began to hike up the hill away from the beach.

"Where are you going?" asked Victoria, splashing

through the water in an unsuccessful attempt to grab a crab.

"I'm gonna see if there are any fish on the other side of the island."

"Not by yourself, you're not. You can barely swim."

"I can too swim!" Miguel lied.

"I'll go with you," volunteered Isa.

"Fine," said Victoria. "But be careful." Her stomach rumbled with glee when she imagined eating fresh fish for dinner. As Miguel and Isa hiked away, Victoria stared into the water. Her hunger inspired an idea.

She yanked up a handful of seaweed and sniffed it optimistically.

MIGUEL AND ISA wriggled through the tangled jungle to reach the far side of the island. The underbrush was dense, and they couldn't see more than a few feet in any direction. They ducked under vines, hopped over fallen trees, and slowly made their way toward the sound of the sea, which grew louder and louder in the distance.

The jungle ended suddenly. Miguel and Isa found themselves standing at the edge of a cliff, which plunged to the water below. Massive waves crashed hard against the jagged rocks. It seemed nearly impossible that any fish could be swimming in the churning surf without getting spun around like a doll in a washing machine. But Miguel was insistent they go investigate more closely.

The cliff was steep, but it looked like there were plenty of little platforms and sturdy handholds, and it seemed possible to make it to the water without too much danger. Miguel got on his belly, dangled his feet over the ledge, and found his footing. He lowered himself and began to descend. Isa followed close behind.

Tiny lizards darted under rocks as the two kids slowly, carefully climbed all the way down to the sea. There was no beach. The water came right up to the cliff. But Miguel spotted a shallow area, waited for a wave to pass, then dropped into the water.

"Be careful," urged Isa.

"Don't worry!" Miguel acted confident, but despite what he'd told Victoria, he had never actually finished learning how to swim. Luckily, the water was only chest deep.

At first, he planned to wade out to a big rock a bit farther out from the cliff. But a swell dunked his head, and when he resurfaced, he eyed the sea with renewed distrust. Powerful waves pounded the rock he had previously considered. He hurried through the shallows and climbed atop a smaller rock closer to the bottom of the cliff.

"Maybe I'll just fish from here," he said.

"Good idea," said Isa.

Miguel opened up the tackle box that held the fishing supplies. He had no idea what he was looking at. Isa offered several helpful suggestions, but Miguel refused to accept any advice.

To catch a fish, all you really need is a line, a lure, and a hook. But Miguel did not know that. He didn't even know how to tie a proper knot. So he overcompensated. He tied three hooks and ten different colored lures to the line. He used five knots for each one to be sure that nothing fell off.

Miguel swung the pole backward and nearly caught the tangle of hooks in Isa's hair.

"Watch where you're swinging!" she shouted, ducking out of the way.

"Sorry," he muttered.

Miguel stood at the edge of the flat-topped rock and tried to keep his distance from his sister, who crouched low on the other side. He swung the pole forward as hard as he could and accidentally let the thing slip from his wet hands. The pole landed with a plop in the water below.

"Cobblestones!"

"Oh no! That's our only pole!" squealed Isa. "I'll swim out and get it."

But before she could dive in, a huge wave snapped the pole in half against a rock.

A gaggle of seagulls swirling above them seemed to laugh.

KA! KA! KA!

"Don't tell Vicky!" pleaded Miguel.

Isa sighed. "Okay, well, maybe we don't need the pole anyway." She poked at the contents of the tackle box. "There's plenty of line left, and whatever these things are." She held up what looked like a pair of shimmering earrings.

A big pelican swooped down and scared the gulls from the rocks. A silvery fish poked its head from the pelican's beak before being swallowed whole.

"Look," Miguel said. "There are definitely fish in there."

He cut off a length of fishing line with the scissors and attached a hook and a weight (only one of each this time, just in case he dropped them again). He swung the fishing line like a lasso and tossed it out into the surf, aiming for the spot below the circling gulls.

Isa got bored waiting and busied herself hopping from rock to rock along the shore, collecting pretty pebbles and shells.

Miguel fished for hours but caught nothing.

WHEN MIGUEL AND Isa returned from their trip empty-handed, Victoria decided to try and stay positive. She had built a blazing fire while they were gone. The coconut husks burned very well. She had found a discarded metal crate washed onto the beach and propped it over the flames like a soup pot.

"Look what I made." She picked up a hollow coconut shell and scooped it full of steaming green broth. She handed the makeshift bowl to Isa along with two twigs to use as chopsticks. "Seaweed stew!"

Isa sipped the broth and then munched on some of the boiled leaves.

"It's really good!" she proclaimed.

At that point, Miguel was too hungry to be picky anymore. They all sat around the fire and slurped ravenously. They could feel the vitamins and minerals restoring the energy in their bodies. It was the first hot meal the kids had enjoyed since landing on the island, and although Miguel was adamant in his belief that "vegetables are gross," even he had to admit that the seaweed stew was pretty darn tasty.

They each ate three bowls.

After dinner, they lay on their backs staring at the stars. Isa began to hum their mother's favorite song, and Victoria soon joined in singing:

"Flash light, red light, neon light, ooh, stop light."

An explosion in the distance startled them into silence.

"We've gotta get out of here." Miguel sat up. "We've got to go find Mom and Dad."

"We're safer here," Victoria said, trying to convince herself. "If we set off in the boat, we might starve. Here, at least we've got coconuts and seaweed."

"And fish," added Isa. "It's only a matter of time till you figure out how to catch 'em. Right, Gordo?"

"I don't want gross island food. I want a cheeseburger." Miguel pouted.

"Come on, Gordo," Isa cooed. "That seaweed stew was good—admit it."

Miguel stood up. "I'm sick of this place. Are we just gonna wait here to die?"

"Shut up!" Victoria threw a coconut shell at him, but he ducked out of the way.

"Ow!" cried Miguel.

"It didn't even hit you!"

"Don't fight!" pleaded Isa. "Vicky has a plan. We just have to be patient. Right?"

"Don't call me Vicky!" Victoria hugged her knees to her chest. "We can't go anywhere until you-know-who learns to swim."

"I know how to swim!" Miguel threw his hands in the air, exasperated.

"We'll see tomorrow." Victoria stood up and walked down to the beach to be by herself.

Isa retrieved the coconut-shell bowl from the ground.

"I hate her so much," Miguel growled.

"Aw, don't say that. She's just trying to protect you."

"Do you really think she'll make me swim tomorrow?"

"You've gotta learn sometime." Isa tugged his big ears playfully. "Plus, it might help you with your fishing."

THE NEXT MORNING, the water in the cove was calm and cold.

"It's freezing!" complained Miguel as he waded in up to his knees. He had stripped down to his boxer shorts and left his blankie on the beach. Victoria wore a swimsuit and cap she had brought to keep up with her training. She ran into the water and started doing the backstroke. Miguel watched his sister swim away from him with alarming speed.

"It's not so bad once you get used to it. Dunk your head under!" shouted Victoria from a distance before disappearing below the surface. Miguel didn't have time to panic before she popped up right in front of him and spit an arc of seawater onto his head. "There ya go."

"Gross!" Miguel wiped the water from his face and splashed her.

"I'm just trying to help!" Victoria laughed and took him by the hand. "Come on, show me how you tread water."

"How deep are we going to go?" Miguel stepped gingerly as the slippery seabed squished between his toes. Behind him, Isa gathered clumps of seaweed from below the water.

"Don't worry," Victoria said. "I'm right here with you. Doggy-paddle. Come on, it's easy."

Miguel began to tread water, but his movements were frantic. He looked panicked.

"Relax, you don't have to paddle so fast. You'll tire yourself out. Just go slow. Remember, you float good 'cause you're chubby."

"Hey!" Miguel swallowed a mouthful of salty water. He coughed and started to sink. Victoria slipped her arm around his waist and lifted him up.

"Look, lean back." She let her feet bob to the surface and floated with her face to the sky. Miguel did the same. "See? Easy. No effort at all. Just breathe slow."

Miguel took a deep breath and found himself floating a
little higher in the water. He breathed out and started to
sink again, which scared him. He kicked his legs.

"*Cálmate*, relax . . ." Victoria put an arm under his head
as they rocked in the gentle waves. "You can do this."

Miguel let his body go limp and took another deep

breath. He felt the water embrace him and hold him up, even as his sister let him go.

"See? You're doing it all by yourself now."

"I told you I could swim."

"Floating is not swimming, but Dewsberrys are quick learners. Dad always says that. Or at least, he used to."

Miguel closed his eyes and thought of his parents. "Do you think we'll ever see them again?"

"I don't know," said Victoria. "I hope so."

Miguel began to cry silently. He dipped his chin below the water so the sea would swallow his tears. Victoria pretended not to notice.

They swam back to the beach and lay in the sand watching clouds go by.

Isa was busy arranging driftwood to spell out *HELP!* in giant letters.

"What if I forget their faces?" said Miguel quietly.

Victoria put her arm around her little brother and hugged him close.

"You won't," she assured him. "I'll remind you."

THE DEWSBERRY SIBLINGS decided that if they were going to be stuck on an island for a while, they may as well be comfortable.

They collected moss, palm fronds, and vines from all around the island. Victoria worked as quickly as possible to arrange three "mattresses." The piles of moss and leaves were much softer and warmer than the rocky ground in the clearing.

The girls braided the vines into strong rope. Miguel tried to learn their technique, but his stubby fingers weren't as nimble as his older sisters', so he was tasked with gathering stones to surround the firepit.

Isa figured out a way to weave strips of palm leaves together. She made a basket, which she planned to use for collecting seaweed. But Victoria was intent on eating crab and suggested the basket be used as a trap.

They took turns splashing through the shallows of the cove, but catching a speedy crab was very tricky, and removing one from the trap without getting pinched was nearly impossible.

Victoria rubbed the pinch marks on her fingers as an angry crab scuttled away into the safety of the surf.

"They really don't want to be eaten," observed Miguel. "Pointy claws and rock-hard shells—how would you even chew it?"

"The inside is buttery-soft and delicious," said Isa. "Crab is a delicacy!"

"What's a 'delicacy'?" asked Miguel.

"A special fancy food," said Victoria.

Miguel laughed. "I can just imagine people in tuxedos and gowns with crabs pinched onto their tongues."

The girls giggled.

"I am getting a little bored of seaweed stew and coconuts," Isa complained.

"There's always more nutrient flakes," noted Victoria.

"Ugh, Vicky. That's not what I meant."

"Victoria," she said, correcting her sister.

"Don't worry," Miguel added brightly. "We'll be eating fish for dinner tonight."

"You feeling lucky, Gordo?" Victoria snickered.

Miguel hadn't caught a single fish yet, and his sisters were skeptical that he ever would.

MIGUEL SCRAMBLED HALFWAY down the cliff wearing nothing but his Batman boxer shorts. The fishing line was looped over his shoulder, and his blankie was tied around his neck like a cape.

Isa followed after him while Victoria stayed on the other side of the island, chasing after crabs.

"The waves are much bigger today!" shouted Isa over the roar of the sea. "This seems dangerous."

Miguel threw his head back with a big fake laugh. "Ha! Danger is my middle name."

"Your middle name is Guadalupe."

Undaunted, Miguel pointed at the birds circling patiently above the water. "They know where the fish are."

He baited his hook with a worm he'd found under a rock and then tossed the line as far out into the water as he could. It landed with a tiny splash right under the swirling birds.

"Nice one!" said Isa, cheering him on. She felt the urge

to record the moment, but only after she reached into her empty pocket did she remember she'd left the long-dead meme stone back at camp.

Miguel sat down and crossed his legs. Isa strained to keep sight of the line in the crashing waves.

"What do we do now?" she asked.

"Now we play the waiting game."

Five minutes later, he finally broke the silence. "The waiting game stinks. Let's play Bear, Ninja, Cowboy."

After a few rounds, they pulled in the line to find the bait still on the hook.

"Maybe these fish don't eat worms." Miguel stuck out his tongue. "I don't blame them."

"Don't the big fish eat smaller fish?" Isa drew pictures of a fish in the sand with a stick. "Why don't you use a little fish as bait?"

"I can't catch any fish! That's why!"

"You just haven't caught any yet. If the birds can do it, a human can do it too. Give it one more try. If it doesn't work, maybe Vicky had some luck with the crabs."

"Sea bugs," muttered Miguel.

"They're delicious! I'm telling you. I ate one once."

"Gross!"

Isa laughed.

Miguel spit into his hand and rubbed his palms together.

"Gross!" squealed Isa.

Miguel swung the line in a circle over his head, faster

and faster, as hard as he could. He locked his eyes on the spot below the birds and then tossed the hook with all his might.

WHISH!

The hook flew through the air, pulling the line behind it.

SPLISH!

The hook landed in the water and sank below the surface.

PIP!

The line went taut. Miguel was so surprised he nearly let it go.

"I got a bite!" He wrapped the line around his hand and tugged. The force on the other end of the line pulled him forward, and he nearly stumbled to his knees. "Help!"

Isa jumped up to reach her brother. She wrapped the line around her drawing stick and handed it to Miguel. Then she wrapped her arms around his waist and leaned back for extra weight.

"It's so strong! It must be a huge fish!" Miguel furiously wound the line around the stick.

"Mmm," Isa said. "I can almost taste the fish already."

"Uh-oh," gasped Miguel. "It's not a fish."

A furious seagull burst out of the water and into the air, pulling the line with it. The hook was lodged in its beak. The bird screeched and flapped its wings violently, nearly lifting Miguel into the air. Isa hung on tight.

"What do I do?" shouted Miguel.

"Reel it in!" shouted Isa.

So he did. But as he wrapped the line around the stick, the bird grew closer and closer, angrier and angrier. It swooped to attack, wings flapping, beak pecking.

"Ahhh!" shrieked Miguel as he dropped the stick to cover his head with his hands.

Isa grabbed the stick and held it like a baseball bat.

WHAM!

THAT NIGHT, THE Dewsberry kids had a joyous feast.

Isa and Miguel spent all afternoon plucking the feathers from the bird, and Victoria used the scissors from the tackle box to cut open the belly and remove the organs. Miguel planned to use the guts for fish bait. Isa planned to use the feathers for necklaces.

Victoria built an extra-large fire to roast the gull. They waited until the meat was juicy and the skin was crunchy. Then they split the bird into pieces and served it on palm-frond plates.

"Sorry, bird," said Isa as she prepared to dig in.

"Thank you, bird," said Victoria as she savored a mouthful.

Miguel happily gnawed at a drumstick bone. "I love you, bird!" he shouted at the top of his lungs.

"QUIET, MEAT STICK!" roared Chunk from across the bay.

The kids chuckled quietly while they ate.

IN THE MORNING, Miguel and Victoria woke up with a shock.

Isa was screaming.

Her body thrashed violently on top of her moss mattress, and her legs kicked out in all directions. Miguel and Victoria leapt out of their beds and rushed to her side.

"Isa, wake up!" Victoria tried to give her sister a comforting hug without getting kicked or punched in the process. Isa's eyes rolled back in her head.

"Isa!" Miguel helped Victoria wrangle her spasming arms and legs.

Suddenly, Isa's eyes blinked hard, and she regained consciousness. "What happened?" she asked. Her heart was pounding.

"You had a bad dream." Miguel stepped back. "It was scary."

"That's so weird. I don't remember anything."

"I don't think it was a bad dream." Victoria grew serious. "I think it was a seizure."

"Really?" said Isa.

"What's a seizure?" asked Miguel.

"It's when your body goes out of control," said Victoria. "Something happens in your brain."

"Cool!" said Miguel.

"Not cool," Victoria scolded.

"I've never had a seizure before," said Isa. "Are you sure?"

"I saw it in a meme once. It's a neurological anomaly."

"You made that up," said Miguel.

"No." Victoria looked worried. "This is serious. There's medicine for it, but we don't have any."

Isa sat up. "Don't worry, Vicky . . . toria. I'm fine. It's over now."

Victoria put on her grown-up face. "No. Lie down. You need rest. What would have happened if you were in the cove collecting seaweed? You could have drowned!"

Isa laughed. "You're overreacting. I'm fine. It was probably just a one-time thing. Maybe my body wasn't ready for a bird feast."

"Your body is stupid." Miguel rubbed his belly. "That bird was delicious."

Isa massaged her skull, then measured her pulse on her wrist. "I'm fine." She yawned and stretched her arms over her head. "Sorry I scared you guys. It won't happen ag— AAHCK!"

Isa's eyes rolled back in her head, and Victoria caught her before she fell. Isa started writhing and foaming at the mouth. Victoria lowered her to the ground gently.

"Isa!" Miguel dropped to his knees and cradled his sister's head in his hands.

Victoria was terrified. It was her job to protect her family, and she felt powerless.

"Do something!" cried Miguel. Isa continued to wriggle in his arms.

Victoria could almost see her mom and dad shaking

their heads with disappointment. She wanted to run and hide. She closed her eyes and screamed.

Miguel yelped, startled by her sudden outburst. Isa kept convulsing and began to drool.

Finally, Victoria snapped into action.

"Turn her on her side." She folded Miguel's blankie and placed it under her sister's head. She brushed the hair from Isa's eyes as the convulsing began to subside and she blinked back into awareness.

"Isa?" Miguel was still covering his ears.

Isa sighed. "It happened again, didn't it?"

"You almost hit your head." Victoria petted her sister's hair.

"We need to go for help," said Miguel.

"No," said Victoria. "It's too dangerous."

"But—"

"Miguel!" Victoria's face went red. "Just shut up! We have to take care of Isa right now. We're not going anywhere!"

Miguel went quiet. Isa pleaded with him with her eyes.

"Fine," he said. "You stay here. I'll go down to the beach to fetch her some water from the filter."

Ten minutes later, Miguel had not returned. When Victoria went looking for him, she saw the dinghy was missing.

THE TINY BOAT bobbed up and down in the waves beyond the cove. Water was seeping in through the crack in the bottom, and Miguel couldn't get the engine started, but he still had the oars and he figured if he rowed hard enough, he could reach the shore before the dinghy sank. His arms were already burning from exertion.

"The rock monsters are too slow to catch me," Miguel said out loud, trying to convince himself. "I'll run for help. I'll find Mom and Dad. I'll find a cheeseburger . . ."

A wave crashed over the dinghy and sprayed Miguel in the eyes. He flinched and almost let go of one of the oars by mistake. The bottom of the boat was flooded with an ankle-deep pool of water.

"MIGUEL GUADALUPE DEWSBERRY!" shrieked Victoria so loud she surprised herself. She lowered her voice a few octaves in an attempt to sound more intimidating. "GET YOUR CHUBBY BUTT BACK HERE RIGHT NOW!"

Miguel turned to find his sister running into the surf. He rowed faster.

Victoria dove under the waves and kicked her legs hard. She was a strong swimmer, and the sinking boat wasn't moving very fast with a young boy manning the oars. Miguel tried his hardest, but soon his sister had caught up with him. She reached out of the water and clung to the side of the dinghy. Miguel smacked her hand.

"OWWW!" yelled Victoria. "You little brat, I'm gonna drown you!" She rocked the boat hard, then swam underneath and climbed up the other side while Miguel was off-balance.

"You . . ." growled Victoria, sopping wet, looking more like a crazed beast than a teenage girl. Miguel scrambled backward to the far end of the dinghy. Victoria stalked toward him slowly. "You selfish little . . . stupid little . . . fat little baby!" She pounced.

Miguel screeched.

First, she got him in a headlock. Then he bit her arm. Next, the boat began to tip, and before either of them knew what was happening, they were both upside down in the bay.

Victoria surfaced first. She gasped, treaded water, and coughed seawater from her lungs. "Miguel!" She raged and thrashed in the waves. "Miguel?" She twisted around in search of her little brother. The boat had flipped over and was sinking fast. The tow rope floated toward her, and she grabbed it to keep the boat from washing out to sea. "Miguel!"

Miguel was struggling to keep his head above the water. He was gulping mouthfuls of salty brine, and as panic set in, his swimming techniques flew out of his mind. He sank below the waves with his eyes wide open, wishing he could convince his arms to do something helpful. Instead, they floated uselessly in front of him.

He was stunned by this sudden turn of events, that he, a newly expert swimmer, was about to drown.

The last thing he remembered was sitting on the seabed, admiring the beautiful way the sunbeams danced through the water above his head. The vision was hypnotic, and soon Miguel was lulled into a vivid dream.

AT THE BEGINNING of time, Rock was the sole inhabitant of a land forged in fire and covered in ice.

Rock ruled alone for ages and ages. And then ages more. But slowly, the land grew warmer, and Water was released from its frozen slumber. Water trickled throughout the land. Then splashed. Then crashed. Rock tried to defend the land, but Water flowed under, around, and through.

Before long, Water flooded half the planet. It ran below the ground. It fell from the sky. Rock was furious, and also terrified. But Rock still ruled the land. Or what was left of it.

But one day, Water gave birth to Plant. A tiny floating thing at first, Plant grew bigger and sprouted roots, which burrowed deep and crumbled Rock. Water nourished Plant, and together they transformed the land into soil. Plant flourished far and wide, and the once-barren land became green.

The age of life had begun, and Rock had no choice but to hide. So Rock slept and waited in secret. For ages and ages.

And then ages more.

Until a new age came when the land was barren once again. Plant had grown sick and weak. Water had been poisoned. It was then that Rock returned.

Rock awoke with a fiery vengeance. Explosions of ancient lava swallowed Water and scorched Plant. Rock roared and raged, leaving nothing but flame and destruction in its path.

Once Water had retreated and Plant had been defeated, Rock released a victorious roar so powerful it shook the land. But Rock's celebration was premature, and it soon discovered a bewildering new foe . . .

"MEAT!" CALLED CHUNK from the shore across the bay.

Miguel snorted, and a splash of the sea sprayed from his nostrils. He lay on his side, with his oldest sister kneeling over him, panting with exhaustion. He coughed up a bucket of salt water onto the sand.

"Finally," Victoria grunted.

"You saved me," Miguel whimpered.

"I almost decided not to." Victoria struggled to her feet.

"I'm sorry." Miguel curled into a ball of shame. "I just wanted to help."

"MEAT, COME HERE!" bellowed Chunk. Crag waved, trying to appear friendly.

"Shut up!" shouted Victoria. She made every obscene gesture she could think of, then turned and slapped her butt for good measure.

Isa came running down the hill toward the beach.

"What happened to the boat?" She was still disoriented from the seizure.

Victoria could just barely see the tip of the dinghy sinking into the waves. "The boat is gone."

Miguel grabbed a handful of sand and felt the tiny granules slip through his fingers.

"I'm sorry," he whispered.

"You're sorry?!" Victoria's eyes were wild.

"Calm down," urged Isa. She picked up Miguel's blanket from the sand and offered it to him.

"NO!" raged Victoria. "I will not calm down! This selfish little baby nearly got us both killed, and now we're stranded with no boat, no parents, no nothing!" She glared at Miguel as she violently snatched the blanket from Isa's hand. "When are you going to grow up?!"

Victoria ripped the blanket in half. The worn threads tore like paper. Isa tried to stop her, but Victoria pushed her to the sand. She shredded the fabric until the blanket was in tatters. Miguel wailed in anguish.

The frenzy left Victoria dizzy. Her siblings sobbed quietly, and she found herself disgusted with them. She stormed off.

"Vicky, wait!" Isa ran after her, leaving Miguel alone on the beach.

He cried even harder then. He flopped on his belly, pounded the sand, and kicked his feet. He knew it was childish to throw a tantrum, but he was overwhelmed with sorrow, anger, and fear, and he decided to let it all out since no one was watching.

Or so he thought.

"ROCK! SMASH! MEAT!" said Chunk, startling Miguel from his tantrum.

"LAAAAAAAAND OOOFFFFFFFF ROOOOOOOOOCK!" Crag threw its hands to the sky.

"LAND OF ROCK!" echoed Chunk, caught up in the enthusiasm.

Crag bent down slowly, picked up a boulder, and launched it toward the island.

Miguel watched the rock splash into the water only halfway across the channel. It landed just short of the dinghy, which had already sunk beneath the waves.

AT FIRST, VICTORIA was so angry with Miguel she couldn't even look at him, let alone speak to him. She felt her scalp tingle with rage anytime he was nearby.

But soon, fear began to nibble at her fury.

Without the dinghy, they really were stranded. Despite the giant letters Isa had spelled out on the beach, no one was coming to help. Like it or not, Victoria was responsible for her younger siblings, no matter how bratty or infuriating—or mysteriously ill—they might be. That last thought, more than any other, sent a cold shiver of terror down Victoria's spine. She tried not to dwell on it.

At sunrise each morning, before her siblings were awake, Victoria would go for a swim to clear her head. She would breaststroke at racing speed, kicking her feet and sweeping her arms with all her might. She would swim away from the island as fast as she could, for as long as she could, before she reached the point of total exhaustion. Some days, she fantasized about swimming all the way back to the mainland, leaving her brother and sister behind on the island.

But most days, when she had reached her physical limit, lungs burning, muscles aching, she would simply stop in the middle of the bay, turn over to float on her back, and surrender to the waves.

Floating in the sea was a kind of meditation for Victoria. The sensation of riding the swells up and down calmed her. It required no effort, no responsibility, no planning, no worrying . . . Somehow, the tremendous power of the sea released her from her stress. Every muscle in her body relaxed, and that allowed her troubled mind to do the same.

ISA WOULD PREPARE breakfast while her sister was out swimming. After the second seizure, Victoria had forbidden her from climbing trees to fetch coconuts or wading through the cove to collect seaweed. It was too dangerous, Victoria said. If Isa had another attack, she could fall and break her neck or collapse into the water and drown. Isa didn't want to argue. There was already too much tension between her hardheaded siblings, who were far more similar than they were willing to admit.

Isa filled her newfound free time with foraging and crafts. At first, she mainly searched the island for colorful flowers to decorate her hair (and, much to his dismay, Miguel's as well). She collected enough colored pebbles to make a crude backgammon board. She wove loose blankets from palm fronds to keep them all cozy while they slept. But the more Isa explored the island, the more she began to notice little details that she'd previously ignored.

For example, none of the animals ate the red berries that had made Miguel sick, but other bushes grew berries that attracted hungry little birds. Isa sampled one or two of those same fruits herself to see if they were safe to eat. Some turned out to be quite tasty. When she started looking more closely, she discovered nibble marks on the leaves of certain plants. She wasn't sure what sorts of creatures were munching on them, but she knew it meant those plants could be edible. After careful experimentation, crunchy salads became a daily staple at mealtimes. She even concocted a primitive tea from a blend of aromatic leaves.

Isa's patient observations revealed mushrooms, wild onions, and eventually, the critters who enjoyed the native vegetation as much as she did. A family of little brown mice.

At first, the mice were skittish. But after sharing many berries, Isa gained their confidence, and one mouse in particular became curious, almost friendly. She named him Weenus.

"Yuck! Get that thing away from our food!" shouted Victoria when she returned from her morning swim and spotted Weenus sitting on a stump, watching Isa stir an onion-mushroom stew. The mouse scampered off into the bushes.

"Aw, you scared him," scolded Isa.

"It's a *rodent*, Isa. Gross."

The shouting roused Miguel from his slumber, which was surprising because he normally slept more deeply than a comatose hog. He stretched and yawned as he crawled out from under his palm-frond blanket.

"Good morning, Isa," said Miguel, ignoring his oldest sister. He and Victoria were still not on speaking terms. He leaned over the metal crate that served as their cook pot and inhaled. He greatly appreciated his sister's efforts to improve the island cuisine. The food was much tastier since she'd started adding salt that the solar filter had removed from the seawater.

Miguel sloppily slurped down his breakfast while Victoria glared at him, her face twisted with disgust. Miguel smacked his lips with great satisfaction, just to irk his oldest sister even further. Then he clasped his hands with gratitude and gave Isa a kiss on the forehead.

"Thank you so much, sister," he said with exaggerated sincerity. "I love you."

Victoria fumed.

Isa pushed her brother away, well aware he was only being sweet to get on Victoria's nerves.

MIGUEL SLUNK OFF to the north side of the island, leaving his two sisters alone. Victoria added more coconut husks to the fire while Isa finished her breakfast.

"What's he do over there all day?" Victoria asked. "I don't like him going off by himself."

"He's fishing," Isa replied. "Or trying to anyway."

"No." Victoria pointed to the tackle box by Miguel's bed. "He hasn't taken that stuff with him all week."

"Oh, don't worry. He's not a baby anymore."

"Is that right?" Victoria remembered the torn-up blanket and felt a pang of guilt. "'Cause he's still acting like a spoiled little brat."

"Maybe you could make up. Just tell him you're sorry."

"I'm sorry? *I'm* sorry?! I'm not the one who sank the boat and nearly got himself killed. I saved his life, and I'm the one who should be sorry?!"

"Never mind. Forget I said anything." Isa made herself some tea. "But I do wonder what he's doing out there by himself."

Victoria sat down to braid vines into rope. She was planning to make a ladder for collecting coconuts. Isa came over to help. After a few minutes of working in silence, Victoria spoke softly. "This reminds me of how Mom used to braid our hair."

Isa laughed. "She was terrible at it!"

"She really was." Victoria tried to smile, but there was

sadness in her face. "Sometimes I worry I'll forget what she looked like."

Isa leaned over and stroked her sister's head. "We'll see her again. Don't worry. You worry too much."

Victoria choked up. She pretended to find something interesting in the clouds, and turned away so Isa wouldn't see her eyes glazed with tears. Isa threw her arm around her sister and kissed her head.

"It's okay," she whispered. "Let it out."

Victoria wept gently and felt great relief that her little brother wasn't around to see it.

MIGUEL WAS BUSY fishing. Or trying to anyway.

It's hard to learn anything without a good teacher, and Miguel was on his own. He had tried and failed a thousand times to catch a fish, and a thousand times he had wished for someone who knew what they were doing to come along and show him what he was doing wrong. On the thousand and first try, Miguel had a breakthrough.

As his hook splashed into the sea under the swirling birds, he realized that he was surrounded by fishing experts. They just happened to have wings and beaks. Miguel couldn't fly, but he did think of a way to attack the fish from above—just like the birds.

He used the scissors to carve a pointy spear from a stick of bamboo. The spear was strong, light, and super sharp. He would have loved to brag about the tool to his sisters, but they would have asked too many questions, told him it was too dangerous. Miguel knew his new approach was risky, but he was determined to prove he was not just some helpless little kid.

Spearfishing is different from line fishing. It requires much closer proximity to the fish. Miguel carefully waded out to the rocks that protruded from the water beyond the breaking waves. Victoria had taught him how to dive under the swells, and he tried to follow her instructions, but he still got water up his nose.

The important thing was that he hung on to the spear and managed to reach a flat rock. He hoisted himself up the side and perched on top, with his spear at the ready.

At first, he tried throwing the spear, but each time he missed, he had to jump into the water and swim out to retrieve the floating stick of bamboo. Next, he tried jabbing the spear, but the fish were too fast. By the time the pointy tip of his weapon hit the water, the fish had already escaped.

Miguel watched the birds carefully. They didn't always strike successfully either, which made him feel a little better. Even the experts missed from time to time.

After a week of failure, Miguel made a very important observation: The birds didn't strike directly at the fish; they aimed at an empty spot in the water. They anticipated where the fish were going.

Miguel studied his prey for hours. He paid careful attention to how the fish darted and dodged out of the way to avoid getting gobbled by the hungry birds. They never moved backward. They tended to follow the group.

Miguel tried to think like a fish and act like a bird.

He sat perched on top of his rock, deep in concentration, waiting for the perfect moment . . .

SPLISH!

He jabbed the spear into the water speedy-quick—just ahead of a fish. Suddenly, the spear was heavy. A wiggling fish was impaled on the tip, and when Miguel lifted it from the water, he was filled with such triumphant joy he couldn't help but shout at the top of his lungs.

"Booyah!" The fish nearly wriggled free. "Oh, no, you don't!" Miguel changed his grip and pinned the fish to the rock with his spear.

But his happiness faded when he remembered how far he was from the island. There was no way to swim back without losing his catch. Miguel punched the rock with frustration.

"Ow!"

Hungry birds started circling his head.

"Hey, get out of here!" He waved his arm, and the birds squawked as they dispersed. He could almost hear them saying, "Well, if you're not gonna eat that fish, we will!"

He glanced jealously at a bird picking apart a fish carcass on a nearby rock. "You birds are lucky you don't have to cook your food."

The bird looked up, shrugged, and continued eating.

Miguel held the slippery fish to his chest to protect it from the would-be thieves in the air. It had been days since he'd had any protein, and he was salivating at the thought of a hearty meal. He licked his lips.

"I can't believe I'm doing this," he muttered. Then he took a big bite out of the silvery flesh of the fish.

He squeezed his eyes shut and began to chew.

"Mmm," he mumbled with his mouth full. "Pretty good." The raw fish tasted kind of like a sardine sandwich, without the bread. He devoured almost all of it but decided to leave some behind as a gift for his teachers, the birds. They squawked their thanks and squabbled over who got first dibs.

Miguel felt reinvigorated. He patted his spear proudly and licked his lips. Then he waited fifteen minutes before swimming back to the cliff. After all, he had just finished eating and he didn't want to get a cramp.

"WHAT ARE YOU grinning about?" asked Isa over dinner that night as they sat around the fire.

"Oh, nothing." Miguel was eating his salad with twig chopsticks.

Victoria eyed her brother suspiciously. "Must be nice to screw around all day and not help with any of the chores."

Miguel scoffed. "Isa," he said sweetly, "will you ask Vicky if she needs any help . . . yanking the stick out of her butt?"

Victoria growled. "I wonder what your leg will taste like roasted over the fire."

"Get bent!" Miguel tossed his coconut-shell bowl at Victoria and escaped into the darkness.

"Come back here, you spoiled brat!" She chased after him into the trees, but he knew the path to the north side of the island much better than she did, and soon, she'd lost sight of him.

Victoria returned to camp and ignored Isa's attempts to calm her. She stormed off to the cove to be alone. She hadn't been on the beach at night since they first landed on the island. Most days when the sun went down, she was so exhausted from collecting food, supplies, and water she fell asleep before the stars came out.

She sat in the sand and buried her bare feet. Then she looked up at the sky and tried to find a familiar constellation. But as she was staring out into the cosmos, she noticed an unusual light flashing in the distance. It was too close to the horizon to be a star and too far out in the water to be coming from the shore.

Victoria got excited. She thought it might be a boat. She ran around the beach, trying to gather enough wood to make a bonfire to attract attention. Maybe someone would come and rescue them! But after a while, she realized that the light wasn't moving. It couldn't be a boat. No one was coming to rescue them.

They had no choice but to rescue themselves.

ISA WAS HUNTING for mushrooms under a log when Victoria approached her with a plan.

"Don't tell Gordo." Victoria made her promise.

"I won't," swore Isa.

Not five minutes later, Miguel approached Isa with a secret plan of his own.

"Don't tell Vicky," he whispered, glancing over his shoulder to make sure his oldest sister wasn't anywhere nearby.

"I won't," swore Isa. She couldn't help but crack a smile.

"What are you grinning about?" asked Miguel.

"Oh, nothing," said Isa.

FOR ALMOST A week, Isa's two siblings were so engrossed in their own secret plans that they never noticed she was playing double agent. She would help one in the morning, then go "rest" for a while so she could help the other.

It was impossible for Isa not to notice their similarities. Victoria and Miguel both focused like a laser to the exclusion of all logic or reason. Both were racked with guilt over a "mistake" they had made and obsessed with redeeming themselves in the eyes of the other. And of course, both were so donkey-dang stubborn that, to them, every helpful suggestion felt like an insult.

"I think it might be easier if you try it this way," Isa offered sweetly.

"I know that," grumbled Miguel. "Let me do it."

"Maybe it will be stronger if you do it crosswise," Isa proposed gently.

"I know that," said Victoria. "I'll do it. You rest."

"Don't tell Vicky," said Miguel. "I want to surprise her in the morning."

"Don't tell Gordo," said Victoria. "We'll show him tomorrow."

And so Isa laughed with great relief when they both woke up the next day and said in unison: "Come with me. I want you to see something."

Miguel and Victoria stared at each other slack-jawed for

a moment while Isa dumped her water cup to extinguish the fire. "Gosh, it's almost like you're related or something." She started walking to the cove. "Let's do Vicky's first—sorry, *Victoria's*."

"You fink!"

"You sneak!"

"What?" Isa threw up her hands. "You both asked me not to tell, so I didn't."

Miguel shouted with excitement when he saw the raft on the beach. It was pretty impressive for a desert-island construction job. The craft consisted of a double-layered base of bamboo stalks bound tight with vines. Victoria had made oars from branches and palm fronds. A simple mast supported a small sail of old clothes that Isa had sewn together with a fishing hook and line.

"I knew it!" said Miguel as he jumped on the sturdy raft and rocked it back and forth with admiration.

"You had no idea," said Victoria.

"He had no idea," confirmed Isa.

"I had a suspicion . . ." Miguel said weakly.

"Well, you were right, Gordo." Victoria put her hands on her brother's shoulders and pressed her forehead to his. "We can't stay here forever. We've got to go find the other survivors. Maybe we'll find Mom and Dad. Maybe we won't. But we're not the only ones left and"—she squeezed him tight—"together we're stronger."

Miguel wrapped his arms around his big sister.

"I'm sorry about the boat," he whispered.

"I'm sorry about your blankie," she whispered back.

Miguel sniffled. "It's okay. I'm too old to have a blankie anyway." He puffed out his chest and stood tall. "I don't need it anymore."

"Actually"—Victoria reached up to unroll the sail—"I think it might come in handy."

Stitched among the shirts and pants of the makeshift sail were patches of Miguel's old blankie.

He tried his best to hold it in, but he couldn't help crying. He covered his face with his hands, and Victoria gave him another hug.

"I saw a light in the distance," Victoria explained. "I think it was people. Someone is out there." She pointed west, across the water. "There's another island, but it's pretty far away. I think it will take a few days, even if we take turns rowing and the wind is blowing in the right direction . . . so we need to stockpile enough food to last the journey before we can set sail." She pulled out a piece of bark with a rough calendar scratched into it. "If we stick to the plan, we can leave next Tuesday."

Miguel jumped down from the raft. "Well, I have a surprise for you too." He ran off into the jungle to retrieve his secret stash.

"Where's he going?" asked Victoria.

"No spoilers," said Isa.

Miguel returned with a long bamboo pole strung with a dozen smoked fish.

"Holy crap!" blurted Victoria.

"Isn't it amazing?" Isa clapped her hands. "He caught them all by himself."

Victoria was astonished. "How?"

"With this!" Miguel tapped the end of the pole, which had been split into four prongs and sharpened into points.

"You speared all of these?"

"Yup." Miguel beamed with pride. "But it was Isa's idea to smoke them."

"They'll stay good for weeks," Isa said.

Victoria sniffed one of the crispy dried fish.

"Try it," said Miguel.

She took a bite. "Wow! It's tasty!"

"Right?"

Isa pulled out a piece of cardboard she had cut from the box of nutrient flakes.

"What's that?" asked Miguel.

"I have a surprise too." Isa revealed a detailed portrait of a smiling man and woman. The woman had Victoria's speckled eyes and wide nose. The man had Miguel's freckled skin and big ears.

"Mom!" said Miguel.

"Dad!" said Victoria.

"I made it with charcoal from the fire." Isa admired her own drawing. "I know you were both worried that you might forget what they looked like, so I decided—"

Isa couldn't finish her sentence because her face was smushed between her two siblings hugging her as tightly as they could.

EVERYTHING WAS PACKED onto the raft. The Dewsberry
kids had waited an extra day for the waves to die down, and
now they were ready to row.

"Come on, let's go!" complained Miguel. He jabbed his
spear in the air.

"Careful with that thing!" Victoria ducked as she
adjusted the sail.

Miguel plopped down and swapped his spear for an oar. "I'll row first," he proclaimed.

"Me too." Isa sat beside him and picked up the other oar.

"Are you sure?" Victoria looked worried.

"I'm fine." Isa rolled her eyes. "I haven't had an attack in forever. I think it was just a vitamin deficiency."

Victoria sighed and tightened her backpack straps. "Fine, but let me know as soon as you get tired, and I'll take over. Don't be stubborn."

"Ha!" Isa laughed. "Look who's talking."

"Shut up." Victoria smirked. She shoved the raft out into the waves and climbed aboard.

"Goodbye, island!" Miguel waved. "Thanks for all the fish!"

"Thanks for the coconuts and the seaweed!" added Isa.

"And the bird and the wood and that one tiny crab!" Victoria laughed.

Miguel and Isa rowed to the edge of the cove and into the current. The waves were strong, but the wind was with them, and soon the sail was full. The island was shrinking in the distance. Victoria reached for a coconut to take a swig of water.

"Yeeeek!" she screamed. A little brown mouse crawled out from the pile of fruit. She smacked it away, and it landed in the sea with a tiny plop.

"Weenus!" yelped Isa.

"I'm sorry!" Victoria grimaced. They both rushed to the side of the raft in a panic.

"Whoa!" Miguel leaned backward as the raft lifted him into the air.

"Careful!" Victoria dove back to the middle of the raft to set it level again.

"Weenus!" Isa peered into the water, worried that her little friend might have drowned. She froze, and in an anguished moment of silence, her siblings prepared for the worst. But then she started giggling.

"I didn't know that mice can swim!" Isa crawled to the middle of the raft so Miguel and Victoria could lean over to take a look.

Weenus was paddling casually in the water.

"Look at that," marveled Victoria. "He swims better than you."

"Shut up." Miguel scooped the mouse from the water. "Try not to throw him into the ocean this time."

Victoria accepted the soggy mouse at arm's length, still a bit skeeved by the idea of touching a rodent. Though she did find it pretty cute when Weenus shook himself off to dry out.

Miguel and Isa took up the oars and started rowing again. They all felt a surge of hope about the fate that awaited them on the unknown island in the distance.

But then a strange shadow cloaked the raft in darkness.

Victoria was the only one facing the shore, so at first Miguel and Isa didn't know what had caused her mouth to drop open with terror. All they knew was that it made a sound so loud they couldn't even hear themselves scream.

"LLLAAAAAAAAAAAAAAAANNNDDD..." A TREMENDOUS rock monster roared from the shore. It was larger than any the kids had ever seen. It towered over Crag and Chunk, its head covered by the clouds. "OOOOOOOOOOFFFFFFFFFFFFFFFF..." Crag pointed at the boat, and the living mountain slowly bent over with an enormous stone claw extended. "RRROOOOOOOOOOOOOOOOCCCKKK . . ." The monster lifted Chunk from the ground like a baseball and slowly cocked back its arm.

"CHUNK GO BYE-BYE," Chunk uttered with horror.

The mountainous monster catapulted the living boulder into the air with the force of a volcanic explosion. Chunk soared through the sky like a cannonball—aimed directly at the Dewsberrys' dinky raft.

"Row!" shouted Miguel.

"I'm trying!" Isa paddled as hard as she could, but the flying rock monster loomed closer and closer.

"CHUNK SMASH MEAT!" roared Chunk, filled with the satisfaction of glory and sacrifice, thrilled with the chance to finally contribute to the great and honorable victory of his ancient Rock brethren.

Of course, the simpleminded rock monster could not express any of these deep and powerful feelings verbally, so instead, once again, Chunk roared as it prepared to crash down upon the raft and destroy the three squishy humans on board.

"CHUNK SMASH MEA—"

ZZZZZZPLOW!

A beam of brilliant purple light ripped through the boulder, vaporizing its core. Chunk exploded into a thousand pieces, and tiny pebbles rained down into the water.

Victoria stood motionless, both arms extended to the sky, the blaster grasped tightly in her hands. A wisp of smoke curled out from the barrel. She coolly brought the blaster to her mouth and blew the smoke away like an action hero.

"You had a blaster this whole time?" Isa was stunned.

"I said I would keep you safe, and I meant it."

Miguel dropped his oar. "Let me see that for a second."

Victoria laughed. "No way, Gordo."

"Come on, Victoria! I'm responsible. I'll be safe. I just want to shoot it once."

"No way." Victoria held the blaster out of reach above his head.

"Come on!"

"Play with your spear!"

"I don't want a stupid spear!"

"Sit down, you two!" said Isa. "You're rocking the boat, and if either of you falls in, I'm leaving you behind."

FOUR DAYS LATER, a woman on crutches was scanning the horizon with binoculars when something floating in the water caught her attention.

The woman had the same speckled green eyes and wide nose as Victoria.

She smacked her husband on the shoulder and pointed at what looked like a raft approaching the island from the north. He took off his radio headset and borrowed the binoculars to get a better look.

The man had the same freckles and big ears as Miguel.

Boats full of survivors were arriving every day, but this raft was different. It looked homemade. And as it got closer, they both agreed that something about the sail looked surprisingly familiar.

IV.

THE HUMAN KABOOM

(the one with the world's greatest circus)

illustrated by

DANIEL GRAY-BARNETT

Before the accident, the Flying Zamboni Brothers were widely considered the finest trapeze act in all of Europe. Their whole family had worked in the circus for three generations, striving for greatness, and despite the name of the act, it wasn't just the brothers who went spinning, flipping, and soaring through the air (eighty-six feet above the ground, without a net). Sisters and aunts, cousins and uncles, eleven Zambonis in all, performed death-defying feats that earned standing ovations from every crowd lucky enough to witness their aerial acrobatics.

There was only one member of the Zamboni family who didn't perform with the rest. She had the same alabaster skin, jet-black hair, and sharp widow's-peak hairline as everyone else in her family, but unlike her relatives, Zuzana Zamboni was hopelessly clumsy.

She had tried her best to learn the familial tradition of the flying trapeze, but she simply didn't have the coordination required. Zuzana experimented with other circus arts, but she couldn't juggle, she couldn't ride a unicycle, and she couldn't do cartwheels or handstands or pat her head and rub her stomach at the same time.

By the time Zuzana was twelve, her relatives had given up on pushing her to develop any sort of athletic prowess. The girl had enough trouble just getting through the day without tripping over her own two feet. But she was sweet and funny and smart as a whip, so the Zamboni clan simply accepted her for who she was, and anytime they heard a small crash in the distance, they would chuckle lovingly and say, "There goes Zuzu . . ."

So while her younger brother and her half-deaf grandmother and all the rest of her family basked in the adulation of adoring crowds as the star attraction of the Wunderheim Traveling Circus, Zuzana earned her keep by ripping tickets, sweeping sawdust, cleaning costumes, and, on occasion, shoveling elephant dung.

Even still, Zuzana loved working in the circus. She loved the excitement, the colorful characters, the infectious joy. She couldn't imagine living a normal life in a normal house, having normal relatives who never did backflips and didn't know how to juggle flaming torches. She loved the circus

as she loved her family, and for Zuzana, they were one and the same.

The circus was like a traveling village. Every night, the big top would fold up like an umbrella, roll through the countryside by train, and unfurl in a different place the next morning.

But for the people who lived in each place, Circus Day was a deeply special event that happened only once a year. All the other days, they would wake with the sun to milk the goats or harvest the grain or lay bricks or do paperwork or go to school. But not on Circus Day.

On Circus Day, everyone in their family, everyone in their town, pretty much everyone they had ever met would put on their finest clothes and gather at the big striped tent that had sprung up overnight in a previously empty field at the edge of town.

Old men became children again as they entered the big top, and children were filled with such overwhelming spasms of joy that their hearts nearly burst from their chests. This was the power of the circus in an age when radio was new and television had yet to be invented.

But one fateful night in southern Spain, while Zuzana was watching the show from the back of the audience, her life changed forever.

A powerful earthquake struck in the middle of the closing act, while the Zambonis were still flying high above the crowd. The ground began to shake violently. Zuzana fell down the stairs and spilled a tray full of popcorn all over the spectators. The grandstands nearly tipped over. The support wires shook loose, and a section of the big top collapsed.

When Zuzana finally wrestled her way out of the deflated tent, she felt as if she had stumbled into a bad dream. The earthquake had tossed the flying Zambonis from their perches and sent them plummeting eighty-six feet to the hard ground below. A beloved circus dynasty was brought to a sudden and tragic end.

Zuzana was the only Zamboni left.

THE IMMEDIATE AFTERMATH of the earthquake was chaotic. The wounded were rushed to the hospital while the town doctor did his best to treat minor injuries on-site. Sirens wailed, and firefighters arrived to help rescue the people still trapped under the tent. Luckily, none of the children in attendance were hurt, but it was soon confirmed that all eleven of the Flying Zambonis had perished.

Zuzana cried, of course. Everyone in the audience cried too. And the whole cast of performers—even the elephants.

Late that night, when the crowds and the ambulances were gone, the circus family held a tearstained candlelight vigil. They surrounded young Zuzana and tried their best to comfort her. The clowns and belly dancers, the horse riders and acrobats, all gathered around and sang songs and lit candles to grieve for their dear departed friends.

Under a blanket of stars, Professor Umschlag Wunderheim

climbed upon a soapbox and called everyone to attention. He was the visionary ringmaster who had built the show from the ground up, starting as the sole performer—magician, singer, tumbler. He had slowly grown the spectacle until it was the biggest traveling circus in Europe. He was admired by the public as well as his employees. Even the people who ran rival circuses liked and respected him.

"Poor Zuzu . . ." Wunderheim bellowed. He had an ample belly, a booming voice, and a twelve-language vocabulary to match. "*Pobrecita, mon pauvre, armes Ding!* I am so very sorry, my dear. My heart is torn asunder, and my spirit hangs heavy with woe. The most sorrowful poem fails to capture the depths of despair we now suffer.

"Only the fates know why tragedy befalls such beautiful, talented, and gentle souls. But remember this: We will always be here for you." The dozens of performers cheered and whistled in agreement. "And your family will never be forgotten—they live on through stories of their miraculous feats told lovingly by adoring fans." Wunderheim grew quiet and leaned close to Zuzana. "They live on because true legends never die."

The trio of elephants caressed Zuzana's head gently. Mongo was the biggest, Mary was still quite large, and Mabel, the baby, tucked her trunk under Zuzana's arm to give her a hug.

Wunderheim continued. "I will be adding a memorial oratory to each performance, during which I will regale the audience with tales to commemorate the greatness of the

Flying Zamboni Brothers. In this way, we will keep their memory shining bright for years to come. But also, with these."

Wunderheim removed the cap from a large cardboard tube and slid out a roll of huge colorful posters that had been used to advertise his circus over the years. Each poster conjured romantic fantasies of excitement and danger. All the fabulous attractions of the show were lavishly illustrated, and Zuzana recognized her friends, captured in their most impressive poses: Mongo playing chess against an Oxford professor; Wacko, Wawa, and Wowza the clowns making mischief, much to the amusement of the children in the audience; Equilibrio balancing a sword on his nose; the graceful Egyptian belly dancers swirling strands of silk; Lazlo the lion holding a live rabbit in his open mouth while the fuzzy little creature contentedly munches on a carrot . . .

WUNDERHEIM was emblazoned across the top of each poster, the biggest and brightest of all the names. But just beneath, illustrated larger than any of the other acts, were the Flying Zambonis, the whole family frozen in action, mesmerizing the crowd pictured below.

Zuzana had seen some of those promotional posters before. But in all those years, she had never thought to keep any for herself.

"These advertisements go back before you were born." Wunderheim leafed through the stack for Zuzana to see. Some of the older posters were mounted on canvas to protect the delicate paper. "Here's your grandfather Zachariah. Here's your great-uncle Zed. And many other Zamboni legends." He rolled them carefully and slipped them back in the tube. "I want you to have these."

Zuzana was touched that Wunderheim would give her

such a valuable collection. It had clearly taken him many years to assemble it. She hugged him tight and felt just a tiny bit better.

The circus performers wiped their tears and clapped their hands.

AFTER THE TRAGIC accident, Wunderheim and the clowns helped Zuzana pack her family's possessions from their wagons. Everyone in the circus lived and traveled in colorful covered wagons.

During the winter, they set up camp to repair props, practice new tricks, and prepare for the next season. But at the first hint of spring, they would load their wagons onto train cars and hit the road for a forty-city tour across Europe.

Life on the road did not afford the luxury of collecting many objects, so in the end, all the worldly possessions of the late Zamboni family fit into a half-dozen cases for storage. Wunderheim thought it best that Zuzana not spend too much time alone with her grief, so he arranged for her to move into a wagon with two roommates, who might help comfort her.

"You poor, poor darling," said Itsy, who was four feet tall.

"Don't crowd her, sister," said Bitsy, who was seven feet tall. The twins wore identical powder-blue dresses and matching blue bows in their long blond hair.

"Let me help you with your things." Bitsy plucked the heavy sack from Zuzana's arms with two fingers.

"We've made up your bunk right here." Itsy patted a feather mattress that was draped with a velvet blanket and fresh flowers.

"Thank you," said Zuzana. She had only ever shared a

bed with her little brother (who'd had an unpleasant habit of kicking in his sleep), but now she would enjoy a cozy bed of her own.

She crawled inside and lay down. It was so comfortable she giggled. And no sooner had the laugh escaped her lips than she started sobbing. Not because she missed her family, but rather because, for a split second, she had almost allowed herself to forget to miss them. Tears rolled down her face and pooled on the pillow.

"The poor thing," said Itsy.

"I can't imagine what she must be going through," whispered Bitsy as she embraced her tiny sister.

"You-know-who can, though . . ." said Itsy.

"I thought we promised we weren't going to talk about him." Bitsy stiffened and pushed her sister away.

"Well, he's coming, like it or not. So we're going to have to talk about it."

"I saw him first!"

"Ha!" Itsy threw up her hands. "You only spotted him before me because I couldn't see over the crowd!"

"You flirted with him!" Bitsy wagged a giant painted fingernail.

"Can you blame me?" Itsy smiled. "He's so handsome."

"And daring," Bitsy added. She smiled too.

"And that hair . . ."

The sisters giggled.

Zuzana was eavesdropping from her bed. She had no idea who they were fussing over. She didn't know that a promising young performer from a rival circus had already been invited to join Wunderheim's show as the new grand finale. She didn't know that he also came from a famous circus family and that he had also been orphaned as a child.

ZUZANA SLEPT FITFULLY, haunted by dreams of her deceased relatives, waking every few minutes disoriented, forgetting where she was. She would sit up sweating and panting, her cheeks wet with tears.

Itsy climbed into bed with her in the middle of the night and massaged her head to calm her down. Bitsy would have come to comfort her too, but she couldn't fit in the bed.

Having someone to snuggle with helped Zuzana finally fall asleep. But only an hour after sunrise, she woke to a thunderous explosion.

KABOOM!

Zuzana opened one eye. From the animal wagons, the elephants trumpeted grouchily. Clearly, they were not pleased to be woken so early.

Itsy and Bitsy bolted upright in bed.

"He's here!" they exclaimed.

While the twins were busy gussying themselves up like they were going to the opera, Zuzana wandered over to the big top. Loud noises were coming from inside.

A high wire had been strung between two tall poles, and a wild-haired, olive-skinned man was checking all the support wires by doing pull-ups. Despite the fact that the sun had barely risen and the lights in the big top were off, he wore sunglasses.

Wunderheim was sitting in the stands, sipping a cup of tea and eating burnt toast with apricot jam. He noticed Zuzana enter the tent, snapped his suspenders, and approached the little girl gingerly.

"Zuzu, my darling. Please understand, I know our grief is still fresh . . . but the show must go on!" He spread his arms wide. "The public demands a grand finale. We cannot embark upon our tour without a spectacular feat that inspires the people to share stories with their grandchildren."

Zuzana shrugged sadly. As much as it pained her to imagine anyone else closing the show, without a big finish, the circus could never be a success.

The ringmaster called to the man in the sunglasses. "Hugh, there's someone here I'd like you to meet."

When the young man turned to face her, Zuzana felt her belly go fluttery. He walked over and knelt with a calloused palm extended, his sleeves rolled up around his powerful forearms.

"You must be Zuzu," he said with a hint of a Slavic accent. Zuzana's distaste for her nickname suddenly vanished. He took her hand and leaned in closer. *"Tahn-khoo-MEEN."*

Zuzu could sense the deep compassion in his voice, but she didn't understand what he'd said.

"What does that mean?" she asked quietly.

Hugh bit his lip. "I'm not sure, actually . . . but that's what people said to me."

"It is a Hebrew expression of condolence," interjected Wunderheim. "Hugh here also lost his family at a young age. He traveled with us for a spell, but you were too young to remember. You and Hugh are but two lonely souls united in unspeakable tragedy. I only hope you can both make a happy home here with us."

Hugh rubbed the back of his neck, searching for words. "I don't talk so good as the professor, but . . . I know how you feel, kid. And . . . uh . . ." He patted her hand gently. "It will get better."

Zuzu felt the heat from his palms warm her whole body.

"Well," said Hugh, "I better get to it. First show tonight."

Zuzu nodded.

"Can I get my hand back?"

Only then did Zuzu realize she was squeezing with all her might. She let go.

"Good grip," Hugh joked. Then he cartwheeled backward as effortlessly as taking a sip of water.

"Incredible, isn't he?" marveled Wunderheim.

Without breaking his stride, Hugh leaned over, picked up a canvas satchel full of jangly metal instruments, and slung it over his shoulder. He dropped a pie tin at the foot of a ladder, then climbed up, two rungs a time. He rummaged inside his bag for a steel marble, which he balanced on the wire. A flick of his finger, and the marble fell to the pie tin on the ground with a clang. Hugh nodded.

Wunderheim leaned in and whispered to Zuzu, "Hugh's family, the Mankebaums, had a friendly rivalry with the Zambonis for many years. They traveled with the Periwinkle Circus. Through Eastern Europe, mostly. They suffered from disease and political persecution, but their final downfall was a loose wire, set improperly by a lazy roustabout. That's why Hugh insists on setting all his equipment himself."

Hugh slid down the ladder like it was a fire pole. He jogged over to a gleaming steel cannon at the edge of the ring and loaded it with a sack of potatoes.

"His new stunt is hair-raising," continued Wunderheim. "Shot out of a cannon and onto the wire. No one's seen anything like it. Myself included. I've insisted he prove he can actually do it before I present such a dangerous feat to the public."

Hugh struck a match against the bottom of his shoe and lit the fuse of the cannon.

"It's sure to look fantastic on the poster." Wunderheim waved his hands through the air, envisioning the artwork. *"The Human Kaboom!"* He raised an eyebrow at Zuzu. *"The explosive blind daredevil! That'll draw 'em in."*

"Blind?" asked Zuzu.

KABOOM!

The sack of potatoes flew through the air and rattled a bell strung above the high wire.

Hugh smiled at the sound of the shot hitting its target. Hidden behind his dark glasses, the cloudy white orbs of his eyes saw nothing.

THE COSTUME TENT was abuzz with excitement that evening. Wunderheim hadn't had time to print up new posters yet, so the audience had no idea they were about to see the debut of something special. But the other performers did. They gossiped breathlessly as they gathered in front of the dressing mirrors, getting ready for the show.

"Can you believe it?" squealed Itsy.

"He's so brave!" Bitsy shivered.

"He's gonna get himself killed," said Wacko the clown.

"Don't say that!" said Wawa the clown.

"It's bad luck!" said Wowza the clown. "Say it backward three times fast and spin in a circle to reverse it."

Wacko shrugged, then did just that—a perfect triple reverse recitation followed by an elegant jumping pirouette. Immediately upon landing, he grabbed hold of a nearby glass of water, splashed it in his face, and honked his nose.

Itsy and Bitsy laughed.

"Are you happy now?" asked Wacko.

"Not exactly," said Wowza. "I was using that water to shave."

Meanwhile, the crowd filed into the tent, and excitement filled the air. The big top was illuminated with electric lightbulbs, which very few people had in their homes in those days. For many, it was the first time they had seen such a large space so brightly lit.

A ten-piece band of mismatched misfits played a raucous ragtime as spectators bought sugar-dusted fried dough and cotton candy, then dashed off to find their seats, where they waited, buzzing with anticipation, for the show to begin.

Then the lights faded, the band became quiet, and suddenly, a booming voice rang out in the darkness: "Ladies and gentlemen, children of all ages, favored beasts and benevolent spirits, welcome, *willkommen, bienvenidos,* and *bienvenue* to the world-famous Wunderheim Traveling Circus!"

A spotlight revealed Professor Umschlag Wunderheim in a sparkly red tuxedo and a black velvet top hat, his

mustache lovingly waxed into splendiferous swirls.

Wunderheim tapped his cane, and a burst of flame exploded from the tip. Cymbals crashed, and the band roared back to life. Wacko, Wawa, and Wowza the clowns dashed into the ring and began to stir up mischief—stumbling, tumbling, and stealing people's snacks.

"My friends, you are in for a treat this evening," crooned Wunderheim. "A cascading cavalcade of entertainment the likes of which have never been seen before and may never be seen again."

One by one, the performers paraded into the ring to give the cheering crowd a small taste of the show they had in store. The trick riders from Mongolia galloped in, some standing upright on the backs of their gorgeous white horses. The acrobats flipped in behind them, seven powerful athletes from China who seemed to defy the laws of gravity with their gymnastic tricks.

Bitsy entered with Itsy held on the palm of her hand. Itsy contorted one foot over her head while standing en pointe with the other. The jugglers followed, with balls, hats, and flaming clubs flying. The scantily clad Egyptian belly dancers waved and blew kisses to the crowd, causing many cheeks to blush red. Equilibrio balanced a sword on the tip of his nose. Leslie the lion tamer cracked her whip, and Lazlo roared with enthusiasm from the wheeling platform behind her. They both had luxurious manes of honey-brown hair.

Finally, Mongo, Mary, and Mabel greeted the crowd by tossing flowers with their trunks. The audience squealed in collective glee.

"But a small taste of the wonders in store for you this evening, my friends!" Despite the cacophony, Wunderheim's tremendous voice could be heard by all. "The show has only just begun!"

He tapped his cane, and there was another flash of fire. When the puff of smoke cleared, Wunderheim had disappeared. The audience gasped and applauded wildly.

Then the band put down their horns and picked up violins. The drummer gently tickled a vibraphone. Three giant white ribbons dropped from the rafters, and a trio of silk climbers gracefully floated out to meet them, like dandelion seeds on the wind.

For the next two hours, the circus cast its intoxicating spell over the audience, who marveled at the beauty of the dancers, cackled at the antics of the clowns, and gasped at the skill of the acrobats.

Lazlo the lion struck fear into the pits of their stomachs. (Though in truth, Leslie had trained him so well that the big cat had made friends with the speedy white rabbit he captured during his act each night.)

Equilibrio balanced a sword on his nose for a while. It was not the greatest act in the show, but he was a very nice man and Wunderheim knew it was important to give the audience an opportunity to go to the bathroom.

Many of the kids in the audience had the chance to pet Mabel. They would hold out a different coin in each hand, and the baby elephant would take the more valuable of the two. In return, she would offer the donor a chance to pet her trunk, to feel real live elephant skin, a texture unlike anything else in the world.

The trick riders amazed all, shooting bows and arrows with their feet while their magnificent horses were mid-gallop.

If the show had ended there, the audience would have been happy. But the unsuspecting spectators had no idea that they were about to witness the birth of a legend.

Wunderheim silenced the band and removed his hat.

"*Queridos amigos estimados*, my dear esteemed friends, this is a very special moment for us all." He gestured to the other performers, who had returned to watch the final act. "What you are about to see is a stunt so spectacular, a feat so formidable, a deed so dangerous, that I must warn you— there is a terribly high chance of failure, and even death. But one courageous man dares to defy gravity, dares to slice through the night, dares to fly BLIND. I give you: the Human Kaboom!"

Hugh entered from one side of the ring as the cannon was wheeled into position at the other. He wore a black cape, black tights, and a black blindfold. His hair was wild, and his chest was bare.

An ominous, slow drumroll began, and the audience held its breath.

Hugh checked the support structure, jingled the bell on the high wire, and adjusted the position of the cannon slightly.

Zuzana, watching from the back of the tent, felt her heart skip a beat.

Wunderheim masked his fear with bravado. "This trick requires precise measurements, superhuman agility, incredible strength, and nerves of steel." He wiped the sweat from his bald head with a handkerchief. "Kids, please: Don't try this at home."

Hugh climbed into the mouth of the cannon, struck a match, and lit the fuse. He waved to the audience and saluted the ringmaster before crouching into the barrel. His head disappeared from sight.

The fuse burned slowly, and no one said a word. The tent was so quiet that even the ticket taker outside could hear the gentle hiss of the spark traveling closer and closer to the point of ignition.

The hissing stopped, and there was a brief moment of absolute silence before . . .

KABOOM!

A blur exploded from the mouth of the cannon and shot through the air.

It was a young man named Hugh Mankebaum, a little-known circus performer, who was brave enough—and perhaps foolish enough—to try something so outrageously dangerous that it had never been attempted before. It was Hugh Mankebaum who climbed into that cannon. It was Hugh Mankebaum who soared across the tent and performed a perfect front flip. But the second he landed on that high wire, gathered his balance, and waved to the crowd, he was no longer a mere mortal. He had been transformed forevermore into the legendary superman known around the world as the Human Kaboom.

After the audience recovered from the initial shock, they screamed, cheered, and carried on until they were hoarse. When Kaboom slid down his ladder, they swarmed the ring and hoisted him onto their shoulders, certain they had witnessed the impossible.

Even the other performers clapped so hard their hands hurt the next day. The ovation turned into a sing-along, and the celebration that followed lasted well into the night.

WORD OF THE Human Kaboom and his death-defying feat spread like a blazing fire throughout southern Spain. People traveled from miles away to see Kaboom take flight.

Zuzu couldn't blame them. She had watched the act every night for a week, and it never got any less thrilling.

Each day, Zuzu would finish her chores early to watch Kaboom set his equipment, which to her was nearly as impressive as the high-flying stunt itself. Since he couldn't see, he arranged all his props by feel and sound, using clever techniques he had devised himself.

One afternoon, as Zuzu was playing backgammon with Mongo and watching Kaboom make his preshow arrangements, he called to her, somehow aware that she was present on the other side of the big top, even though she hadn't made a peep.

"Zuzu." He turned to face her. "If you're going to watch me do this every day, you may as well give me a hand."

She wasn't sure whether to feel embarrassed or honored.

"Come over here."

Zuzu stood too quickly and knocked the backgammon board to the floor. She hurried to tie her hair back in a ponytail and managed to knot one hand behind her head in the process.

Kaboom held out a small leather pouch. "It'll save me a

lot of time if you can help me measure the powder. The formula requires a precise ratio."

Zuzu accepted the pouch nervously and struggled to free her other arm from her hair.

Kaboom patted the cannon. "Most of the oomph comes from a big hidden spring." He put a finger to his lips as he divulged the secret. "But that's not very theatrical, is it?" He smiled and opened a hatch below the fuse. "Four parts flash powder for the burst of light, three parts smoke powder for the pooferoo, and a small pinch of bang powder— just enough to get your ears ringing. Especially if they are extra sensitive, like mine."

Zuzu grunted as she finally managed to pull her hand free from her ponytail.

Kaboom closed the hatch on the cannon. "All the chemicals are in the tool chest in my wagon, along with a balance scale, which is much easier to read with a pair of working peepers." He lowered his sunglasses and winked an unseeing eye.

Zuzu swooned.

"Kaboom!" Wunderheim burst in wearing rainbow boxer shorts and eating a sardine sandwich. "Your new costume is ready." He carried a black cape adorned with zigzagging gold sequins that shimmered and radiated like exploding fireworks. Kaboom took the cape and held it up for Zuzu to see.

"How does it look?" he asked.

"It's perfect," said Zuzu.

Kaboom looked pleased. "Will you put it in my wagon? And get rid of the old one while you're at it."

Zuzu ran off to hang the new costume. As for the old one, instead of tossing it in the garbage, she folded it up neatly and squirreled it away in her trunk for safekeeping.

ZUZANA ZAMBONI WAS officially hired as Kaboom's personal assistant. She quickly proved herself indispensable. She helped him set his equipment, arrange his clothes, and stay on schedule. After each show, she would shoo away the overenthusiastic admirers who gathered outside his wagon.

"The Human Kaboom needs his sleep!" she would bark at the crowd of late-night well-wishers hoping to gain access to his personal quarters. "Proper concentration cannot be achieved without sufficient rest."

Zuzu smiled as the fans dispersed. She tried her best to act professional, but she was more enamored with the olive-skinned daredevil than anyone.

THE CIRCUS WOULD soon embark upon a whirlwind summer tour, and the days leading up to its departure were busy with packing and preparation. The animal wagons were stocked with food. The big top was disassembled and reassembled many times, by local kids who had decided to run away with the circus. Wunderheim watched his new hires carefully with a stopwatch in hand, offering hard-won insights as to how to improve their speed.

Zuzu rode her bicycle into town to fetch some confections from the candy store. Kaboom had an insatiable sweet tooth and loved nothing more than sampling a wide variety of local candies from every country he visited. When Zuzu returned to the circus grounds, she was laden with sacks of azucarambas, candied fruits, and a kaleidoscopic array of other colorful treats.

Kaboom sat on the steps of his wagon, washing his socks in a wooden bucket. He held out his hand, and Zuzu gave him a few candies to hold him over till dinner. Then she climbed inside to organize the rest into jars for their trip. The circus would hit the road the next morning.

There was a cardboard tube lying on the bed.

"What's in the tube?" called Zuzu to Kaboom.

"I think it's the new poster for the show." He tossed an azucaramba high into the air and caught it in his mouth. "Apparently, I'm on it."

Zuzu unrolled the poster. It was a huge three-sheet—seven feet tall. She gasped when she saw it unfurled.

"How does it look?" asked Kaboom.

Zuzu was speechless. Gone were the many small vignettes of various acts, the multiple proclamations of ASTONISHING FEATS, BEAUTIFUL DANCERS, and MAGNIFICENT BEASTS. Instead, the dramatic new design was simple and bold.

At the top, it said, WUNDERHEIM PRESENTS. Below that, a bright-yellow explosion arced through a void of deep purples and blues. A glowing human figure wearing a cape and a blindfold was visible in flight. At the bottom, there were giant flaming letters spelling out just three words: THE HUMAN KABOOM.

EVEN AN AIRPLANE pilot will tell you that the best way to travel across Europe is by train. Trains are speedy and convenient. Every major city and even most small towns had a train station long before anyone had ever heard of an airport. Some of the train stations were big and beautiful. Others were small and charming. They all had a giant clock to help keep things running on time. The ticket agents and train conductors wore matching uniforms and synchronized their pocket watches to avoid leaving early or showing up late.

In a classic train station, you could walk right on to the platform to say farewell to a friend before they took a trip. And on the day that the Wunderheim Traveling Circus departed from Valencia for its summer tour, a dense crowd of well-wishers put on their fanciest clothes and gathered at the station to wave goodbye.

At the very front of the train was the locomotive, the powerful steam engine that burped white puffs of smoke and pulled the line of cars behind it. Just behind the locomotive was the tender, full of coal to power the engine.

Toward the back were the first-class cars—plush, spacious cabins with dining service and big glass windows. Before that came the second-class cars, which were a little more crowded, with slightly smaller windows, and seats that were a bit threadbare. The cars before second class were for cargo. They had no seats or windows at all.

The circus folk didn't ride in any of these cars. Wunderheim had worked out an ingenious system that allowed them to travel in the same wagons they lived in. They simply rolled them up a ramp and onto flatbed cars at the back of the train.

Everyone knew when the circus was aboard. The normal cars at the front of the train were gray or rust-colored. But the circus wagons were decorated with colorful murals that served as advertisements for the acts. The performers rested in comfort while the train chugged through the European countryside on the way to their next destination.

The first stop on the tour was Barcelona, and when the train arrived, there were pictures of Kaboom everywhere. The advertising boys had pasted hundreds of posters in advance of that night's show.

Zuzu described the scene to Kaboom as they searched for the local candy shop. Without his signature cape and blindfold, he was not easily recognizable. But whispers swept through the streets, and soon there was a crowd of children following his every move. He entered the sweet-shop and bought four big bags of sugary confections.

"Who wants candy?" he asked the crowd of tittering kids.

"*Yo!*" they all screamed.

Kaboom tossed out handfuls and laughed.

At that moment, a photographer from the newspaper happened to be passing by, and the next morning, an image

of the circus star sharing candy with his adoring young fans was printed on the front page of the early edition. Zuzu bought a copy and added it to her trunk.

Over the next few weeks, she began to gather quite a collection of newspaper clippings: rave reviews, editorial illustrations, gossip reports of dates with famous actresses (Zuzu didn't enjoy reading those, but she kept them anyway).

However, nothing drew more publicity than the blindfolded motorcycle rides.

Each day, when the circus arrived in a new city, Kaboom would ride through town on a motorcycle while wearing a blindfold. Even Zuzu wasn't sure how he did it, but every time, he would end the same way, by "accidentally" crashing into a fruit stand that Wunderheim had arranged to be left in a convenient location.

Zuzu would then retrieve the motorbike and wash off the smashed bananas and watermelons while Kaboom signed autographs and posed for photos for every newspaper and magazine in town.

By the time the circus arrived in Paris, the Human Kaboom was drawing a crowd of reporters wherever he went. Even as he took his morning coffee at a sidewalk café.

"How do you set your equipment if you can't see?" asked one journalist.

"How do you use the toilet in the middle of the night?" retorted Kaboom. "By feel and by sound!"

The reporters laughed.

"Aren't you afraid of death?" asked another.

"I'd rather go out in a blaze of glory than fade to darkness and be forgotten." Kaboom did a handstand on a chair. Flashbulbs popped all around.

"Are you really blind?" asked a skeptic.

"If I could see"—Kaboom smiled—"do you think my hair would look like this?"

A chorus of young girls whistled loudly.

Zuzu returned from the candy store with a mix of local sweets and handed the sack to Kaboom.

"Ah, the breakfast of champions!" Kaboom climbed down from the chair and thanked the crowd as it dispersed with a little encouragement from Zuzana.

"Kaboom must prepare for his performance this evening! Please, a little space and privacy before the show."

She barely noticed as a lithe, creeping figure slid past her like a gust of cold wind.

"Young Mankebaum," said a slim gentleman with a thick Swiss accent. "My, how you've grown."

Kaboom recognized the voice immediately, and his smile faded. "Zephyr Mephisto."

"Ah, but I am flattered that you remember me. It is so easy to forget the little people when you become a big star." Mephisto circled him silently, like a tiger stalking its prey.

"What do you want?" asked Kaboom.

"Do I detect a hint of suspicion? But whatever for, *mon ami*?" Mephisto slithered closer, placed his hands on Kaboom's shoulders, and squeezed. "I live so near I simply had to come wish you luck on your performance this evening. Good luck. *Bonne chance.*" He curled his upper lip and laughed silently.

Zuzu scowled. Everyone in show business knows that wishing someone "good luck" is actually bad luck. In the circus, the tradition was to wish someone the worst luck possible. "Break a leg," they would say. If the act was especially dangerous (as the Human Kaboom's most certainly was), fellow performers would joke even more darkly to signal their admiration and well-wishes. In Italy, they would say, "*In bocca al lupo,*" which means "Into the mouth of the wolf." In Spain, they would say, "*Mucha mierda,*" which means "Lots of poop."

Zuzu gave the stranger the stink eye, and he slunk off into the shadows.

"Who was that?" she asked.

Kaboom reached into his pocket for his bag of candy and pulled out a handful. "That was Zephyr Mephisto, the best wire walker in the world."

"But you're the best wire walker in the world!" protested Zuzu.

"I most certainly am not." Kaboom shook his head. "Drama and spectacle are no substitute for true artistry." He popped the candy into his mouth, chewed briefly, then spit a gooey wad into his palm with disgust. "Bleh . . . Is this black licorice?"

Zuzu knew better than that. It was the only kind of candy Kaboom didn't like. She always made sure to avoid it. But when she examined the sack that he pulled from his pocket, she saw it was full of nothing but black licorice.

She must have grabbed the wrong bag at the store. At least that was the only explanation she could think of.

Kaboom wiped his tongue on his sleeve.

A few blocks away, Zephyr Mephisto dropped a sack full of colorful candy into the gutter and snickered.

HARDENED SOLDIERS WERE known to cry while witnessing the elegant artistry of Zephyr Mephisto dancing on the wire.

His wire was not strung very high, his routine was not death-defying in any way, and his costume was a simple white leotard, but his technique was so fluid and refined that it felt more like a miracle of nature than a demonstration of skill. Some compared him to a spider, dancing across its web.

It took years of study and constant practice to make something so difficult seem effortless. Mephisto refused to use a balancing tool like a pole, an umbrella, or a fan—considered it cheating, in fact. He rehearsed six hours a day, six days a week. On Sundays, he would read the newspaper while bouncing on a trampoline.

Zephyr Mephisto did not enjoy touring the countryside, so after years on the road, hopping from circus to circus, he had signed a contract securing him a permanent position as the featured act at a burlesque show in Paris.

Mephisto had never been beloved by his fellow performers. He was unfriendly and pretentious—he looked down his nose at anyone he felt was not sufficiently dedicated to their artistry (which was everyone but him). Though the other performers did not enjoy socializing with the slender, pointy-eyebrowed acrobat, they all agreed he was the most inspiring wire walker they had ever had the pleasure to witness.

Zephyr Mephisto was also a favorite of Princess Poppinlock of Monaco, and every year, he was invited to give a command performance at the birthday celebration of Her Royal Highness. A wire was strung up across the grand hall of the palace, and while guests enjoyed a dessert of fresh berries and cream, they were treated to a demonstration of otherworldly agility and technical perfection.

This is what Zephyr Mephisto's performance entailed:

He entered slowly, as if wading through syrup. Every movement of his willowy limbs rivaled the grace of a prima ballerina. He approached the wire with love and admiration. One hand caressed the cable, and after grabbing hold firmly, he levered himself off the floor with such strength and control he appeared to be lifted by invisible strings.

Up on the wire, Mephisto never wavered, never trembled. His actions were impossibly smooth, like a cool mountain stream. Backbends, splits, and somersaults—at no time did he seem to be exerting any effort at all. And at the end of his performance, when he balanced on the wire on one open palm, his legs perfectly vertical, his toes pointed directly at the sky, it was the stillness that drew the applause.

For minutes on end, he would remain frozen in place, as still as a statue, while the audience rose to their feet and shouted, *"Bravo!"*

Zephyr Mephisto loved nothing more than the pursuit of technical perfection, and nothing drove him to rage like the freewheeling antics of his brash young rival Hugh Mankebaum.

As THE WUNDERHEIM Traveling Circus crisscrossed the continent by rail, stories of the Human Kaboom spread to even the smallest villages in Europe. The spectacular act and its daring star helped the circus sell more tickets that summer than any season before.

Every few weeks, Wunderheim would commission a new poster to celebrate the stunt that was described in dramatic typography as IMPOSSIBLE! GRAVITY DEFEATED! A MIRACLE OF MIRACLES!

Despite his growing reputation and newfound status as an international celebrity, Kaboom kept a level head. He did negotiate a raise for himself, however, and one for Zuzana as well.

Zuzu was thrilled. She did not miss shoveling elephant dung at all. Plus, her harmless crush on the handsome daredevil had flourished into full-blown infatuation. She kept saving press clippings, along with ticket stubs and life-size lithographs, all under the guise of "professional duties." But really, she was keeping them for herself. When she opened her trunk to gaze at the collection of memorabilia, she felt dizzy with glee.

Aside from assisting with setup for the act and supervising the loading of equipment, Zuzu ran Kaboom's errands and prepared his meals (to ensure he ate some vegetables in addition to all the candy). She also made sure he wore matching socks.

One of her favorite responsibilities was helping him answer fan mail. A packet of letters would arrive nearly every day—letters that had chased after the show from town to town, sometimes for months, and eventually found their way to the constantly shifting location of the Wunderheim Traveling Circus.

Zuzu loved reading the letters to Kaboom, because they often said things she wished she could say herself, if only she had the courage.

"Mr. Kaboom, I love you," she read to him one day. "Will you marry me?"

"Dear HK, you are the most incredible creature I have ever laid eyes on. Will you do me the great honor of sending a personal photo?"

"Kaboom, I wanted to write you this letter to say you are my favorite performer in the circus, but how will you read it? Are you really blind? My mom says you are, but my dad says you ain't. Please send candy."

Kaboom laughed. "That one deserves a response."

"Very well." Zuzu pulled out a fresh sheet of paper and a pen. The stationery had been custom-made by a printer who was a fan. An illustration of Kaboom shooting out of an inkwell decorated the top of the page. Beneath, it read: FROM THE DESK OF THE HUMAN KABOOM.

Zuzu prepared to take dictation and write down whatever Kaboom said. Which was difficult under any circumstances, because he tended to get excited and talk very quickly when responding to fans. It was especially difficult that day with the added distraction of Kaboom doing hand-stand push-ups without a shirt on.

"Dear Kid," he began. "Kaboom here. Well, not technically." He laughed. "Owing to the fact that I am blind

(really and truly) my intrepid personal secretary, Zuzana Zamboni"—he smiled at Zuzu—"is writing this letter as dictated. I have included a sugar toffee from Austria for your enjoyment."

Zuzu snapped open an envelope and held still. From six feet away, Kaboom tossed a piece of candy, which landed inside.

ONE NIGHT IN Brussels, Kaboom hit the high wire funny and twisted his ankle. He winced and fell but caught hold with one hand to keep from plummeting to the ground below. When he pulled himself back up onto the wire, he was rewarded with even more thunderous applause than usual, and from that night on, the "slip" became a part of the act.

The outrageous danger of the stunt was what fascinated people. From the moment the Human Kaboom entered the ring, it was impossible to look away. A blind man shot from a cannon onto a high wire was the most thrilling entertainment that anyone could ever hope to witness.

But for some, the death-defying daredevil took on a deeper significance. He represented boundless bravery, embodied the notion that with proper determination and skill, anything was possible. The Human Kaboom became a symbol, a metaphor for overcoming adversity through sheer gumption—and maybe a little insanity.

Of all Kaboom's fans, the most passionate were blind

children. They looked to the circus star as proof that they too could accomplish their wildest dreams. Kaboom would often invite one of the kids to sit on the back of his motorcycle as he circled the fountain in the town plaza. These lucky children would never tire of telling that story for the rest of their lives. Though sometimes their concerned mothers fainted with worry before the ride was over.

In private, Hugh was reclusive. He rebuffed the advances of even the most glamorous admirers. He turned down dinner invitations from powerful politicians and sports stars. He simply preferred the company of his fellow circus performers.

He would spend lazy afternoons joking and singing with the clowns, lifting weights with Bitsy, and playing backgammon with Mongo the elephant. Despite his explosive fame, inside the bubble of his circus family, he was still just Hugh Mankebaum, the only remaining member of a well-loved circus family. Everyone in the show had worked with at least one of his relatives, and some even remembered Hugh from his days as a child acrobat, back when he was embarrassed to admit he was going blind. Hugh had worked hard and made something special of himself. The other performers were proud of him.

But there was someone who looked upon his success from afar and grew sick with envy.

In fact, Zuzu was not the only one collecting articles about Kaboom. Zephyr Mephisto was too. He used them for knife-throwing practice. Especially the one titled WORLD'S GREATEST WIRE WALKER.

ON A BRIGHT, sunny morning in the Tuscan countryside, a special letter arrived via royal messenger. In a way, it was fan mail for Kaboom, but more specifically it was an invitation to give a command performance in Monaco, at the royal palace of Princess Poppinlock in honor of her birthday, the following Tuesday.

A second letter had also been dispatched via royal messenger. That one went to Zephyr Mephisto, informing him that his services would not be needed on this particular occasion, despite a five-year-long tradition. Mephisto raged, and darted the messenger's cap to the door with a throwing knife.

The terrified boy ran screaming from the room.

THOUGH WUNDERHEIM WAS certain his audience that night would be sad to miss the star attraction of the show, he was willing to risk their disappointment in order to reap the rewards of the international publicity that would come from Kaboom's performance at the princess's private birthday soirée.

So Zuzu and Kaboom packed up the steel cannon and the wire and booked a train bound for Monaco. Itsy and Bitsy drove them to the station in a wagon pulled by Mary the elephant.

"Don't you go falling in love with the princess," warned Itsy.

"I just couldn't stand it if you became royalty," joked Bitsy. "Imagine that blindfolded face printed on money."

"It's the only place it hasn't been printed," teased Itsy.

The station was covered in posters emblazoned with the image of Kaboom. He and Zuzu climbed aboard the train while Mary helped Bitsy load the trunks with the other cargo. They all waved goodbye as the locomotive started chugging away.

"See you tomorrow!" shouted Zuzu over the train whistle as she leaned out the window.

Kaboom had already settled into his seat to take a nap, but she was too excited to sleep. She had never been to a palace before, never met any royalty. Itsy had even loaned her a fancy floor-length yellow dress for the occasion. Though when Zuzu wore it, it came up to her knees.

KABOOM AND ZUZU were greeted at the Monaco station by a royal welcoming committee. Footmen unloaded their luggage, and a chauffeur directed them toward a private automobile that would whisk them to the palace, where they could begin making preparations for the show that evening.

"Be careful with that!" scolded Zuzu. One of the footmen

had nearly dropped the crate with the cannon inside. "The back end is much heavier than the front."

The servants stared at Zuzu, their mouths agape. They were not used to taking orders from a young girl.

"Do as she says," instructed Kaboom. "This young lady is my eyes and ears, and most of my brain too."

Zuzu crossed her arms and nodded emphatically.

"Am I clear?" asked Kaboom. The men nodded. "Am I clear?" he asked again, this time with his head turned toward Zuzu.

"The ceiling is a bit low, and there's a cart at your seven o'clock."

Kaboom adjusted his feet slightly. He then executed a perfect backflip, avoiding the ceiling and the aforementioned cart. He bowed, and the onlookers applauded with enthusiasm. People gathered around to form a crowd.

"It's the Human Kaboom!"

"THE Human Kaboom?"

"The human KABOOM!"

"You'd better go ahead," whispered Zuzu.

"Follow me, sir," said the chauffeur, gesturing to a fancy white car. The circus star was scheduled for a private pre-show meeting with the princess.

"I hope these rubes don't slow you down," said Kaboom as he mussed Zuzu's hair. "You'll need time to get ready for dinner. I know you'll look resplendent in your special yellow dress!"

Zuzu's cheeks turned pink, and though she was sure he couldn't see her, she felt confident that Kaboom could feel the heat radiating from her face.

THE ROYAL SERVANTS proved obedient and efficient in following Zuzana's instructions. They even helped her to her feet when she tripped on her way up the stairs to the palace.

The wire was strung in the garden outside the grand hall, which, despite the name, was not quite grand enough to accommodate a cannon shot. The first part of the show would be performed indoors after dinner, and then the guests would retire to the open air to watch the much-anticipated finale under the stars.

The stage was set, and Kaboom arrived to double-check the equipment before changing into his costume. Zuzu followed close on his heels.

"What was she like?" she asked.

Kaboom played dumb. "Who?"

"You know who! The princess! Is she as beautiful as they say?"

"How would I know?" said Kaboom.

Zuzu rolled her eyes.

"I'll tell you one thing," he said, grinning. "She smells fantastic. Like lilac and lavender."

Zuzu didn't like the way he complimented her rival for his affection.

"Well, not everyone around here smells so sweet." She wrinkled her nose. "You should wash up before the show, and a little cologne couldn't hurt. It's the round bottle in your shaving kit."

"What would I do without you?" he asked. Then he spun on his heel and headed back inside, accompanied by a royal valet to guide him through the palace.

Zuzu was keen to go get ready herself, but out of the corner of her eye, she noticed a hooded figure lurking a little too close to the supports of the high wire.

"Excuse me," she called. "What are you doing?"

Peering beneath the hood, she recognized the long nose and pointy eyebrows of Zephyr Mephisto. He stepped back silently.

"What are you doing here? You're not in the show tonight."

"I know that," spat Mephisto, betraying his secret rage. He regained control of himself and removed his hood. "I am merely a fan, here to enjoy the *spectacle*." He struggled through his clear distaste for the word.

"You should know better than to touch another performer's equipment."

"How right you are, young lady." He knelt and put a hand on her shoulder. "Young Mankebaum is lucky to have such a loyal assistant." He squeezed her arm and put his face too close to hers. "Your parents would be proud. They were real circus artists, not a crass sideshow attraction."

Zuzu shook free of his grasp. "You don't know what you're talking about."

Mephisto sneered, then threw the hood back over his head.

"Well, I'm sure this evening's performance will be one to remember," he said ominously.

Zuzu watched him slink away, then triple-checked the equipment to make sure he hadn't messed with anything.

"Guard!" she called to one of the foot soldiers in the garden. "Keep an eye on this equipment until showtime." The guard nodded. "It's a matter of life and death."

Just beyond the palace walls, Zephyr Mephisto dropped a pouch full of powder into the gutter and hurried out of sight.

ZUZU PUT ON the yellow dress and tried her best to walk in the heels that Itsy had loaned her. After tumbling to the carpet twice, she decided to spend the rest of the evening barefoot. No one seemed to care.

The birthday feast was twelve courses long, each expertly prepared by the royal chef. Zuzu stuffed her face with glee. Kaboom ate nothing, as was his preshow superstition.

"This chicken is delicious!" mumbled Zuzu with her mouth full. "And these potatoes!"

Kaboom spun his empty dinner plate on the table, somehow aware that the princess could not take her eyes off him.

After some breathless introductions and royal pomposity, an elaborate cake was served, and the show began.

Zuzu had never seen a collection of talent equal to the intimate performance she witnessed that evening.

First, Lady Jumbojingle, the famed prima donna of the Vienna Opera, sang arias from Mozart and Wagner. Her vibrato was hair-raising, and her high notes could shatter glass.

Next, the Cockamamie Cuckoos performed. The masked clowns were acclaimed for their acrobatic tumbling and hilarious antics. They worked on a teeterboard, a kind of oversize seesaw. One clown would stand on the low end of the board, and two others would leap from a tower onto the high end, launching the first one into the air to perform flips, twists, and other impressive tricks.

Last came Dr. Woofenstein, the celebrated dog trainer, whose clever canines danced on two legs, jumped through flaming hoops, and solved mathematical equations by barking. *"The dog that chases its tail will be dizzy!"* he declared with great authority.

At the conclusion of his act, Dr. Woofenstein made a puppy appear from an empty box, and presented the adorable pooch to the princess as a birthday gift.

With the inside portion of the show concluded, the guests were invited to the garden for the finale. Tea was served while Zuzu and Kaboom made their last-minute preparations. The wire was perfectly tight, the cannon was aimed precisely on target, and Zuzu carefully measured the powder from her pouch to load the charge. In the darkness, she did not notice that the color was different than usual.

Kaboom did his warm-up stretches and waited for the band to play his intro music.

"Break a leg," said Zuzu. She straightened the blindfold on his face while he lowered into a front split.

"Thank you, my friend. There's no one I would rather share this moment with than you."

Zuzu giggled and kissed him on the forehead.

THE BAND BEGAN the overture, and Kaboom strode out to a round of enthusiastic applause. He waved, climbed into the cannon, and struck a match. He lit the fuse and disappeared from view, into the barrel.

The band stopped playing. The audience of aristocrats held their breath with anticipation. Aside from the crickets in the grass, the only sound audible was the fizzling hiss of the burning fuse. Then there was a brief silence before . . .

KABOOM!!!

The sound was deafening. The explosion toppled tables and lit the grass around the cannon on fire.

Zuzu knew immediately that something had gone terribly wrong. She looked to the sky and watched her beloved companion fly higher than ever before—over the wire, over the walls of the cliffside palace, and out to sea. He arced in front of the moon, flipped gracefully one last time, and then dove with perfect form into the turbulent waters below.

He was never seen again.

NEWS OF THE incident spread quickly. Grisly rumors were splashed across the front pages of papers around the world.

While dozens of boats searched the bay, with grim expectations, the police launched an official investigation. Their first suspect was poor Zuzana Zamboni. When they brought her in for interrogation, she was inconsolable, sobbing so hard she couldn't speak.

Zuzu was sure she had checked the equipment and that everything had been set correctly. She had mixed the powder herself the night before: four parts flash powder, three parts smoke powder, and just a tiny pinch of the highly explosive bang powder.

The police were kind but firm. They confiscated the props to be kept as evidence. All the attendees were questioned, including the princess herself, but there was no clue as to what could have gone wrong. It wasn't until the powder was tested by a chemist that the mystery was solved.

The flash and smoke mixture had been switched for pure explosive powder. Zuzu was sure it was the work of Zephyr Mephisto. When the police arrived at his apartment for questioning, he had vanished without a trace. But the knife-stabbed photos of Kaboom that lined the walls were incriminating, to say the least.

The police returned the confiscated evidence to Zuzu, and the princess provided a first-class train ticket for her to return home to the circus.

WHEN ZUZU ARRIVED, her entire circus family was waiting at the train station to greet her. Once again, they hugged and cried and told stories about their dear departed friend, just as they had after the earthquake that took the lives of the Zamboni family. But this time, the outpouring of grief spread far beyond the big top to every corner of the globe.

Kaboom's tragic death was mourned by countless fans, and even strangers who had never seen him perform. Candlelight vigils, musical tributes, and heartfelt memorials celebrated his legacy.

At the end of the season, Kaboom's cannon was placed in the town square of Valencia, and thousands of admirers came to adorn the machine with flowers in honor of their hero, whose blazingly passionate life was cut short by a nefarious rival.

Somewhere, on a stank-filled sheep farm, deep in the mountains of Switzerland, Zephyr Mephisto seethed with rage, especially when the royal proclamation was issued, officially declaring Hugh Mankebaum to be "the greatest wire walker who ever lived."

Mephisto was driven mad with jealousy. He remained in

hiding for the rest of his life and never performed again. As the years passed, the once-famous Zephyr Mephisto faded from public memory until he was totally forgotten.

MEANWHILE, KABOOM'S LEGEND only grew.

In each retelling of Kaboom's tragic story, the wire grew higher and higher, the cannon farther and farther away, until his stunt reached mythic proportions.

Zuzana grew up and rose through the ranks of the circus until she was managing the whole business. Eventually, she married a kind and talented juggler, known for his preternatural coordination. They traveled happily with their circus family and enjoyed life on the road for many years.

After retirement, they settled down and bought a farm in southern Spain. They adopted a menagerie of circus animals who had grown too old to perform.

Zuzana brought her circus memorabilia collection with her. She had never stopped collecting, and had become world-renowned for her expertise on the subject.

So when the British Museum began planning a special exhibit about the history of the European circus, the curator knew just who to call.

All of Zuzana's posters, letters, and paraphernalia were presented for thousands of visitors to admire. It was almost as good as seeing a golden-age circus in person.

There were photos of Lazlo the lion gently teasing a live rabbit with his enormous paw, Mabel the elephant plucking a silver coin from the palm of an archduke, Mongo and Mary setting a table for dinner with their trunks, Egyptian belly dancers and Mongolian trick riders and Chinese acrobats performing their amazing feats.

Itsy's and Bitsy's costumes, Equilibrio's sword, and Wunderheim's top hat were displayed under glass. Ephemera like ticket stubs, popcorn bags, and business cards helped people appreciate even the smallest delights of Circus Day.

Three generations of the Flying Zamboni Brothers troupe were represented with portraits and biographical information that Zuzana had researched herself.

The whole exhibition was a smashing success, but the most popular part was the room dedicated to that legendary blind daredevil, the Human Kaboom.

Elderly visitors told unbelievable stories to anyone who would listen about the time they had seen Hugh Mankebaum shot from a cannon to land on a high wire. Skeptical teenagers ate their words after watching grainy film footage that proved the tales to be true.

Zuzana Zamboni was incredibly proud of the way the museum exhibit turned out. Her favorite part was the collection of comic books, video games, and movies inspired by the Human Kaboom. It reminded her of the wise words Wunderheim had shared with her those many years ago: *True legends never die.*

So the next time you do something scary like dive off a cliff, or jump out of an airplane, or try to eat a weird new food, think of old Hugh to make yourself feel brave. And if you need an extra dose of courage, you might find it helps to shut your eyes and shout out "KABOOM!"

V.

The Human Kaboom

(the one with the cursed pirate treasure)

illustrated by

MARTA ALTÉS

*T*hunder crashed through the darkness of the night, and monstrous waves tossed the mighty pirate ship across the Caribbean Sea. The first mate clung to a mast for dear life and screamed at the captain over the roar of the storm.

"¡Tíralo!" he begged. "Throw it overboard!"

"Never!" The dapper captain clutched a golden coin in one hand and drew his sword with the other.

"It's cursed! You'll kill us all!" pleaded the desperate sailor. A flash in the distance lit the terror in his eyes.

"Cursed?" The captain threw back his head and erupted in a fit of crazed laughter. "There's no such thing as a cur—"

Lightning ripped from the sky and blasted the wooden ship, which was loaded with barrels of flammable rum.

KABOOM!

Marco McEnroe dreamed of pirates and sunken treasure almost every night, even though he lived in Iowa, a thousand miles from the sea. The landlocked location hadn't stopped Marco from hunting for hidden valuables. In fact, he'd filled a whole tackle box with "treasures" he'd found by scrounging around in the dirt.

Mostly they were rocks: colorful agates, sparkly quartz, speckled jasper, and a few chunks of petrified wood. The special stones were stored alongside a variety of other tiny prizes Marco had discovered: glass marbles, a plastic dinosaur, a skeleton key, an old New York City subway token, and a genuine arrowhead.

Marco's parents had surprised him with a ticket to go visit his older sister over spring break. Some kids might have been nervous to take an airplane all by themselves, but Marco was too excited to be scared. His sister had moved to an island, which meant he was going to see the ocean for the very first time. He was sure he'd find tons of new treasures like seashells and sea stars and sea glass and probably other kinds of sea stuff he'd never even heard about before. He made sure to pack his snorkel and plenty of sunscreen.

But the island where Layla lived was in northeastern Canada, which isn't exactly known for fun in the sun. Not many palm trees there. And even during spring break, the weather can be quite chilly.

So when Layla pulled up in front of the airport and found

her little brother shivering outside in a Hawaiian shirt and shorts, she couldn't help but laugh.

Layla had purple hair, face piercings, and so many tattoos she'd lost count. At one time, she'd toured the world playing with a rock band called Thunder Snow, but that was before she decided to go back to school and get a doctorate degree in maritime archaeology.

Layla was a full fifteen years older than Marco. Sometimes they joked that he was an "oops baby," though their parents never laughed at that joke.

Marco liked having a much older sister. She taught him about cool music and movies, gave good advice, and never picked on him the way some older siblings tended to do.

Layla got out of the car, and Marco ran over to give her a hug.

"I missed you!" he said.

"I missed you too, stinkball!" Layla picked him up and spun him around. "You're getting big!"

Marco beamed as he hoisted his suitcase into the trunk. "I've been working out."

"Oh yeah? You do look buff." Layla chuckled. "You also look cold. Here." She took off her tattered leather jacket and draped it over his shoulders.

"Can I drive?" asked Marco.

Layla rolled her eyes.

Marco's flight had landed in a storm, with dark clouds spoiling the view out the window. The drive home from the airport wasn't much better, and he couldn't spot the coast through the rain, no matter how hard he tried. When they pulled onto the rinky-dink ferry to reach the island where Layla lived, Marco jumped out of the car and leaned over the railing of the boat, confident he was about to get his first glimpse of the water. But when he looked down, all he could see was a thick white mist.

"That's why they call it Fog Island," Layla explained. "Some people think it's gloomy, but I love it. There are only a couple dozen houses, but some old-timer just passed away and the bank decided to rent the place while they figure out what to do with the property." She snapped her fingers. "I snatched it up as soon as I heard. Wait till you see."

Marco couldn't see much of anything. It was like driving through a thick cloud as they exited the ferry, climbed a steep hill, and pulled into the driveway of Layla's new home.

The fog parted just enough to reveal a crooked little house with a bloodred door.

"Isn't it great?" asked Layla as she grabbed Marco's suitcase from the trunk.

Great is not how Marco would have described it. The word *creepy* came to mind. As they climbed the creaky stairs to the porch, the front door suddenly swung wide open, emitting a rusty whine that sounded like a demon screaming. Marco gasped.

"Relax," said Layla when she saw the terrified look on her little brother's face. "It does that sometimes. It's an old house."

That didn't seem like a sufficient explanation to Marco, but he didn't want to spoil his sister's enthusiasm.

"No one locks their door here," she added. "How cool is that?"

They stepped inside, and the floor groaned beneath their feet.

"I'm still getting settled," said Layla as she turned on the lights, which flickered when she closed the door behind them, "but the place came furnished."

The walls of the house were covered with hundreds of old paintings of sailboats. The couch, carpet, and curtains were decorated with vintage nautical patterns. The wooden tables looked like they belonged in a museum. Marco smelled mothballs and heard strange noises coming from the basement.

"What was that?" asked Marco nervously.

"That's just the radiator," said Layla. "You'll get used to it."

Marco shivered. "Don't you think it's kinda spooky to live in a dead person's house?"

"Don't be such a wuss," Layla said, laughing. "I think it's cool! The former resident's name was Marion Lantutsky, and I think she had excellent taste." She took a life preserver off the wall and tossed it over Marco's head. "Though she was a bit of a hoarder."

Layla opened a cabinet to reveal a hundred mismatched coffee mugs.

"I stashed all the junk in the extra bedroom. The good news is, you're welcome to keep whatever you find in there. The bad news is, there's hardly any space to move around. So you get to pick: You can sleep on the couch down here or upstairs in the bed with me."

"I'll take the couch," said Marco. "I'm way too big to share a bed." He flexed his muscles.

"Whatever you say, stinkball."

"Can I go rummage through the junk room?" Marco kicked off his shoes.

"Of course," said Layla, "but don't get your hopes up."

It was excellent advice, which Marco didn't take. His head filled with visions of rare antiques and expensive jewelry. Instead, what he found were stacks of old books, towers of magazines, and dozens of garbage bags stuffed with unused promotional T-shirts.

He dug through the bags for a while, hoping to at least find a shirt in his size.

"They're pretty much all XL," admitted Layla. "But if you need a new bag . . ." She opened up a box full of canvas totes branded with the names of various stores and radio stations.

"Thanks," said Marco joylessly.

But that first night wasn't a total bust. Unlike at his parents' house, Marco was allowed to stay up late. He and Layla watched three Jackie Chan movies in a row and ate four plates of spicy nachos for dinner.

MARCO DIDN'T SLEEP so well. It could have been indigestion. It could have been the lumpy couch cushions. It could have been the spooky noises coming from the basement throughout the night.

⚓

He would have preferred to snooze for a few more hours, but Layla had a student coming over that morning. When she wasn't busy studying maritime archaeology at the local university, she taught music lessons to make money.

Given her appearance, most people wouldn't guess that Layla played the accordion. And typically, there isn't much demand for accordion lessons. But she had recently started a weekly jam session at the local seafood shack, and suddenly, everyone in town wanted to learn to play the squeeze-box.

Layla was a talented musician. Unfortunately, most of her students were not. Marco stuck around for her first lesson, but after suffering through the hour-long session of off-key warbling, he was highly motivated to flee the house and avoid the noise of the remaining lessons that day.

It was raining outside and he hadn't brought the right clothes for the weather, so he rummaged through Layla's closet to borrow a sweater, a waterproof jacket, and a pair of green galoshes. None of it fit quite right.

"Going somewhere, stinkball?" Layla was organizing sheet music in the living room, preparing for her next student to arrive.

"I'm gonna go down the hill and check out the pier."

"Do Mom and Dad let you wander around strange towns by yourself?" Layla asked.

Marco shrugged.

"Well, okay, then." She zipped up his coat. "I'm sorry I have to work while you're here, but tuition doesn't pay itself, you know? Tonight we can make lasagna, and I'll teach you how to play backgammon."

"Okay," said Marco.

"Tomorrow, I'm free all morning. We can do something fun. Maybe visit the lighthouse?"

Layla pointed out the window, and at that very moment a bolt of lightning flashed through the sky, illuminating the looming tower in the distance.

"Whoa," said Layla. "Did you see that?"

"Yeah," said Marco. "Creepy."

"Ah, don't be such a scaredy-cat," teased Layla. She punched his arm and went to the kitchen to fill her mug with tea.

"Yeah, right," muttered Marco. "I'm not scared."

A sudden bang on the door startled him so badly he nearly jumped out of his galoshes. Luckily, his sister didn't see.

"That'll be Drummond," said Layla. She dropped her voice to a whisper. "Only started playing two weeks ago, so I suggest you skedaddle quick if you don't want your ears to bleed."

"*Skedaddle.*" Marco giggled at the word. Like many little brothers, he was convinced his older sister was the funniest person in the world.

He opened the door for a wet little kid lugging a large accordion case.

"Have a good lesson!" shouted Marco as he hopped down the front steps into the rain.

LAYLA'S HOUSE WAS perched on a hill overlooking the ocean. There were a dozen other little houses on the hill, and each of the doors was painted with a different bright color. Layla told Marco it was so that sailors could spot their homes on Fog Island as they sailed into port through the haze.

The rain fell in fat globs as Marco trotted down the hill, but when he heard the screeching of a novice accordion player in the distance, he knew he had made the right decision in venturing out of the house to explore.

He skipped through a puddle, curious to test out his new galoshes.

Splash! Splish! Sploosh!

"Pretty good." Marco wiggled his toes and admired how his socks remained dry. He spotted a shiny white rock on the pavement and shoved it in his pocket to add to his collection.

When Marco reached the main road at the bottom of the hill, he noticed a bucket full of orange safety flags attached to a pole. Layla had warned him about this.

They didn't have any stoplights on the tiny island. So to avoid accidents, pedestrians were supposed to borrow a reflective flag from the bucket, wave it around as they used the crosswalk, and then place the flag in the bucket on the other side of the road. Supposedly, cars could see the brightly colored flags, even through the fog, and slow down to avoid hitting anyone.

This sounded like a ridiculous system to Marco. He had assumed that Layla was making the whole thing up. But apparently, in Canada, it was real. He grabbed a flag and waved himself across the street.

There Marco finally got his first good look at the ocean. It wasn't sparkly, blue, and inviting like he'd seen in the movies. It was dark and foreboding. The churning waves were almost black. And, much to his surprise, the vast expanse of water filled him with dread.

But Marco had three hours to kill and nowhere else to go, so he marched onto the pier in hopes of discovering an adventure. And if not an adventure, perhaps some entertainment. And if not entertainment, well, something distracting, at the very least.

The pier was shaped like an E. There was a broad wooden walkway closest to the shore, and three thinner docks that stuck out into the bay. The docks were crowded with all sorts of boats: big fancy sailboats, tiny old rowboats, sports boats, fishing boats, even a few Jet Skis for summertime. The boats were tied to the docks with thick knots of rope so they wouldn't accidentally float off into the ocean when no one was looking. Though there was no risk of that at the moment. It was low tide, so the watercraft sat awkwardly on the dry ocean bed.

The main part of the pier was lined with a handful of shops, and it looked like the whole structure was built to bob up and down with the tide. For now, it rested on the dry rocks of the ocean floor, and the stores sat slightly askew.

The most promising-looking shop was called Fog Island Souvenirs, and Marco decided to check that one out first. The bell on the door woke the teenage clerk, who was sleeping, face flat on the counter.

"Can I help you?" said the clerk, without lifting her head.

"Oh, uh . . . I'm just poking around," said Marco.

The girl sat up and wiped the drool from her mouth. A receipt was stuck to her cheek.

"You're new." She peeled the paper from her face and rubbed her eyes. "That's pretty cool, I guess. Don't get many new kids around here."

"I'm just visiting. I'm Marco, Layla's brother."

"Oh, cool! I'm Trish," said Trish. "Layla rocks. She plays the accordion. You know that. She plays in the band at the fish 'n' chip on Tuesdays. Now everyone wants to play accordion because they saw her play. And because she's pretty cool. So, yeah . . ." Trish had lost her train of thought. "Pretty cool."

Marco started poking around the store. The shelves were crowded with ships in bottles, seashells with googly eyes, and novelty beer cozies with cheesy jokes printed on the sides. The whole place reeked of scented candles.

"So, um, is there anything fun to do around here?" Marco asked hopefully.

"Yeah, sure!" Trish brightened. "This place is pretty cool. You can go fishing, or fry up some fish, or take out a fishing boat . . . Mostly fishing stuff, I guess."

"Sounds . . . pretty cool." Marco tried to hide his disappointment unsuccessfully.

"Say . . ." Trish leaned over the counter. "Is that old house really haunted?"

"Which house? Layla's house?" asked Marco.

"Yeah." Trish nodded. "Crazy Carl says it's haunted. I don't know. Crazy Carl is pretty crazy. Says he's seen ghost ships in the bay. But I've never seen any ghosts around here, and I've lived on this island my whole life. So, yeah . . ."

The perfumy smell in the shop was starting to make Marco light-headed, and Trish's rambling didn't help.

"I'm gonna get some fresh air," he said. "It was nice to meet you."

"Yeah, the candle smell." Trish took a deep breath. "People say it stinks in here, but not as bad as the bait shop next door. Grimey, who works there, he doesn't shower and he chews tobacco, so it's gotta stink even worse in there. But, yeah, the candles. I can't smell 'em anymore." She took a whiff and shrugged. "I guess I got used to it, so it doesn't bother me, which is pretty cool, I guess . . ."

Marco waved politely, then slipped out the door before Trish could start talking again.

Once he was gone, she folded her arms into a pillow and put her head down on the counter for another nap.

MARCO PEEKED INSIDE the bait shop, but it really did reek like fish guts, and the surly teen behind the counter looked anything but friendly, so he walked past without going inside. A sign at the candy shop offered saltwater taffy, but the store was closed on Sundays during the off-season. As was the burger joint, the ice cream shack, the whale-watching stand, and the kayak rental place.

Marco strolled to the far end of the pier and stared down at the ocean floor. The tide was so low he could see bare rocks with little tide pools scattered in between. He lay on his belly and peered over the edge to get a better look at the tiny crabs that scuttled from puddle to puddle. Marco spotted a spiral-shaped seashell that would make an excellent addition to his collection. He stretched out his arm in an effort to reach it.

"Might want to wait for high tide if you're thinking of

going for a swim," called an old man from in front of a small café. The sign above the door read POSEIDON'S POT and had a picture of a crowned merman holding a steaming cup of coffee.

Marco had walked right past the place without noticing it.

The old man wore an apron tight around his bulging belly. He had his hands on his hips, and his eyes were squeezed shut. "Course, you'll have to watch out for the nipple-biting fish!" He chuckled. "They'll get ya every time."

"Excuse me?" Marco turned to face him.

The old man seemed taken aback for a moment, almost like he hadn't expected Marco to hear what he'd said. "You must be new in town."

"Yeah, I'm Marco."

"It's a real pleasure to meet you, Marco. I'm Toots." The man thumbed over his shoulder at the ramshackle café. "This is my place."

"Toots?" Marco asked.

"Yeah, like 'foots' or 'schmutz'—good ol' Toots. That's me." Toots smiled. He looked at Marco like he was squinting into the sun. "Say, I couldn't help but notice you seem like a curious sort of fella. A seeker of that which does not wish to be found, one might say."

"Sure." Marco crawled to his feet. "I guess."

Toots nodded. "Would you mind giving an old pack rat a hand with something?"

Marco considered the offer. He wasn't sure what Toots had in mind, but whatever it was would probably be the most interesting option he'd find all day. He set his expectations for "distracting, at the very least."

"Actually, I am a bit bored," Marco admitted.

"That's terrific! Not that you're bored," clarified Toots. "That you're here. That you're interested. That we're having this conversation! You're just the kind of person I've been

waiting for." Toots tried to snap his fingers, but they didn't make a sound. He tried again, failed, and frowned. "Never mind that. Follow me. I need to unpack some boxes, and this old bag of bones don't work like it used to." Toots wheezed, and Marco realized it was a laugh. "I'll give ya ten bucks for your help, and all the coffee you can drink."

Marco shook his head. "I don't drink coffee."

"That's okay," said Toots. "More for me." He wheeze-laughed again.

THE INSIDE OF the café was dusty and dark. The front area had two simple tables and some wooden bar chairs scattered about. The walls were crowded with signed photos of local fishermen and sailors from around the world. Ornate frames displayed dozens of different kinds of knots tied with rope.

On the far wall was a door that led back to the kitchen area, and next to that was the counter where the coffee was served. But the coffee machine didn't look like anything Marco had ever seen before. It looked more like a science experiment.

Rubber tubes formed loops and spirals that resembled a roller coaster track. Bubbling brown liquid circulated through the tubes and dripped into beakers. Scales, thermometers, and pressure gauges measured the conditions of the apparatus in various places. The aroma of fresh-brewed coffee filled the room.

"My prized possession." Toots opened a nozzle, and a steaming stream of coffee filled his mug. "Are you sure you don't want a taste?"

Marco was intrigued. "Do you have any cream or sugar?"

"Ha!" barked Toots. "And ruin the rich bouquet and clean flavors I've worked so hard to cultivate?" He put his nose over the mug and inhaled deeply. "This is pure kopi luwak."

"Kopi what?"

"The finest coffee in the world!" explained Toots. "Small catlike creatures called civets pick the ripest berries from the tallest trees in the jungle, and then coffee hunters pick the digested berries from the civets' dung to be roasted and ground for gourmet consumption."

Marco frowned. "Are you saying you're drinking poo?"

Toots wheezed. "Well, that's a bit of an oversimpli-fication, but . . ." He took a long sip, swallowed, and licked his lips. "Yes."

Marco's nostrils flared as he failed to hide his disgust.

"Are you sure you don't want to try?"

Marco shook his head vigorously.

"Too bad," said Toots. "I roast it myself in the back. And the brewing technique is of my own design. I built this percolator from scratch. You won't find coffee like this anywhere else in the world." Toots gestured proudly at his machine, and a splash of coffee spilled from his mug. "People used to sail from miles away just to try a cup . . ."

"Used to?" asked Marco.

Toots cleared his throat. "Ah." He clutched his mug with both hands and shrugged. "Business has . . . slowed down lately."

Marco felt bad for making the old man sad, but Toots quickly changed the subject.

"You ever use a crowbar before?"

"Um." Marco thought about it for a moment. "No."

"Well, everybody should learn how to use a crowbar at some point." Toots nodded at a long piece of metal with curved ends that was lying by the door. "You still keen to help me sort through my collection?"

"Why not?" said Marco. "I've got literally nothing else to do."

"Terrific!" Toots raised his mug with satisfaction.

Marco retrieved the crowbar, and Toots instructed him

to stomp around on the floorboards until he heard the hollow sound he was looking for.

"There it is!" He looked around the room suspiciously and lowered his voice to a whisper. "I hid my most valuable stuff under there."

"What kind of stuff?"

"Oh, all kinds of wonderful stuff." Toots swayed as he reminisced. "Sailors would pass through with treasures from faraway lands, and we would barter and trade. Rare stamps, signed books, baseball cards, Beanie Babies . . . Pry up these boards, and you'll see. Probably fifteen boxes full of treasure down there."

Now Marco was excited.

The boards were nailed down tight, so it wasn't easy. But Toots offered some helpful suggestions, and eventually, Marco managed to loosen three wooden planks to reveal a hidden chamber under the floor.

Toots clasped his hands together as Marco dragged the boards out of the way. "That's good work, my boy. Very good. But I'm afraid the hard part is yet to come."

Marco wiped the sweat from his forehead.

"I'd love to help, but—my back." Toots rubbed his back and made a pained face.

"It's okay," said Marco. "You want me to hoist all the boxes out from under there?"

"Hardworking *and* smart! I knew I liked you." Toots wheezed.

Marco lowered himself into the hidden chamber. It was

bigger than he'd expected, and packed with boxes made of reinforced plastic—waterproof, fireproof, and sealed airtight. They looked heavy.

Marco giggled with excitement. He had found an adventure after all. An adventure involving strenuous physical labor, but an adventure nonetheless.

"Where do you want me to put these things?" asked Marco.

"Oh, just pile them anywhere." Toots glanced over his shoulder. "I'm expecting some company to arrive, and I don't want them to get in the way, so . . . I'm gonna see if I can meet them somewhere else." He nodded at his own idea. "If I'm not back before you finish, just grab ten dollars from the register before you go."

"Wait, what?" Marco was slightly confused, but Toots hurried out the door without answering. So Marco rolled up his sleeves and ducked below the floorboards to get to work.

It took him hours to lug all the boxes out from their hiding spot. It was dark and slippery down there, and there wasn't much room to maneuver.

By the time he was finished, the sun hung low in the sky, and the tide was coming in. Marco knew it was getting late, and he figured he'd better get going. Layla would be expecting him.

He stepped outside to look for the old man, but Toots was nowhere to be found. So he returned to the café to collect his pay like he'd been told.

The cash register was unlike any he'd ever seen before—a

beautiful, ornate antique machine made of brass. There was no screen, and it didn't even have a plug.

It must have been built before electricity was invented, Marco thought.

Each button had its own little stem, like an old-fashioned typewriter, and made a satisfying clack when he pressed it. The display for dollars and cents at the top looked like the spinning wheels of a slot machine. Marco spent a few minutes poking at the buttons, but it wasn't until he tried turning the crank on the side of the register that the drawer in the base popped open with a DING!

The drawer was full of colorful cash. Marco had never seen Canadian currency before. The twenties were green, like normal, but the fifties were red, the fives were blue, and the tens were purple! It looked like Monopoly money. But Marco figured it was no stranger than the crossing flags, so he grabbed a purple bill and shoved it in his pocket.

"WHERE HAVE YOU been?" shouted Layla from the kitchen. Old-school funk music was blasting from the record player, and Layla was singing along. *"If you hear any noise, it's just me and the boys. Hit me!"*

Marco kicked off his galoshes and dropped his coat by the door. "I got a job," he said.

Layla laughed. She was dance-sliding across the tile in thick woolen socks and dropping raw sheets of lasagna into a pot of boiling water.

Marco slapped the purple ten-dollar bill onto the kitchen table.

"Oh, you were serious?" She stopped dancing.

"For my share of the groceries." Marco washed his hands and grabbed the biggest knife from the rack to start chopping the vegetables for the salad.

"What kind of job did you get?" asked Layla.

"Some guy needed help hauling boxes." Marco started hacking the lettuce apart with a meat cleaver.

"Some guy?" Layla gently replaced the cleaver in her little brother's hand with a smaller knife so he wouldn't accidentally chop off one of his fingers.

"He seemed nice!" added Marco.

"I hope when you go back home, you don't tell Mom and Dad I let you wander around the docks by yourself, hanging out with random strangers."

Marco zipped his lips.

Layla demonstrated a proper chopping technique, and then Marco sliced the carrots like an expert.

They choreographed an elaborate dance routine to one of Layla's favorite songs while they waited for the pasta to bake in the oven. The whole meal turned out to be delicious.

After dinner, they left the dishes to soak in the sink and set up the backgammon board on the kitchen table.

"Want to see something weird?" asked Layla.

"Of course," said Marco.

She put a kettle on the stove and dropped a bag of tea in her cup. "If I'm making tea, the burner won't light." She turned the knob, but no flame appeared. "But if I'm making coffee . . ." She removed the tea bag and took down a bag of coffee beans from the cupboard. Then she turned the knob on the stove, and the burner ignited right away.

"Are you messing with me?" asked Marco.

"No," protested Layla. "I swear!"

"That is weird," admitted Marco.

"You want some coffee?" asked Layla.

"No!" Marco stuck out his tongue. "Why is everybody always trying to get me to drink that stuff?"

"Jeez," said Layla. "Overreacting much? Sit down, stinkball. I'll teach you how to play."

AFTER ANOTHER LONG night of sibling revelry, Marco woke up to the smell of blueberry pancakes. "Good morning, sleepyhead," said Layla as she sat down by his feet on the couch. "You slept late, but I think we'll still have time to hike to the lighthouse before my first lesson."

Marco rubbed the sleep from his eyes and sat up. Layla dropped a plate of pancakes in his lap and handed him a fork. "Eat up, stinkball."

It was a sunny day, finally. Layla wore shorts and sunglasses, but Marco felt chilly even in a jacket.

"You think it's cold now?" Layla said. "You should visit

in January. I love this early spring weather. The mosquitoes haven't come out yet."

The path to the lighthouse was a narrow squiggle which wound past the houses that dotted the rolling green hills of

the island. Friendly neighbors recognized Layla from afar and came out to say hello.

The hillside smelled like grass and cows, a warm, earthy aroma. But as Marco and Layla approached the beach, the air began to change. The breeze from the ocean was crisp and cool. It smelled like shimmering fresh fish, dark-colored vegetables, and salt. Marco was reminded of the uneasy feeling he'd gotten when he first saw the ocean.

A staircase had been carved in the stone of the hill leading down to the beach. The stairs were steep and covered in moss. Layla descended carefully.

"Watch your step," she warned.

"I know!" protested Marco, just a second before he slipped and nearly lost his balance. Luckily, his sister didn't see.

The beach was rocky and scattered with busy little creatures. Hermit crabs scuttled between puddles, where sea stars watched tiny shrimp swim in circles as they waited for high tide. Marco immediately began hunting around for treasures to take home with him.

Clumps of seaweed littered the shore, and while Marco stuffed his pockets with shells, Layla stooped to scoop up a handful of the green stuff. She offered some to Marco.

"Sea lettuce. Try it."

Marco shook his head. "I'm not falling for that."

"Seriously!" Layla shoved the wet green leaves into her mouth and started to chew. "It's delicious. Reminds me of Japanese food."

Marco waited for her to swallow, still suspecting a trick. But after Layla gulped down the sea greens with a grin, he pinched a tiny wad of seaweed from the ground and gave it a whiff. He touched it with the tip of his tongue.

"Don't be a weenie! Just try it!"

So he did. Much to his surprise, it tasted pretty good.

"These over here are called limpets." Layla pointed to some rocky-looking white shells. "You can eat them too. But they're a little slimy."

"I think I'll pass," said Marco politely.

"And you see that big rock?"

Marco nodded.

"That's a leavitrite."

"A leavitrite?"

274

"Yeah. As in, we're just gonna leave it right there."

Marco groaned. "That's the stupidest joke I've ever heard."

"Why are you laughing, then, stinkball?"

The lighthouse towered above the beach. It looked like a white fang wearing a red wizard's hat. At the top, an eerie light spun in slow circles.

"Does somebody live in there?" whispered Marco.

"Not anymore," said Layla. "The locals say it's haunted . . ." She twinkled her fingers to be spooky. "But sailors say everything's haunted. Want to climb up and check it out?"

Marco hesitated. The lighthouse gave him the willies. Plus, he wasn't keen on climbing all those stairs. He'd be perfectly content digging through the sand to find more treasure. But before he could protest, Layla squeezed through a gap in the boards that blocked the entrance and disappeared inside.

Marco hurried after her. It was creepy on the misty beach all by himself.

The stairs spiraled up four stories, and by the time Marco reached the top, Layla was already leaning halfway out the window.

"Look!" she said. "I didn't want to get your hopes up, but there they are!"

Four humpback whales swam through the waves just off the coast. Marco boosted himself onto the window ledge to get a better view. One of the enormous sea creatures blasted a massive fountain of water from its blowhole.

"Whoa . . ." whispered Marco. He'd never seen animals so big before. "Hello, whales!" he shouted, waving from the window.

Almost as if they could hear him, the whales began to leap into the air.

"They're breaching!" said Layla.

"Breaching?" asked Marco.

The whales propelled their gigantic bodies clear out of the water, twisted, and then crashed back down with huge cannonball splashes. Marco couldn't believe it. The animals were so big it almost seemed like they were moving in slow motion.

"They're sending messages to other whales with the sound waves from the splashes," Layla explained.

Marco smiled. "It looks like they're just having fun."

"It does seem like a good time, doesn't it?" Layla said. "You want to jump in too?" She reached for Marco's waist, but he darted away from the window.

"Yeah, right!" he scoffed. "That water must be freezing!"

"Oh, it's not so bad." Layla chased after him. "Come on, give it a shot!"

"You'll never catch me!" taunted Marco as he ran down the steps of the lighthouse.

They gave the whales names as they watched them disappear into the ocean, and Marco collected more colorful shells on their walk back to the house.

Layla made a late lunch of bacon grilled cheese while she danced to a Brazilian bossa nova album.

"Are you sure you don't want to stick around while I give this lesson?" asked Layla. "Mrs. Doohickey was actually a pretty good player back in her day. Before the arthritis . . ."

"No, no." Marco plugged his ears. "I'm gonna go down to the pier and watch the tide change. I still can't believe the water goes up and down so high."

"Suit yourself," said Layla.

MARCO ARRIVED AT the pier just in time. It was high tide. All the boats he'd seen lying awkwardly on the rocky sea-bed at low tide had righted themselves to float proudly in the water. The ocean had crept up thirty feet in six hours. Marco jogged out onto the pier, which was now floating as well. Then, at the exact time predicted on the chalkboard outside the souvenir shop, a foghorn sounded, startling Marco so badly he nearly fell into the water.

The current suddenly switched directions, and Marco observed the tide change with great fascination. The water swirled in little whirlpools for a moment and then began its retreat back out to sea. Marco tried his hardest to see the boats sinking as the water receded, but the tide moved so slowly he eventually got bored and gave up.

He headed over to the café, curious to see what sorts of

treasures the old man had unpacked from all those mysterious boxes.

As Marco approached the door, he heard shouting inside.

"You're cheating!" said a woman with a thick Romanian
accent.

"It's part of the game!" retorted a British man.

"Calm down!" urged an American.

"*Ave María*," muttered a Spaniard.

"Marco!" shouted Toots as he entered. "You're back!"

Four eccentric characters were seated around one of the
tables, playing cards.

The Romanian woman wore a thick fur coat with rabbit's
feet dangling from the shoulders. An ivory cigarette holder
hung from her frowning lips.

The British man wore a brown vest and a bowler hat.
He looked quite proper except for a black eye and a broken
nose.

The American wore a Dodgers cap, a white T-shirt, a
Bluetooth headset, and black jeans.

The Spaniard wore a feathered helmet and a costume
with a frilly collar, like an actor in a Shakespearean play.

They all turned and stared at Marco.

"This is the young treasure hunter I was trying to tell
you about," said Toots, his eyes squeezed shut, as per
usual.

"Nice to meet you," said Marco. He waved sheepishly.

The card players exchanged puzzled glances.

"Some manners," muttered Toots. "That's Madame Silva, Lord Stanley, Zeke Steineker, and Don Frisco San Fanfisco," he said, pointing to each one. "This is Marco."

The card players kept staring.

"He's just a kid," said one of them under their breath.

"Never mind them," said Toots to Marco. "Uninvited guests. Just sit around all day and never buy nothin'!"

Steineker, the American, slurped from the straw of a Jumbo Gulp that was almost empty. "Maybe if you sold anything aside from black coffee," he said.

"Tea would be nice," added Lord Stanley, winding a gleaming gold pocket watch.

"Or champagne," suggested Madame Silva.

Toots waved his dishrag at them. "Go jump off the pier and play in the ocean, why don't ya?"

"Maybe I should come back later," offered Marco.

"No!" urged Toots. "Stay, stay! I need your sharp eyes and nimble fingers to help me sort through my collection. Some very valuable items in these boxes."

"Like what?" Marco asked.

"That's what you're here to find out!" Toots turned to the card table and stuck out his tongue. "The boy seeks that which does not wish to be found. What did I tell ya?"

Marco felt a pang of pride.

"You never know," said Toots. "We might find a long-lost treasure."

Someone at the card table cleared their throat.

Toots rubbed his hands together with excitement. "Why don't you start over here?"

The boxes were still piled next to the hole in the floorboards where Marco had left them the day before. He peeled off the duct tape and unclasped the latches on one of the boxes to open the lid. It was full of clumps of old newspapers. He unwrapped one of the paper wads to reveal a porcelain teacup. A second wad contained a saucer.

"Ah, yes," said Toots. "That's what they call a tea service—cups, saucers, sugar bowl, teapot, et cetera."

"But don't you drink coffee?"

"Yes," confirmed Toots. "But this is a complete set made by Chanticleer. Very precious, and only gets more valuable with time. The stuff in these boxes is kind of like my life savings."

"That's one way to put it," muttered Steineker.

"Indeed," mused Lord Stanley.

"*Órdago*," said Don Frisco, the Spaniard, laying down his cards. The other players groaned.

"He wins every time," complained Madame Silva.

"They are his cards," noted Lord Stanley.

"Maybe they're marked," proposed Steineker.

Marco examined the card players. There was something unsettling about them. They didn't fit together. They didn't even seem to like each other.

"Ignore them," Toots whispered to Marco. "They're just bitter old pirates."

Marco set the tea service aside and reached back into the box.

He peeled Bubble Wrap from a fancy-looking bottle. "Wine?"

"Actually, it's sherry," said Toots. "What else have we got?"

Marco unpacked a few more bottles and a bunch of canned sardines. Nothing he'd consider treasure.

"Drat." Toots glared at the empty box. "Those tins of salty fishies are worth a pretty penny, though. Would you like to try some?"

"Really?" Marco examined a tin with a dancing octopus on the label.

"Sure! Take 'em home with you. Nothing beats a sardine sandwich."

"Thanks," said Marco.

"Let's open another box, shall we?"

"What's your rush, old man?" asked Steineker. "You've got nothing but time."

"You're one to talk about rushing," Toots replied. "Remind me what happened to your rocket-powered racing yacht again, hotshot?"

Steineker frowned. "We've all been burned by fate in one way or another," he said gravely.

"What's he talking about?" whispered Marco.

Toots put his hands on his hips. "Well, it's a bit of a bad-luck club around here, I guess you could say."

"*Cursed* is more like it," said Lord Stanley with a wry grin.

"Destiny is a cruel mistress," mused Madame Silva, stroking her rabbit-fur coat. "I used to dine on caviar in castles, and now . . ." She looked around at the dusty café and almost choked with disgust.

"*Otro juego?*" Don Frisco began to deal a new game.

Marco noticed that the cards did not have the kind of designs he was used to. They were more colorful, with different symbols. Some had elaborate characters on them.

"What kind of cards are those?" asked Marco.

"It's an antique Spanish deck," replied Steineker. "We're playing a game called mus. Don Frisco is a bit old-fashioned, if you couldn't tell."

The Spaniard made an elaborate bowing gesture without standing. Marco realized he had a sword hanging from his belt.

"But even the charmed conquistador had his fortune run out," Lord Stanley explained. "His beloved ship caught fire and sank."

"And his precious treasure with it," added Madame Silva.

Don Frisco glowered at her.

"In a way," noted the American, "this is all his fault. He took something that didn't belong to him, and the rest of us were foolish enough to go chasing after it."

Madame Silva sucked her cigarette. "And unlucky enough to find it." She snorted a cloud of stinky blue smoke.

"That which does not wish to be found . . ." sighed Lord Stanley.

The room grew quiet.

Marco turned to Toots with a puzzled expression on his face.

"Oh, you know how sailors love to tell tales." Toots dismissed the card players with a wave of his hand. "Let's get back to it, eh?"

"What are we looking for anyhow?" Marco asked as he struggled to open another box.

"*El encanto de oro*," said Toots. "The golden charm."

"Just because we're stuck here doesn't mean it's nearby," tutted the Brit without turning his head. "Moneybags found it ten miles from where we three were waiting."

Steineker sucked at his Jumbo Gulp and sneered.

Madame Silva clicked her tongue. "It's back at the bottom of the ocean somewhere. Hopefully lost for good this time."

"No!" said Toots. "It's in here somewhere. I can feel it! Maybe this one . . ." He bent over to look into the newly opened box, and his back cracked like the ice on a winter lake.

He froze.

"Are you okay?" asked Marco.

Toots wheezed. "I'm gonna have to lie down." He shuffled toward the bar, wincing after each tiny step. "Keep going without me," he grunted through gritted teeth. "This might take a while." He slowly lowered himself to the floor and started rocking back and forth, trying to straighten his spine.

Marco kept digging through the boxes, but he didn't find any golden charms. He did, however, find a bunch of baseball cards, several unopened *Star Wars* action figures, a stack of comic books, and an envelope full of old Dutch stamps. None of it seemed too valuable to Marco.

He opened a new box and pulled out a rubber chicken.

"So much for treasure," Steineker said with a laugh from across the room.

"That's what happens when you only take what comes to you," scoffed Madame Silva.

"You mean when you don't just *steal* whatever you want?" Toots retorted, still recovering, flat on the floor, facedown.

"'Steal' is such an ugly word." Lord Stanley hooked his thumbs in his vest. "Everything I took, I *earned*." He winked his black eye.

Madame Silva turned up her nose. "Violence is so unsophisticated."

"And deception is so despicable," Steineker said coolly.

"Oh," said Madame Silva, "and I'm sure your methods were wholly honorable."

"I was merely persistent, thorough, and highly motivated." Steineker sounded defensive.

"And how many millions of your shareholders' dollars did you waste in your persistence?" Madame Silva blew a stream of smoke at Steineker to spite him.

"Enough!" shouted Toots. "Quit your endless bickering. It's driving me mad!"

"I think I'm gonna go," said Marco. "It's getting late."

Toots tried to sit up. "Ack!" He grimaced and lay back down. "But I haven't paid you for your trouble."

"It's no trouble," said Marco. "It's been . . . interesting. Plus, you already gave me these." Marco held up the fancy tins of fish.

"But—but—" Toots stammered.

Marco patted the only box that remained unopened. "I'll leave this one for you," he said, putting on his coat. "Whatever you're looking for must be in here."

"It's not in there," said Madame Silva.

"You don't know that!" protested Toots.

"*El encanto de oro*," said Don Frisco dreamily.

"The long-lost treasure," added Steineker.

"Just be glad you'll never find it, kid!" said Lord Stanley.

They all started chuckling. Then the laughter grew infectious, and eventually they fell into breathless hysterics. Except for Toots, who lay pouting on the floor.

Marco wasn't sure what was so funny. But as soon the door shut behind him, the dusty café fell silent.

"I GOT YOU some fancy sardines." Marco dumped the tins onto Layla's kitchen table.

"Thanks, I guess." She slid a frozen pizza into the oven. "Maybe we can use them as toppings."

"Let's try 'em first," said Marco. "Before we ruin the whole pie."

In the end, Marco was glad they decided not to put the

salty little fishies on the pizza. But as they sat on the couch scarfing slices and watching *Mr. Bean*, Layla could tell that something else was bothering her little brother. He wasn't snort-laughing like usual.

"What are you thinking about?" she asked.

"What makes something a treasure?" asked Marco. "Like, a real treasure, officially."

"Well, that depends." Layla lowered the volume on the TV. "All the little rocks in your collection, for example, they were just lying around. No one wanted them. But you do. Why?"

"I like them."

"Yeah, but why?"

"I just do, okay?"

"Fine. But if you can explain *why* you like something, why it's important or beautiful or rare, and enough people agree with you, that thing could be considered a treasure—officially."

"What about shipwrecks and pirates and stuff?"

"Sure. That stuff might be considered treasure if it's old or made of valuable material. Or—and you know this is my favorite—if it gives us some new information about the past."

"Ugh." Marco covered his face with his hands. "Please, I don't want to talk about spoons."

"Why not?" said Layla, pretending to be offended. "That's my specialty!"

Marco groaned. "Spoons are boring!"

"Spoons are boring?!" Layla leapt to her feet. "How DARE you!" She smacked Marco with a pillow.

"Shut up." Marco rolled his eyes and turned the volume on the TV back up.

Layla started hula dancing in front of the screen.

"Hey!" Marco squirmed to try and see around her.

"You just don't realize what you're missing. I'll take you to the library tomorrow morning and show you some of the fascinating research I conducted last semester. Plus, the archives there are amazing. Tons of dive photos from old shipwrecks full of the sparkly kind of treasure you love so much."

Marco tried to shove his dancing sister away from blocking the screen.

"I'm on vacation! I am not going to the library!"

THE NEXT MORNING, they went to the library.

"Don't be such a grump," said Layla. Marco fumed in the passenger seat as they rode the rinky-dink ferry across the bay to the mainland. "You're gonna love it. The library is really cool. You'll see."

Marco harrumphed and stared out the window into the soupy fog. He was supposed to be on spring break, yet somehow he'd found himself on the way to a school to *learn*. He shuddered at the thought. It started to rain.

They drove through the town and into the woods until they came upon a stone building that looked like a castle.

⚓
289

"Here we are." Layla smiled as they passed through the gates of the university.

"This is a school?" It looked more like a medieval kingdom to Marco.

"Pretty nice, right? Why do you think I moved so far away to go here? Well, I guess the scholarship money didn't hurt either."

Layla parked in front of a gleaming white structure that didn't look anything like the old stone buildings that decorated the rest of the campus.

"What is this place?" asked Marco.

"This is the library," Layla replied. "It's modern architecture."

The university library bore little resemblance to the single room of plastic-wrapped books at Marco's middle school. First of all, it was huge. Three stories tall. On top of that, the whole building looked like it was made from giant sheets of folded paper. When they walked into the lobby, Marco couldn't help but gawk at the soaring white walls arranged at strange angles overhead.

"See?" said Layla. "I told you it was cool."

In the gallery on the first floor, old swords, reading glasses, and logbooks were displayed under glass next to photos of the sunken ships where they were recovered. A big map showed the whole bay with dots to indicate the locations of known shipwrecks.

Marco found Fog Island and pointed at one of the dots on the map.

"Isn't this where the lighthouse is?" he asked.

"Yeah, but it wasn't always," said Layla. "They put it there in 1904 to stop boats from crashing into the rocks."

Marco examined the contents of the display cases and stopped in front of a collection of spoons. Layla was beaming.

"I analyzed these," she said proudly. "There were covered in citric acid, which means the Mi'kmaq people must have used these utensils to make some sort of wild berry concentrate. Or *maybe* they had established trade routes with Indigenous tribes to the south who had access to highly acidic fruits like oranges or lemons. Or *maybe* the Mi'kmaq had already developed hothouse cultivation techniques, which is equally amazing and only raises further questions as to the agricultural technology that—"

"Okay!" Marco threw up his hands. "I get it. Spoons are very interesting. But don't they have any *real* sunken treasure around here? Like, wooden trunks full of jewels or something like that?"

Layla was distracted by a scarecrow-like man in a plaid suit struggling through the revolving doors of the lobby with his arms full of books, and a guitar case slung over his shoulder.

"Professor Binkerhoff!" She picked up a book he had dropped and plopped it on top of the pile in his arms. "This is my brother, Marco."

Binkerhoff put a knee under the books and extended a hand to shake.

"Nice to meet you, young man."

"Nice to meet you too," said Marco.

"Professor Binkerhoff is a brilliant archaeologist, geologist, and historian." Layla beamed. "But more importantly, he shreds on electric guitar."

Binkerhoff grinned. "Our little bar band has gained quite the cult following since your sister joined."

Layla bowed.

Binkerhoff turned to Marco. "So, have you come to bask in the knowledge?"

"Um, I guess," replied Marco.

Binkerhoff turned to Layla. "Did you show him the spoons?"

Marco crossed his arms. "I'm not here to learn about spoons!"

"Well, whatever your preferred topic of study, if you're half as sharp as your sister, you'll make a formidable researcher!"

Layla tussled Marco's hair. Binkerhoff chuckled and nearly dropped all his books.

LAYLA NEXT LED Marco to the basement, where they sat in front of a computer terminal with three screens.

Marco was unimpressed. "I can look up pictures on the internet at home, you know."

"Calm down, you persnickety whippersnapper!" said Layla in an old-timey voice. "This is an academic archive that goes back to the 1700s. You can't find this stuff on your newfangled interwebs."

She punched in some keywords, and a collage of black-and-white images filled the screen.

"Here." She zoomed in on a photo. "Treasure chest."

A jeweled chalice sat atop a pile of golden coins, which had spilled out from a wooden trunk.

"Whoa." Marco leaned closer. "That's what I'm talking about."

"I guess," Layla grumbled. "I prefer to study objects that aren't so cliché."

"Speaking of which, can you search for something called the 'golden charm'?" asked Marco.

"Golden charm?"

"Actually, try it in Spanish: *el encanto de oro*."

Layla tickled the keyboard, and soon images of vintage newspaper ads filled the screen. "It looks like an old brand of cheap powdered coffee."

"That can't be right," said Marco.

Layla pecked at the arrow keys. "Hang on."

Marco was confused. Why would Toots, who was so particular about roasting and brewing his own gourmet coffee, consider some cheap canned powder to be "treasure"?

FRONT

BACK

"Ah," said Layla. "This is more like it." She'd changed the search terms and found a drawing of a thick gold coin. One side was engraved with a skull, the other with a jaguar. "This is probably the treasure you were looking for. But it's just a myth."

Layla searched a social media archive on the other screen. "Check this out, though. There's a whole user group about it. These chumps have been searching for this 'long-lost treasure' for years. What a boondoggle! Might as well go hunting for Bigfoot." She clicked a link and scrolled through an old message board thread. "Some billionaire tech bro claimed he found it a while back, but then . . . well, it seems like he disappeared."

Marco couldn't take his eyes off the image of the coin.

"See?" Layla half sang. "I told you the library was cool."

THE RAIN HAD turned into a full-on storm by the time they left the library, and the waves made the ferry ride back to the island slightly nauseating. Still, Marco insisted Layla drop him off at the pier.

"It's pouring! Are you sure you don't want to hang out at home? I've only got one kid coming today. I can give you head-phones. You can chill upstairs, and you won't hear a thing."

Marco zipped up his coat. "No, I've gotta go find out about something."

"You'll catch your death of cold!"

Marco laughed. "You sound like Mom."

Layla grumbled and locked the car doors.

"Hey!" said Marco. "You're telling me I should let a little rain stand in the way of my pursuit of knowledge?"

"Fine." Layla relented and unlocked the doors. "But take the umbrella, at least. And come right home when you're done."

"I looooove you," Marco sang sweetly.

"I love you too," said Layla suspiciously.

Marco grabbed the umbrella and jumped out of the car into the rain.

As soon as Marco opened the umbrella, it blew out of his hands and danced into the air over the water. He pulled the hood of his jacket around his head and tried to jog across the slick wooden walkway of the pier without slipping.

When he reached the café, he took shelter under the awning to catch his breath. Rain spilled from the roof in sheets and a bolt of lightning ripped across the sky over the bay. The thunder that followed came so quickly and so loudly it made Marco jump. The storm was right on top of him.

Inside the café, the four card players were seated in their same positions at the table. They looked bored. So did Toots, who was absentmindedly watching coffee bubble through the swirling tubes of his machine. He nearly toppled over when he saw Marco walk in.

"You came back!" he cried with surprise.

Toots bounded out from behind the counter, his arms held wide and his eyes squeezed shut. Marco could've sworn he was about to hug him, but the old man stopped short mid-step, as if he had just realized he'd forgotten his wallet.

"I thought this lot had scared you off." Toots tilted his head toward the card players. "Can I get you anything? Coffee or uh . . . well, coffee, I guess."

"No, thank you," Marco said. "I just wanted to ask you a question."

"Of course!" Toots laughed nervously. "But first . . ." He hurried over to the one box that remained unopened. "Do you think you could go through this last box for me?" He fidgeted back and forth as if he were fighting the urge to open it himself.

"Sure," Marco said cautiously. He started unlatching the lid, and Toots seemed relieved.

Something didn't add up. The guy was old, sure, but he could certainly open a box without much trouble. If he was so anxious to see what was inside, what was he waiting for?

"Why didn't you open it yourself?" asked Marco.

"Well . . ." Toots said haltingly, "I . . . didn't want to open it without you here. You put in so much hard work. I—I thought you might want to see it through! After all, this is the box with the good stuff."

Toots smiled and encouraged Marco to start unpacking.

Meanwhile, Don Frisco dealt a single card to the table. "El rey de copas."

"The king of cups," said Lord Stanley, rubbing his pocket watch. He looked at Madame Silva. She twirled her cigarette holder, deep in thought.

"That's the old man, of course." She pointed to the details on the card with a violet-painted fingernail. "There's his gray beard, and there's his cup of coffee."

Marco couldn't help overhearing while he dug through the box. He realized they were playing some sort of fortune-telling game.

The Spaniard dealt another card. "El cuatro de espadas."

"The four of swords," said Lord Stanley.

The card showed a dagger in each corner, all four pointing to an empty space in the middle.

"That's us," said Steineker.

"Four hunters with no prey." Madame Silva pouted.

"*Interesante*," said the Spaniard. He dealt a third card.

Marco dug mindlessly through the contents of the final box while listening carefully. He was so distracted he didn't even notice the objects he was finding were actually pretty impressive: a silver statue of an eagle, a bag of rubies, a signed copy of *Catcher in the Rye*. He continued to eavesdrop on the card players, but suddenly, they stopped talking.

When Marco looked up, they were all staring at the card in the middle of the table. It was the *sota de oros*. It showed a boy with a golden coin in his hand.

"*El encanto de oro*," whispered Toots with awe.

The card players turned to the old man with a mix of fear and confusion. There was no way he could have seen what card had been dealt from the other side of the room.

But he wasn't looking at the card. He was looking at the red can of coffee that Marco had pulled from the open box.

FOR THE FIRST time since he'd met him, Marco saw Toots's eyes open wide. He stood perfectly still, pouring coffee into a mug that was already so full it was overflowing.

"Is this what you were looking for?" Marco asked. He

already knew the answer. He just needed to say something to break the awkward silence in the room.

Toots snapped out of his trance and realized he was spilling coffee everywhere. He made a few frantic grunts before he was able to form any words.

"Quickly—bring it here!"

Marco obeyed and set the can on the counter.

Toots lowered his voice and kept a nervous watch on the card players. "Open it up."

Marco peeled off the lid and looked inside. The can was full of powdered coffee.

A strange golden glow filled the room, like the light at sunset. Marco just assumed the storm outside had cleared.

But Toots knew better. He tried to control his excitement. "Pour it out!"

Marco hesitated.

"Anywhere, it doesn't matter—make a mess!" hissed Toots.

Marco shook out the contents onto the counter. The eerie light in the room grew brighter, but the walls of the café began to turn black, and the photos fell to the floor, burnt and smoldering.

The card players seemed unsurprised, their faces slack and expressionless. In the glow of the golden light, the color drained from their skin until it was a sickly shade of pale. Until it was almost transparent. Until the muscle underneath began to show through. Clumps of hair shed from their scalps and wafted to the floor.

Marco saw none of this. He was utterly transfixed by a tiny glimmer of gold poking out from the pile of dull brown powder in front of him.

Toots laughed with a mixture of relief and fear. "*El encanto de oro,*" he whispered.

Marco plucked the golden coin from the coffee grounds. He wiped it off and held it in his palm, enraptured by its shimmering brilliance. "Can I keep it?" he heard himself ask. He closed his fist around the coin, suddenly overwhelmed with desire.

"No!" growled Toots. "We have to destroy it. This treasure is cursed!"

The card players cried out with pain.

When Marco turned around and saw them, he tried to scream. But at that moment, he was too terrified to make his voice work. Instead, he squeaked out a pathetic kind of screech that twisted his throat and made him choke.

Steineker, Madame Silva, Lord Stanley, and Don Frisco had all been transformed into horrifying ghouls. Each one was burned to a crisp, their skin scorched black, their clothing charred, their pearl-white bones protruding from their bodies in places where the flesh had melted away. They stood from the table and started slowly shuffling toward the coin, as if hypnotized.

"Gh-gh-ghosts!" Marco scrambled over the counter and ducked behind it.

"Quick!" barked Toots. "Put the coin back in the can and seal the lid."

Marco did as he was told. "What's happening?" he yelped in a voice that was higher pitched than he would have liked.

"These pirates were blinded by greed." Toots stepped out from behind the bar, placing himself between Marco and the approaching ghosts, who passed straight through the boxes in the middle of the room as if they were made of fog.

"Only the *real* treasure can break their curse," Toots explained. "Until then, their spirits haunt the coin, waiting for the next fool who seeks that which does not wish to be found—waiting to reward him with a fiery death."

The ghosts wailed, and flames burst from their eyes.

"Go!" Toots pointed to the back of the café. "Take the can and lock the door behind you."

Marco crawled on his knees, clutching the can to his chest. He was so scared he wanted to cry. Was he the next fool? Was he already cursed? Was he about to be burned to a crisp by vicious ghost pirates?

"Get back!" Toots hurled a glass jug full of boiling water across the room. It smashed in the scarred face of the notorious billionaire Zeke Steineker. Steineker howled as the piping-hot liquid burned what little skin remained on his head.

"Shake the can!" shouted Toots through the door.

"What?" Marco was trembling so hard the can in his hands was already shaking.

"Shake it!" roared Toots with such fury that Marco was almost as frightened of him as he was of the disfigured ghouls. "And keep shaking it!"

Toots hurled test tubes and mugs and beakers at the ghosts, to ward them off, but it was no use. Soon, Don Frisco had him in his grasp.

"You fool!" cried Toots. "It was right under your nose the whole time." He headbutted the ghost, knocking his helmet to the floor. Don Frisco released his grip, and Toots snatched the sword from the Spaniard's belt. The old man smiled as he pulled the blade from its sheath.

"What do your precious cards say about *this*?" Toots swung the sword and separated Don Frisco's head from his body. The headless ghost staggered backward and fell to the floor. Toots wielded the blade like a man possessed, slicing a leg off Lord Stanley and chopping Madame Silva clean in half.

Toots wheezed out a laugh. "The coin was just a trick! The perfect way to distract greedy pirates. You all thought you'd already found the treasure. And that's the funniest part—you had!" Steineker's ghost lunged forward, and Toots warded him off with a swipe of the sword. "Don't you get it?!"

Marco, for one, did not get it. But he shook the can anyway—as hard as he could. *Tonk! Tonk! Tonk!* The gold coin ricocheted around inside. Marco climbed to his feet to peek through the window in the door and see if Toots was okay. When he saw the old man brandishing a sword and the ghosts all chopped to pieces, his terror was replaced with pride.

But only for a second.

"ORO! ORO! ORO!" the ghosts moaned in unison. The dreadful noise felt like spikes being shoved into Marco's ears.

The ghouls began to glow. They floated into the air and their bodies re-formed—more or less. These Frankenstein versions, with body parts assembled at odd angles, were even more disturbing than before. The four ghosts burst into flames and prepared to attack.

Toots steadied himself and raised the heavy sword above his head.

Crack!

His back went stiff, and his eyes went wide.

"Toots!" cried Marco.

Tonk! Tonk! Tonk!

The cursed treasure bounced around inside the can.

"Stay back, Marco!" groaned Toots, rigid with pain. He dropped the sword to the ground. "It's too late for me."

Marco watched through the window as the ghouls descended upon the old man and Toots was engulfed in a blazing fire.

"No!" screamed Marco. He slammed the can against the window. Then he jumped back to avoid the flames that licked through the cracks around the door.

Marco tried to flee the back room through the emergency exit, but as he fumbled with the handle, he realized it was padlocked shut. He turned and flattened himself against the wall as he desperately searched for another way out.

Before he could reach the window, the ghosts burst into the back room, and all Marco could do was stare in wide-eyed horror. The disfigured, burning corpses of Steineker, Madame Silva, Lord Stanley, and Don Frisco loomed over him. Marco had nowhere to run.

"Here!" He lifted the Encanto de Oro coffee can above his head. "Is this what you want?" The ghosts froze. They were still floating in midair, but they suddenly stopped their terrible moaning for gold and everything went silent.

That's when Marco noticed that the noise in the can had changed. He shook it again to be sure.

Piddly, diddly-dink.

The golden coin inside sounded like it had somehow broken into pieces.

The other three ghosts turned to face Don Frisco. The ghost of the Spaniard crossed himself. He almost looked relieved as his feet began to disintegrate, then his legs, and up to the top of his head, until he was reduced to a neat pile of ash on the floor.

At that point, Marco was no longer shaking the can. The can was shaking him. The ground began trembling. The walls started vibrating. The light from the ghostly fire of the three remaining ghouls grew so bright that Marco had to shut his eyes.

In the midst of the chaos, he heard Toots call out from somewhere in the distance. His voice was full of pain but also hope. "Hang on tight, kid. And watch out for those nipple-biting fish!"

Lightning ripped from the sky.

KABOOM!

WHEN MARCO WOKE up, he thought he'd been dreaming. But he was not in his bed. He was not on the lumpy old couch. He was wet and confused. A wave dunked his head and filled his nose with water.

Marco choked and sputtered and finally realized where he was: draped over a plank of wood, floating in the ocean beside the pier. The red coffee can bobbed up and down

nearby, and Marco lunged for it, splashing in a panic until he had it in his grasp.

Layla's galoshes felt like cement blocks on his feet. He kicked them off and swam ashore with the can. Marco flopped onto the beach, panting with relief.

He smelled smoke. When he sat up, he looked for Toots's café. What he found was a flaming husk of a building at the end of the pier.

The place had been blown to bits.

Layla opened her front door to find Marco sopping wet and shivering.

"Holy schnikes! What happened?" she gasped. Layla stripped off his clothes and wrapped him in heavy blankets. Then she crawled under the covers to warm him with a hug. "What happened, Marco? What happened?"

"I—I—I . . ." Marco's teeth chattered as he tried to speak.

After a few minutes, he warmed up enough to tell the whole wild story. When he finished, Layla furrowed her brow and snorted. "You expect me to believe that, stinkball? Ghosts and treasures and magical explosions? Come on."

"B-b-but—"

"Why would you go swimming in a storm? I knew I shouldn't let you wander around by yourself! The ocean is dangerous. What if you had drowned? Mom and Dad would have been so pissed!" Layla hugged Marco tight. "I'm glad you're okay, but—dang, Marco. I thought I could trust you to be honest with me."

"I—I am. I swear!"

"Cursed pirate treasure? Really?"

Marco pointed at the can lying on the floor by his soggy clothes. "S-s-see for yourself."

Curious, Layla climbed out from under the pile of blankets to investigate.

"*Encanto de Oro*?" she read. "From the internet? This

better not be a joke. If paper snakes pop out, I'm gonna smack you." She opened the lid and removed a golden coin with a skull engraved on it.

Layla flipped the coin over to examine the other side, but it was blank. In fact, it was just one-half of a hollow shell. She pulled the other half from the can. It was marked with a jaguar. When she fit the two pieces together, they formed a thick golden coin with an empty cavity in the middle.

Something else rattled inside the can.

Marco raised an eyebrow.

Layla set down the hollow coin and pulled out the real treasure—the one that had been lost for more than a thousand years.

It was a five-sided medallion carved from stone. But not any sort of stone Layla had ever seen before. It was incredibly dense, much heavier than a rock. It almost felt like metal. The surface was pocked like the moon, as if it had been forged by intense pressure and heat. Layla turned the thing over in her hand.

Two sets of symbols were carved into the face of the object, shining in silver where the dark, rocky surface of the material had been scratched away. "It looks like this was carved from a meteorite."

Marco shrugged. "Whatever it is, it's been hiding for a long time, and people were literally dying to find it. It could be important. It was probably stolen. I think it might be really valuable. But the only thing I know for sure is, it was definitely cursed."

LAYLA WAS SKEPTICAL, as any good scientist would be. So the next morning, when Marco had recovered, they drove to the university to talk with an expert.

Professor Binkerhoff examined the stone under a microscope and nearly fainted. He began shouting in French and insisted that Marco show him where the object had been found.

They piled into Layla's car and drove to the pier. Binkerhoff sat shotgun, and his guitar rode in the back seat with Marco.

"I still can't believe what I'm looking at! Mayan glyphs

mixed with Old Norse script?" Binkerhoff had secured the artifact in a plastic case, which he held tightly in his hands. "The trick will be validating the age of the engravings, but if this medallion is what I think it is, it could rewrite history."

"Do you really think so, Professor Binkerhoff?" Marco asked.

"Yes, I do," he replied. "But please, call me Binky."

"Why does it matter that there are two different languages?" asked Marco.

"Well"—Binkerhoff dangled one foot out the window as Layla drove—"it would prove that Mesoamericans had contact with Europeans hundreds of years earlier than we previously thought. It might even help explain the sudden downfall of the Mayan Empire—Vikings might have infected them with an exotic airborne disease!"

Layla pulled up to the pier and parked abruptly. "Okay, stinkball. Show us *exactly* where you found this thing."

"Fine!" said Marco defiantly. It bugged him that his sister still didn't believe he was telling the truth. "Follow me." He stormed out of the car and onto the pier, past the souvenir shop with Trish sleeping soundly inside, past the smelly bait shop, all the way to the far end, where the burnt-out café stood lonely and forgotten. "I got it from the owner of this café yesterday, right before the place exploded."

Layla crossed her arms.

The professor laughed heartily. "Marco, my boy, this place burned down last year."

"No, it didn't," said Marco. "I was here yesterday. It got hit by lightning last night."

"I used to come here often," Binkerhoff said, reminiscing. "The old man who ran the place made exceptional coffee. Unlike anything I've ever tasted."

"Toots," Marco said.

"Yes, Toots." Binkerhoff nodded. "That was his name, but . . . how did you know that?"

For the first time, Marco noticed the CONDEMNED sign nailed to the side of the building. The front door was rusted, and all the windows were caked with dust.

"Did you tell him?" Binkerhoff asked Layla.

"Me?" she said. "I had nothing to do with this. I have no idea who this Toots guy is."

"But you live in his old house," said Binkerhoff. "Marion Lantutsky. Toots."

Marco's arms tingled with gooseflesh.

Layla's mouth fell open. "I thought Marion was a woman."

"No, he was a gruff old sailor type," Binkerhoff recalled. "An insatiable collector, and quite knowledgeable."

"And he laughed like this—" Marco made a wheezing sound.

"Exactly!" said Binkerhoff.

"That's the noise my radiator makes at night," said Layla quietly. "At least, I thought it was the radiator . . ."

"Oh my," murmured Binkerhoff.

"Let's get out of here," said Layla. "This place is giving me the creeps."

"You want to go back to that spooky old house?" asked Marco.

"Why don't we return to the university instead?" suggested Binkerhoff. "There's no better place for questions that need answering."

The professor held the five-sided medallion in his outstretched palm. Marco and Layla stared at the mysterious treasure, and they all huddled in silence at the end of the pier. Indeed there were many questions left unanswered.

When was the object made, and by whom? thought Professor Binkerhoff.

Is the pirate curse real? Is the house haunted? wondered Layla.

"What was that noise?" asked Marco out loud.

It could have been the wind. It could have been the squeaky wooden boards of the pier shifting with the rising tide. Heck, it could've been the nipple-biting fish zipping through the water below. But whatever it was, it sounded like an all-too-familiar wheezing laugh, and when they heard it again, all three of them ran from the pier as fast as they could, jumped into the car, and locked the doors.

VI.

The Human Kaboom

(the one with the mysterious mountain man)

illustrated by

ADAM DE SOUZA

Henry discovered his paranormal abilities one Tuesday afternoon when he was twelve. His older brother, Rod, refused to share his cookies, and when Henry pounded on the table with outrage, the force shattered all the windows in the kitchen. The whole family was stunned. Not least of all, young Henry.

They had heard of paranormals before, but only in the big cities. No one knew exactly why, but there had been a sudden surge in Canadian children exhibiting extraordinary abilities. Jealous American scientists theorized it might have something to do with drinking milk out of bags, a Canadian custom rarely seen in the United States.

Henry had always had a bit of a temper, but his burgeoning powers made his mood swings especially dangerous.

His parents urged him to control his emotions, but after an outburst at school knocked three other students unconscious, Henry got expelled.

Fortunately, there was a special boarding school in Canada for children with mysterious abilities. Tuition was free, the facilities were state-of-the-art, and the instructors were specially trained. Henry's parents tried to explain what a privilege it was to attend such an elite educational institution, but it didn't feel like a privilege to Henry. It felt like a punishment.

THE SCHOOL WAS operated by a shadowy government agency charged with Paranormal Learnings, Operations, and Planning—or PLOP for short. The location was classified as top secret and couldn't be found on any map.

Henry's parents didn't know exactly where they were sending their son. They weren't even allowed to visit. But they did keep in touch with frequent letters and gift boxes, which were delivered to the training facility via a PO box north of Vancouver. Henry's brother, Rod, never wrote.

The other kids in the PLOP training program seemed perfectly content. They were excited to learn how to control their powers. They idolized famous Canadian paranormal heroes like Captain Canada and Super Hoser. They felt safe, protected from the outside world and surrounded by people who understood their unique challenges. Henry seemed to be the only one who felt imprisoned against his will—stuck in a secret government facility in the woods, surrounded by concrete walls topped with barbed wire.

He acted out, refused to cooperate, and threatened the staff when he grew frustrated. The administrators were forced to take disciplinary action. Within a month of his arrival, Henry wound up confined to his own quarters.

Though he was not a model student, Henry was clearly very gifted—more so than most of the other kids in the facility. For this reason, he was given personal instruction by Dr. Vachee Manoogian, lead scientist at the PLOP training facility.

"Good morning, Henry," said Dr. Manoogian, reviewing his notes from the previous day's session.

Henry sat on a stool behind a table lined with weighted metal cubes of various sizes. The walls of the otherwise barren room were covered in thick rubber. A blinking camera in the corner recorded his every move.

"I'd like to try building upon our experiment from yesterday."

Henry crossed his arms. "Whatever you say, Dr. Manoo-GEEN."

Dr. Manoogian's eye twitched despite his best effort to remain unperturbed. "It's pronounced Ma-NOOGIE-un," explained the doctor, "as you well know."

Henry shrugged.

"Why do you insist on antagonizing the instructors? We are merely trying to help you learn to manage your considerable abilities."

Henry yawned. "Sorry, I don't know what 'anti-agonizing' means."

Dr. Manoogian's eye twitched again. "It means, why must you be so difficult? The other students are quite content."

"The other students are chowder heads."

Dr. Manoogian set down his clipboard and clasped his hands. "Henry, I hope you understand that bad behavior only hurts your chances of getting what you want." Henry stared at the floor. "What is it that you want, Henry?"

"I've told you a million times."

"Tell me again."

"I want to go home."

"Yes. Well, we cannot have an untrained and emotionally erratic level-nine paranormal roaming about the streets of Canada, now can we? You will remain in the custody of PLOP until you learn to control your violent temper. It's too dangerous. Do you understand?"

Henry's face flushed red, and his knuckles turned white as he squeezed the seat of his chair.

"Do you understand?"

Henry slammed his hands against the underside of the table.

KABOOM!

The weight-covered table flipped through the air and flew across the room, directly at Dr. Manoogian's head. The scientist flinched as the objects crashed into the safety shield that separated him from Henry. Previous outbursts had motivated the instructor to take extra precautions with his most unpredictable student.

The disappointed doctor collected his things and left the room.

"Let me out of here!" shouted Henry. The air throbbed with invisible waves of power.

"HE'S TOO DANGEROUS."

"He could harm the other students!"

"Please"—Dr. Manoogian tried to calm the room full of concerned instructors. He had called an emergency staff meeting to propose a new approach to dealing with Henry. "We've tried discipline and isolation for over a year. Obviously, it's not working. And he's only growing stronger. Perhaps the key is socialization."

"He's clearly a red folder."

"Don't give up on him yet," Dr. Manoogian pleaded. "He has too much potential."

HENRY WAS A little confused as to why he was suddenly allowed out of his quarters during recess. He hadn't done his assignments. He hadn't improved his behavior. In fact, he'd had another violent outburst earlier that morning and destroyed half his bedroom. Despite his suspicion, he embraced the opportunity to get some fresh air and take a walk around outside.

As soon as he stepped out onto the playground, he regretted his decision. All the other kids stopped playing and stared at him. Then the whispers began.

"They let him out!"

"What's wrong with him?"

"He's a red folder."

Henry pretended to ignore them. He walked off to stand by the far end of the yard and leaned against the concrete wall that fenced in the facility. He stared up at the surrounding woods and inhaled deeply. The air smelled like sugar maple.

A big blond girl carrying a lacrosse stick approached Henry. Her name was Pam Thompson, but everyone called her Pinky. "Hey," said Pinky sweetly. "Are you a psycho or something?"

Henry took a deep breath before answering. "No."

"Are you sure?" Pinky crossed her arms.

A group of kids had gathered behind her. They were just as curious but not quite as brave.

"Yes," replied Henry wearily. "I just want to go home."

Pinky scoffed. "But don't you want to learn how to use your powers?" She briefly transformed into a puff of pink smoke.

"I know how to use my powers," said Henry.

"Dr. Manoogian says we'll never reach our full potential without proper training," retorted Pinky.

"I'm gonna learn to fly!" shouted a kid named Todd.

"Yeah, right!" said another kid. "Not even Captain Canada can fly without a wingsuit."

"It's still flying!" protested Todd. "The human body is not naturally aerodynamic."

"Shut up, Todd," snarled Pinky. "Captain Canada is a level eight. You're a level four."

Todd shut up.

Pinky turned back to Henry. "I heard Dr. Manoogian say that you're a level nine."

The crowd of curious kids drew closer.

"Dr. Manoogian doesn't know his ass from his elbow," said Henry.

The onlookers all broke into hysterics. Pinky hushed them with a withering glare.

"You're pretty funny, eh?" she said. "You like jokes?"

"I guess," said Henry.

"Knock, knock," said Pinky.

"Who's there?"

"I eat mop."

"I eat mop who?" asked Henry.

"Gross," said Pinky.

"I don't get it," said Henry. "I eat mop who?"

"You could get sick," said Pinky, smirking.

"I eat mop who?" Henry repeated the words, trying to understand. "I eat mop who?"

The other kids fell about laughing.

"He eats his own poo!" they squealed.

Henry finally got the joke. But by that point, Pinky and the other kids had already run off giggling.

AFTER THE HUMILIATING incident with Pinky, Henry decided to remain in his quarters during recess, even though he was technically supposed to go out and play. His instructors allowed it because, much to their surprise, he had suddenly started to engage with his training program. He began to take his lessons seriously and even practiced on his own between classes. His progress was dramatic. Dr. Manoogian was very pleased.

Henry was quickly learning to focus his abilities into more concentrated and intense gravitational bursts. He became aware of the subtle vibrations of an invisible energy field from which he could draw additional power. He discovered he could aim his explosions by pressing his hands together and pointing at a target.

After one particularly productive training session, the teaching staff convened to congratulate Dr. Manoogian on successfully rehabilitating a borderline red folder. They brought ginger ale and Hickory Sticks to celebrate. They made toasts and played music. Little did they know that day's training session would be Henry's last.

The following afternoon at recess, Henry walked to the far end of the playing fields and waited for everyone else to go inside. Then he pressed both hands against the thick concrete wall and concentrated his focus, just like Dr. Manoogian had taught him.

Henry slammed his hands against the wall.

KABOOM!

A violent shock wave ripped through the concrete, blasting rubble into the air and triggering emergency alarms.

Henry climbed through the hole in the wall and ran into the surrounding forest as fast as he could.

HENRY DID WANT to go back home, but as he scrambled through the woods, he worried he wouldn't be welcome. His parents were the ones who sent him away in the first place, no matter how many times he told them he didn't want to go. They were afraid of him, just like everybody else. If he went to them for help, they'd probably send him right back to PLOP. And if they didn't, Rod would for sure. Stupid Rod.

This whole thing was all Rod's fault! Henry seethed as he ran. Stupid Rod and his scaredy-cat parents and that moron Dr. Manoogian and Pinky the bully and her mean little friends and everyone else too. This whole thing was all their fault. Everyone was against him!

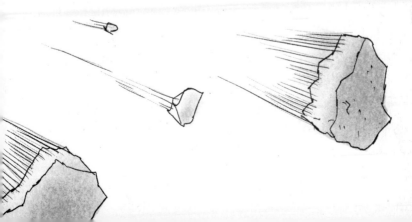

The only option, Henry decided, was to try and make it on his own.

He ran until he reached a small country road. There he crouched in a ditch, trying to catch his breath and make a plan.

At first, he considered hitchhiking. He'd seen it in a movie once. But who would pick up a kid without asking questions? They'd know something was up right away. Henry began to get angry with himself. He should've thought ahead before smashing the wall and fleeing on foot. He didn't think it through. He'd be caught for sure—stupid! Moron! Idiot!

As Henry was busy beating himself up, he heard a car approaching in the distance. It was a silver pickup. The truck slowed to a halt in front of a stop sign. The driver was wildly drumming the wheel and singing along to a Funkadelic song at the top of his lungs.

Henry's feet started moving before he realized where he was going. He climbed out of the ditch, darted across the shoulder of the road, and jumped into the flatbed just as the truck started moving again. The driver thought he heard something and turned around to check, but the music was loud and Henry had already pulled a tarp over his head to blend in with the rest of the junk in the back of the truck.

Henry hid under that tarp for two bumpy hours. He had no idea where the truck was headed, but eventually it pulled off the highway and the engine went quiet. Henry recognized the smell of diesel, so he knew they were at a gas station. He peeked out from under the tarp, and when the driver went inside to pay, he climbed out and scampered off into the bushes to plan his next move.

Henry heard police sirens approaching. He hunkered deeper into the bushes and watched nervously as a police cruiser sped into the parking lot right in front of him. An officer stepped out of the car and checked the license plate number on the silver pickup. When the driver came back outside, he was stopped for questioning.

Henry saw the cop show the guy a picture on his tablet. The guy shook his head. But Henry caught a glimpse of the picture on the screen. It was a picture of him. The cop searched the back of the truck but found nothing.

Henry held his breath, trying not to make a sound. His knees ached from crouching and his stomach growled from lack of food, but he didn't dare move until the police officer, the pickup-truck driver, and all the other cars in the parking lot were gone.

It was well after sunset when Henry finally allowed himself to stretch his legs, but he didn't emerge from his hiding spot until later that night, when he hadn't seen a car pass for hours. He crept along the side of the highway with no idea where to go next. That's when he spotted a billboard for Uncle Buck's Outdoor Supply one exit away.

It was nearly three in the morning by the time Henry reached the store. At first, he tried to be subtle and jimmy the lock on the back door, but it wasn't as easy as they made it look on TV. Eventually, he lost his patience and resorted to using his powers. He patted the door as gently as he could, but—

KABOOM!

The thing broke off the hinges and fell to the ground. Henry winced at the loud crash. He waited for the wail of an alarm, but the night was silent. This was his chance.

Henry crept into the darkness of the store to gather supplies. The place was jam-packed with gear, but he'd never been camping before, and he had no experience in the wilderness. He had no idea what he might need to survive outside on his own.

Henry wandered through the aisles of clothing and sporting equipment, wondering what kind of coat might be best. He considered grabbing snowshoes or skis. He knew he'd need a tent but the options were overwhelming, and squinting at the dimly lit shelves made Henry dizzy with indecision.

But then, in the middle of the store, up on a little pedestal, he saw a sign:

**GUESS HOW MANY ACORNS ARE IN THE JAR AND
WIN THE ULTIMATE OUTDOOR GEAR PACKAGE!**
Everything you need to escape into the wilderness.
(Over $2,000 in prizes. One guess per purchase.)

Next to the sign and the big jar of acorns was a mannequin outfitted head to toe in the latest hiking equipment: boots, waterproof pants, a windproof jacket. It had a warm woolen tuque on its head and a pack stuffed with gear on its back. Henry almost shouted with joy at this sudden stroke of luck.

But the good mood didn't last long. His less-than-subtle entrance had attracted the attention of a nearby security guard. She pulled her golf cart into the alley behind the store and got out to investigate.

"HELLO?" CALLED THE security guard as she stepped over the smashed-in back door. She was shining her flashlight around the store with one hand and pointing her Taser with the other.

As quickly as he could, Henry had put on the boots and the pants and the pack and the toque, and tossed the naked mannequin out of sight. He took its place on the pedestal, mimicked the pose, and tried his best to remain perfectly still.

"Come out with your hands up! I don't want to tase you." The security guard was shaking with nerves. She had never tased anyone before. She paused next to the prize display to listen for any signs of an intruder.

Henry held his breath.

The security guard slowly turned in a circle, searching the store up and down with her flashlight.

Henry was sure she would hear his heart beating through his chest. The fear of being caught was more than enough to make him sweat, but the winter gear and heavy back-pack made things much worse. A thick bead of perspiration dripped down his temple. He tried not to move, but the drip tickled terribly as it traveled down his cheek and clung to the tip of his chin.

"Hello?" The security guard didn't know it, but she was standing right under Henry's nose. For a moment, she thought maybe whoever had broken into the store had already left. Until she felt a tiny droplet of sweat fall onto the top of her hat.

She spun around and shined her flashlight right in Henry's face. He couldn't help but flinch with the bright light in his eyes.

The guard gasped. "You're just a kid! P-p-put your hands up!" she sputtered. "You're coming with me."

"You don't understand," protested Henry.

"No, you don't understand," barked the guard. "Breaking and entering is a serious crime. And where do you think you're going with all this gear, eh? That's burglary, buddy boy. You're in a LOT of trouble."

She pointed her Taser at Henry's chest. He put his hands in the air.

"That's right. Nice and easy," said the guard. "I don't want to hurt you."

"I'm sorry," said Henry. "I don't want to hurt you either."

He clapped his hands above his head.

KABOOM!

The explosion knocked the guard off her feet and into a rack of shelves, which tipped over on top of her.

Henry ran before he had time to think. He slipped on

spilled acorns, but he made it to the back door. He ran to the edge of the parking lot. He ran into the woods.

Henry kept running as fast as he could with such a heavy pack on his back. And as he ran, he felt the gnawing pain of regret. What had he done to that poor woman? Was she going to be okay?

THE PLOP COMMAND center was buzzing with activity. Monitors lined the walls, showing satellite photos, complex charts, and news feeds from countries around the world. Dozens of analysts wearing headsets worked diligently at computer stations. Everything was bathed in a dim blue light, and the only sound was the constant pecking of keyboards.

"Deputy Director Dodson?" said a humorless man in a crisp white shirt and a shiny black tie as he entered the room. In his hand was a red folder.

The deputy director stood in front of the wall of screens with a weary expression on his face. He had short, curly blond hair that circled a growing bald spot on the top of his head. His white shirt was rumpled; his sleeves were rolled up. His black tie—more of a dark gray from repeated washings—hung loosely around his neck.

"What is it, Agent Fearson?" said Dodson. His mustache was damp with coffee. In his hand was a mug that said GO PLOP. He took a sip.

"A red-folder subject has escaped from the junior training facility."

"PFFFFFWHAAAA?" Dodson spit out his coffee in shock.

The hot spray of liquid covered the face of the now-frowning Agent Fearson. He handed over the red folder as coffee dripped from his nose.

The deputy director opened the file and began to read aloud: "Code name Boom Boom, et cetera, et cetera . . . Gravitational manipulation abilities . . . Dramatic increase in power over the last ten months . . . Profound anger management issues . . . Oh boy."

An image of Dr. Vachee Manoogian appeared on-screen.

"Manoogian," barked Dodson. "What are we dealing with here?"

"He's a level nine, sir. Very young, barely trained, but with terrifying potential."

"How did the little hoser get loose?"

"He blew a hole through the perimeter wall."

"Good Gretzky! That wall is half a meter of solid concrete!"

Dr. Manoogian removed his glasses. "It seems the subject

was underplaying his abilities. I should have recognized the deception."

Dodson shook his head. "Doctor, your record speaks for itself. Every so often, there's a bee in the poutine. That's what the PLOP tactical squad is here for. When was the last sighting?"

"Six hours ago, sir," said Agent Fearson. "The boy was spotted on security footage breaking into a sporting goods store near Muckluck. Made off with a load of camping supplies. Nearly killed a security guard."

The doctor chimed in. "I take full responsibility for—"

"Save it, Manoogian," Dodson said. He sipped his coffee, hard. "Planning to hide out in the bush, eh, kiddo?" He scanned the wall of screens. "Agent Tremper, bring up a fifty-kilometer radius around the crime scene."

A young woman with her hair pinned up with a pencil slid her rolling chair across the floor and tickled her keyboard until a detailed map of the region appeared on the display. "Here it is, sir. I've marked the area by elevation, density, and water sources."

"Nice work, Tanya," said Dodson. "Put out an alert to nearby rest stops, restaurants, and grocery stores. When the kid gets hungry and hikes out for a cheeseburger, we'll nab him."

Agent Fearson frowned at the coffee stains on his formerly white shirt. "Sir, the FBI called. They offered to help out with any resources or information that—"

"For the last time: We don't need help from those Yankee keeners at the FBI!" Dodson had turned pink and was shoving his finger in Fearson's face. "We're the gosh dang department of Paranormal Learnings, Operations, and Planning—Canada's finest. If anyone can find a paranormal hiding out in the bush, it's us. Eh?"

Dodson pressed his mug against the agent's chest and growled, "Now, get me some more coffee, ya chowder head."

HENRY HAD RUN all through the night. Well, he'd started off running. By morning, it was more like a labored jog. His feet hurt from the new boots. His shoulders ached from the loaded backpack, which felt like it was somehow getting heavier by the minute.

Once he couldn't hear any cars in the distance, he decided it was safe enough to stop for a quick rest. Henry stripped off the pack and groaned with relief when it thudded to the ground. He stretched, and his back cracked in three places.

The forest was remarkably beautiful in the early morning light. Henry could see his breath, but the jacket and hat kept him warm. He opened up the backpack to see what other supplies he'd swiped in his heist. The image of the security guard's frightened face flashed before him, but he pushed it to the back of his mind.

Henry felt like a kid on Christmas morning as he unpacked the stolen items: a tent, a sleeping bag, a flashlight, a knife, a folding saw, a cooking pot, matches, a water filter, a water bottle, paracord, a compass, and a box of peanut butter protein bars.

He immediately ripped open the box and devoured four of the bars. Only afterward did he realize he should probably conserve his limited food supply.

The truth was, Henry had no idea how to stay alive in the woods. Lucky for him, at the very bottom of the backpack was a thick little book called *How to Stay Alive in the Woods*. He sat down below a maple tree and opened the book to try to distract himself from the overwhelming desire to eat another protein bar.

The book was written in 1956, and at first, Henry was worried that the information might be outdated. But as he flipped through the pages, he realized that the survival techniques the book described probably hadn't changed much for a thousand years. People had been living in the woods long before books had come along. Life must have been so much simpler back then, Henry imagined. He pictured himself alone in a peaceful meadow, surrounded by tall trees near a sparkling lake with happy birds singing, a rainbow in the sky, a juicy cheeseburger in his hand . . .

Fat raindrops splattered onto the pages and woke Henry from his dream. He rubbed his eyes and quickly repacked his supplies. There was no time for dozing. PLOP was hot on his trail.

It rained for two days as Henry continued to trek deeper into the wilderness. Every part of him was cold and wet, but he forced himself to keep walking. When the sun finally emerged from the clouds, Henry was so tired he could barely stand. He had hardly slept since escaping from PLOP, but he used every last ounce of strength he had left to hike up a ridge and get a look at his surroundings.

From the top of the ridge, he could see for kilometers in every direction. Dense forest and craggy mountains stretched to the horizon. He couldn't spot a road anywhere.

Henry decided he was safe. At least temporarily. He stripped off his pack, his hat, and his jacket, and sat against a rock to dry out in the sunshine. He was asleep before he finished untying his boots.

WHEN HE WOKE, Henry ate another peanut butter bar and admired the vast panorama. He watched vultures soar in lazy circles, searching for dead animals

to snack on. Henry was determined not to be their next meal.

He cracked open the survival book to a random page. It showed pictures of various primitive shelters that could be built from scavenged materials. But Henry had a brand-new tent. He just had to decide where to set it up. He read all the requirements for a good campsite: flat, dry ground, far from any animal tracks or potential hazards like dead trees or loose rocks, but close to a convenient water source (though not so close as to risk flooding).

Henry hiked around until he found a suitable location.

It took him a few tries to get the tent set up properly. He struggled with the foldable poles and got tangled in the ropes before eventually assembling it to match the diagram in the instructions. He unrolled the sleeping bag inside and crawled in to test out his new bed. It was surprisingly cozy.

Henry briefly entertained the possibility of an afternoon nap, but as soon as he had snuggled into the perfect position, he realized he was too thirsty to sleep. He put his boots back on and hiked down to the stream to fill his filter bottle. The sound of the rushing water reminded him of something else he needed to do . . .

Henry had not considered the lack of bathrooms in the wilderness.

Going number one was easy. Enjoyable, in fact. He went number one on a tree, on a rock, even over the side of a cliff.

Going number two was a different story. The book

advised collecting soft leaves to use as toilet paper, digging a hole to do your business, and then burying said business (and said leaves) in said hole. But the book did not explain how to squat properly without losing your balance. So the first time Henry tried pooping, he nearly fell onto his own turd. He had to waddle over to a stream with his pants down to wash the mess from his backside. The water was shockingly cold.

A soggy bottom inspired Henry to build a fire. He had always wanted to learn to build a fire, but he wasn't even allowed to play with matches back at home. His closest experience with pyrotechnics was blowing out the candles on a birthday cake.

Henry opened the book to the fire section and tried his best to follow the instructions. He had a full box of matches and a bunch of leftover protein-bar wrappers to get the fire started. But the wind kept snuffing out his matches, and the paper wrappers didn't seem to burn hot enough to light the sticks Henry laid on top. The wood was still wet from the rain.

After a few unsuccessful attempts, Henry's determination gave way to impatience. Then his impatience gave way to frustration. By the time it got dark, Henry was shouting mad and almost out of matches.

"Come on!" he yelled at no one when his pile of skinny twigs refused to catch fire yet again. "Stupid wet wood." He slid open the matchbox, but he accidentally had it upside down, and the few remaining matchsticks spilled out onto the damp ground.

"Come ON!" he kicked the pile of twigs across the clearing.

"Grrrrrrr." Rage bubbled up at the base of Henry's skull. Like a shook-up bottle of warm soda, he was ready to explode. And when a cold gust of wind blew the empty matchbox from his hand, he came unscrewed.

"*Gaaahhh!*" Henry let out a furious scream, dropped to his knees, and pounded his fists on the ground.

KABOOM!

Henry's little tantrum sent all his supplies flying off into the bushes. His tent got stuck in a tree.

"Come on . . ." he muttered quietly. Now he was mad at himself, not the matches. Henry hugged his knees to his chest and whimpered. All the stress and exhaustion and fear from the past few days came pouring out in trembling, snot-nosed sobs.

It felt good to cry, and Henry was glad he'd done it. But when he finally calmed down enough to wipe the tears from his face with his sleeve, he realized he was no longer alone.

HAWK STOOD MOTIONLESS at the edge of the clearing. He was dressed in high-tech camouflage, a rifle slung over his shoulder, his black hair pulled into a ponytail. Hawk had lived, trapped, fished, and foraged in those woods his entire life. He knew the names of every tree and bird. He

was familiar with the local hikers and sportsmen, the occasional tourist . . . But he had never seen such a young boy
out by himself, fifty kilometers from the nearest town.

Henry scrambled to his feet and backed away from the hulking stranger. Hawk's eyes glowed in the moonlight. His face was hard and weathered. Henry found him intimidating, yet strangely beautiful.

"Who are you?" Henry squeaked.

Hawk said nothing.

Henry prepared to run.

"Wait," said Hawk. "You'll need a fire."

Henry blinked. "I tried," he explained.

Hawk stepped closer without making a sound. He peeled a curl of bark from a birch tree and crushed it in his calloused hand. Then he stooped to gather a clump of small twigs.

Henry stood frozen in place, watching carefully as Hawk arranged the twigs into a bundle with the crushed birch bark tucked underneath.

"I have a few matches left." Henry picked up a handful from the ground.

"Keep 'em." Hawk knelt and pulled out a knife. He scraped the back of the blade against a metal rod, and white-hot sparks showered down onto the tinder bundle. Within seconds, it was ablaze. The expert woodsman placed some larger sticks atop the fire, then stood. "Do you have a knife?"

Henry nodded. Hawk tossed the metal rod, which landed at the boy's feet.

"Thank you," said Henry.

The fire crackled.

Hawk looked around at the scattered supplies.

"Most people can't survive very long on their own," said Hawk.

"I'm not like most people," said Henry.

"Time will tell," said Hawk.

Henry bent over to pick up the fire rod, and when he stood, the mysterious stranger was gone.

SLOWLY, HENRY BEGAN to figure things out. He had plenty of time on his hands to experiment and learn. He explored his surroundings with the dog-eared copy of *How to Stay Alive in the Woods* in hand, comparing wild specimens to the illustrations of edible plants. Eventually, he found plenty of things to eat besides peanut butter bars. He gathered sweet huckleberries from bushes, lemony wood sorrel from tree stumps, and salty lamb's quarter from meadows. He even managed to hunt down some meaty maitake mushrooms, which were poking out from the base of a dead oak tree.

His fire making improved as well. Henry had learned to keep an eye out for tinder—dry, flammable materials that would catch the spark from the fire rod that Hawk had given him. Papery birch bark, sticky cedar, and cottony cattail fluffs got stuffed into Henry's pockets as he hiked through the woods each day foraging for food.

A small ring of stones served as a pit, where Henry would build his fire every evening. Next to the pit were piles of fuel he had collected. The materials were organized by size: bundles of flammable tinder to catch the spark, thin twigs or kindling to start the fire, thicker sticks to get it nice and hot, and a pile of logs that would keep it burning for hours.

Building a blazing fire with his own bare hands filled Henry with deep satisfaction. The crackle of the burning wood was music to his ears. The smoke smelled like rich perfume.

He would sit there mesmerized, watching the bright-orange embers rise from the fire and float off into the night. Sometimes he imagined that the tiny glowing specks were trying to escape from their earthly burdens and fly up into the sky to join the stars.

Henry found the stars looked very different in the wilderness. Without city lights to interfere, the whole galaxy sparkled overhead, from horizon to horizon, an intricate tapestry of twinkling lights with such depth and definition it made Henry feel as though he were seeing the universe clearly for the first time in his life.

TWO WEEKS PASSED, and Henry's long-simmering anger began to cool. His once-frequent tantrums had almost disappeared. He felt at peace surrounded by nature. He liked being on his own. Though sometimes he missed conversation. Chatting with the babbling stream was the closest he could get.

"Good morning," said Henry, addressing his reflection in the glimmering surface of the water.

Blub, blub, blub, went the stream.

"Well, yes," replied Henry, "it certainly is a beautiful day." Henry admired the way the sun shone through the leaves above. Birds argued with chipmunks in a nearby tree, and he found himself chuckling at their antics. At times like these, he almost forgot he was a fugitive on the run.

He hopped across the water from stone to stone. "What's the difference between a brook and a creek?" Henry asked. "Technically speaking, I mean." The stream didn't seem to know the answer.

SPLISH!

A fish jumped into the air to snag a juicy fly for breakfast. The water was crystal clear, and Henry watched as the fish swam beneath the surface to return to its hiding place in the shadows under a rock.

Fruits and vegetables were tasty and nutritious, but Henry would need a sustainable source of protein to survive. He only had a couple of peanut butter bars left. He consulted the book and found a full-page illustration of a fish being grilled on a stick over a fire. Henry licked his lips. If only he could catch a tasty fish.

He crouched over the stream and dipped his hand into the cool water. Where his wrist broke the surface, circular ripples expanded outward in waves. Henry was suddenly struck with a promising idea.

He stretched his hand out and closed his eyes. He tried to focus his awareness on the mysterious energy waves that surged up from the Earth and into his fingertips. He would only need a tiny blast . . . He tapped the surface of the water with his fingers lightly.

KABOOM!

A tremendous splash exploded into the air. Chipmunks skittered away in a panic. Startled birds fled from the tree-tops, complaining loudly. A dead fish floated to the surface of the water.

Henry danced in celebration. Then he chased after the fish before it washed away downstream.

That night, he grilled his catch on a stick over the camp-fire, just like the illustration in the book. The aroma of the sizzling fish was irresistible. Once the skin was nice and crispy, Henry started plucking off steaming pieces with his fingers. The meat inside was juicy and delicious. He devoured everything but the bones.

It was easily the most rewarding meal of his entire life.

HENRY'S SURVIVAL SKILLS continued to improve through-out the summer. He foraged for wild edibles and dry wood in the morning and went fishing in the afternoon. At night, he built a fire, cooked a meal, and slept better in his tent than he ever had in a bed. He started to think that he might be perfectly happy living alone in the wilderness for the rest of his life. That is, until the leaves began to change.

At first, the vibrant colors in the trees and the crunch

of fallen leaves were beautiful. But autumn weather was brief, and the temperature fell quickly. Soon, the tree branches were bare, the days were short, and Henry felt a chill in his bones that he couldn't chase away, even with a roaring fire. He put on every item of clothing he had with him. He draped his sleeping bag over his head like a cloak and spent most of the day collecting firewood.

The same wood warmed him three times: first, while carrying it through the woods from where he found it; second, while sawing it into smaller pieces to burn; and then, of course, while it was on fire.

Even still, Henry was cold.

His favorite wild edibles had disappeared. The meadow was bare. The forest was preparing to hibernate for the winter. It even smelled different. The sweet aroma of the summer flowers and grass had been replaced with the earthy smell of pine needles and dead leaves. The only foods left to forage were acorns and tiny rosehip berries. Henry began to rely more and more on fish.

With practice, he had learned to control his explosions with great precision. When he released a blast into the water, it was just enough to stun his target. The surface of the stream barely rippled. But Henry felt the connection with his mysterious energy source growing stronger every day.

He eventually realized it was gravity, the same force that pulls objects toward the planet's center of mass and keeps them from flying off into outer space. But for Henry, gravity felt more like some sort of invisible ocean, pulsating with swells of tremendous power. He suspected there might be a way to harness that untapped potential energy, though he wasn't quite sure how.

ONE SNOWY MORNING, when the weather was frigid and icicles hung from the logs that crossed the stream, Henry bundled up and climbed out of bed to use the bathroom. He had developed a favorite spot just a short walk from his campsite.

As Henry squatted, delicates exposed to the elements, he heard a loud commotion coming from near his tent. He rushed to investigate, shuffling, stumbling, hopping through the bushes as quickly as possible with his underwear still around his ankles.

Henry made it back to the campsite in time to watch a hungry grizzly bear finish ripping his tent to shreds. Henry was stunned—literally caught with his pants down. The bear snatched a peanut butter bar from his tattered backpack, then snuffled off into the trees and disappeared.

A cold breeze on his butt cheeks finally roused Henry from his state of shock.

"Hey!" He pulled up his pants and jumped out of the bushes shouting, but it was too late.

Bears have an excellent sense of smell, and as any

experienced camper knows, you never keep food near the place where you sleep. Henry had heeded the warnings in the survival book, eaten his meals and dumped all the fish guts down by the stream. But he'd totally forgotten about that one last peanut butter bar he'd stashed away for a special occasion.

Henry moaned as he picked up the snow-covered remains of his tent and sleeping bag.

"You stupid bear!" Henry yelled. "Why can't you leave me alone?!" He balled his fists, and his face turned red with rage. Henry felt a surge of mysterious power. He felt his anger warm him. At first, he thought it was just his imagination, but then he noticed the falling snowflakes behaving very strangely. They seemed to melt before landing on his body.

Henry realized he had accidentally created some sort of protective force field around himself. He'd never used his powers in this way before. If he could figure out how he was doing it, maybe he didn't even need a tent.

Henry thought back to all the silly techniques that moron Manoogian had tried to teach him. He sat down on the ground and crossed his legs. He pressed his palms together and closed his eyes. He tried to focus on the source of his power, to push his paranormal abilities in a new direction.

It took great effort, but something seemed to be working. Henry felt centered. He felt *uplifted*.

When he opened his eyes, he discovered, much to his surprise, that he was hovering above the treetops—floating cross-legged in midair.

"Holy crap!" blurted Henry. But the moment he broke his concentration, he began to fall.

Limbs flailing, mind reeling, Henry tried desperately to regain focus as he tumbled through the trees. When that didn't work, he tried to grab hold of one of the branches whizzing past his head in a last-ditch effort to cushion his fall. Unfortunately, that didn't work either.

CRACK!

Henry's knee twisted as he slammed to the dirt. The wind was knocked from his chest. He writhed on the ground, gasping for air. Eventually, lungs still burning, he caught his breath. And as he lay on his back panting, the pain was overwhelmed by a single shining thought: He could fly.

Those kids from PLOP were wrong! Flying wasn't so hard. Landing, that was the hard part.

Henry looked at his knee and saw a stark white bone protruding from the skin. He was suddenly struck with agony so intense he nearly fainted. He couldn't stand, couldn't even crawl.

All the warmth drained from his body, and he knew that if he stayed where he was, he would quickly freeze to death. Henry could only think of one way to survive.

He got angry. Angry at his dumb broken leg, angry at the stupid greedy bear, angry at that idiotic hidden peanut butter bar. Those morons! Henry slammed his hands against the ground with all the strength he had left.

KABOOM!

The explosion propelled him back into the air. Much

higher than before. And this time, as he cleared the treetops, he kept his eyes open, scanning the horizon for some sign of life, looking for someone—anyone out there who might be able to help. All he saw was unpopulated wilderness.

Henry felt his stomach rise into his throat, and he knew he was starting to fall back down again. Black tendrils of panic tangled his mind, but just as he was about to give up on his search, he spotted a thin wisp of smoke in the distance. He spread his arms wide and clapped his hands.

KABOOM!

WHEN THE HERMIT heard the crash outside his cabin, he assumed it was a moose. But when he opened his door to investigate, he found a young boy, badly injured and barely conscious. The grumpy old man was faced with a dilemma. He had gone to great lengths to avoid the company of others. A lifetime of heartbreak and disappointment had soured his opinion of his fellow human beings—that was why he had spent the last thirty years living in a remote cabin in the woods all by himself.

The hermit decided not to intervene. Just let nature take its course. The wolves would get rid of the evidence, and no one would be the wiser. He set his jaw, closed the door to his cabin, and returned to whittling by the fireside.

"Please..."

The quiet moan pricked at the old hermit like a thorn in his side. The kid must have seen him. He sat still, hoping that moan was the last drop of life that the kid had in him. Hoping that was the last time he'd have to think about the boy who had dropped onto his doorstep uninvited.

"Please . . ." cried Henry softly.

The hermit squeezed the wooden fox he had been carving and grumbled. He snapped the figure in half, threw the pieces into the fireplace, and reluctantly trudged outside to save Henry's life.

THE HERMIT DID his best to set the broken bones, but he had no medical training and very little sympathy for Henry's cries of pain. He piled blankets in the corner as a makeshift bed and gave the boy a bowl of water and scraps of food, like an unwanted dog.

For weeks, Henry slept almost constantly, racked with fever, as his body tried to heal. The hermit was fairly certain, though not quite hopeful, that the kid would die of infection, but somehow the tough little bugger made it through.

However, once the grumpy old hermit was sure that Henry would survive, his irritation only grew. He couldn't throw the boy out into the depths of the Canadian winter. He was stuck with the kid until spring. He wished he had let the wolves have him.

Henry tried many times to talk with the man, to thank him for saving his life, but the hermit refused to respond. Most of the time, he refused to even make eye contact. Which took a lot of effort in a one-room cabin.

Henry grew accustomed to staring at the hermit's back while he tended the fire and prepared his meals. The old man even turned his reading chair to face the wall and slept on his side in bed so as not to have to face the boy. Eventually, they both settled into a disgruntled silence.

As Henry grew stronger, the hermit treated him more cruelly. He stopped sharing his scraps and instead offered only bricks of dried pemmican—an ancient survival food made from dried berries, moose meat, and fat. At first, Henry didn't mind the strange taste and texture, but after a few months, the aromas of the hermit's fresh-cooked meals made Henry wild with hunger.

"Please, can't you share just a little?"

The hermit didn't lift his eyes from the pancakes and bacon sizzling on the griddle.

"Could've sworn I heard whinging," he muttered as if talking to himself. "Makes no sense. Plenty of pemmican to eat. Ancestors never complained. Kept 'em strong for thousands of years." The hermit picked up a rawhide-wrapped brick, peeled off a corner, and took a bite. "Tastes fine to me."

He tossed the thing over his shoulder toward Henry, then scooped his pancakes and bacon onto a plate and doused them with maple syrup.

Despite his lack of generosity, Henry learned a lot from watching the old man. The cabin was well stocked with dried goods, tools, and supplies. The woodpile outside would last for months. Dozens of smoked fish hung from the ceiling, and hunks of salted meat filled the icebox, preserved for winter meals. Henry realized the vital importance of planning ahead to survive.

Sometimes he wondered how long the hermit had been living on his own. There were no pictures of friends or family in the cabin. It was hard to tell his age. The old man seemed hardened by the harsh elements, weathered into an impenetrable stone. But one night, invisible in the darkness, Henry heard him crying softly when the hermit thought his unwanted guest was asleep.

AT THE TAIL end of winter, the days grew longer, and the hermit couldn't help but let the sunshine improve his mood. He found himself humming old songs and smiling despite himself. The promise of spring was only weeks away.

One evening, Henry was surprised when the hermit set down a plate on the floor beside his makeshift bed. It was a wedge of fresh-baked cake with huckleberry jam on top.

"It's my birthday," said the hermit.

Henry smiled. "Happy birthday."

"What was that?" The hermit pretended to be startled. "Hmm. Must have been the wind." He sat in his chair with his back turned, as usual. But Henry sensed an opportunity.

Using one of the hermit's old walking sticks for support, Henry climbed to his feet and limped over to a shelf above the window. He used the stick to knock down a flat wooden box, which he caught in his waiting arms.

"What's this?" Henry turned the dusty box over in his hands.

The old man froze. He didn't have to look to know what the boy was holding.

Henry undid the clasp and opened the box to reveal a game board lined with brown triangles. Thirty black and white tokens were tucked into special grooves on the sides. Two dice nestled in a slot in the middle. It had all been carved by hand.

"Is it checkers?" Henry asked.

"Backgammon," said the old man flatly. Though as soon as he answered, he wished that he hadn't.

"Backgammon," repeated Henry. He'd heard of the game but never played. "Can you teach me?"

The old man said nothing.

"It's for two players, right? Who did you use to play with?"

The hermit threw his plate of cake across the room, where it banged against the wall and landed with a clang.

"Enough!" he growled. "Put it away."

Henry flinched but pressed on. "We can play if you teach me."

"No!" The old man turned to face the boy. "I've done taught you plenty already." He stood and jabbed a knobby finger at Henry. "I don't want you here. I don't want anyone here. I just want to be left alone!"

Henry avoided his furious gaze and stared at the floor.

"After first melt, you're going back to Mommy and Daddy."

"They don't want me," Henry said quietly.

"Well, that makes three of us," said the hermit. But again, as soon as he answered, he wished that he hadn't.

Henry lifted his head, his eyes wet with angry tears.

"Fine!" he shouted. "I'll leave right now! Why wait?"

"Ha!" The old man laughed. "You'll be dead before sunrise."

"What do you care?" spat Henry. "You're just like everybody else. You don't understand." He shook his head. "Nobody understands."

"Is that right?" The old man suddenly felt like he was looking in a broken mirror. He'd heard himself say those same words in the past. He'd used them to push away all the people he loved most. A familiar sadness fell over him as he watched the hobbled boy struggle to put on his coat. "Wait."

Henry paused, and the hermit proposed a heartfelt

question, one he had asked himself a thousand times before. "Ya ever think it might be you? That you're the one who doesn't understand?"

Henry felt like he'd been slapped in the face and kicked in the groin at the same time. He wasn't sure if he should feel injured or insulted. He just stood there with his mouth open, and his head started spinning. Was the hermit right? Was it all his fault?

Henry squeezed his eyes shut, fighting his doubts with denial. No. He felt his old anger rising. No. Long-simmering resentment doused his brief flash of compassion. No! It was everyone else who was wrong. No! It wasn't him. NO! It couldn't be! NO! NO—

KABOOM!

Henry did not expect the explosion. It knocked him across the room, where he crashed into the door. It knocked glass jars from the shelves to the ground, where they smashed into pieces. It knocked the old man backward over his chair.

Henry groaned with pain. His injured knee throbbed. He struggled to reach the walking stick and climb to his feet.

The hermit didn't move.

IN THE EARLY spring, when the snow had melted enough to traverse the mountain pass, Hawk hiked out to the creaky old cabin to check on his elderly friend. The winter had been a brutal one, and the hermit had grown frail in his old age. So when Hawk knocked on the door of the cabin, he was hoping for the best and prepared for the worst.

Henry opened the door. It was tough to tell which one of them was more surprised. They stood there in silence, staring at each other for quite some time.

"Where's Ricky?" asked Hawk.

"Ricky . . ." said Henry quietly. "He never told me his name."

Henry led Hawk around the back of the cabin. The woodsman couldn't help but notice how the boy was struggling through each step, even with the aid of a walking stick. Henry slowly made his way to a makeshift grave site surrounded by fresh-picked flowers—golden iris and violet crocus, the first blooms of the season.

Hawk knelt by the grave. He picked up a delicate purple flower and crushed it in his hand. He raised the petals to his face and breathed in the aroma deeply.

"He saved my life," said Henry, blinking back tears. "But I couldn't save his."

"What happened?" asked Hawk.

"It was an accident!" cried Henry. "I tried to go for help, but . . ." He jabbed his walking stick into the ground with frustration.

Hawk looked deep into the boy's eyes, then down at his crooked leg, then back to the grave.

"Eighty-two years," Hawk said. "A good run."

"Do you know his family?" asked Henry. "Should we tell someone?"

Hawk shook his head. He leaned closer to the grave and said something in a language that Henry didn't understand.

In that moment, Henry was struck by a strange feeling, as if he were within arm's reach of a rare, wild creature, as if the slightest noise might send it running off into the woods, never to be seen again.

"I don't know what you're hiding from," said Hawk, "but no one will find you here." He stood to leave.

"Wait," said Henry. "Please stay. I have so many questions."

"No." Hawk waved his hand dismissively. "I'm no good with people. That's why Ricky and I got along. Probably why he took a shine to you too."

"Me?" Henry wiped the tears from his eyes. "He hated me."

"Believe me," said Hawk, "if he hated you, you'd be dead." He almost smiled. "Take care of this place."

"Wait!" shouted Henry, limping after Hawk as he walked away. "Wait!"

The man was still a stranger—they'd hardly spoken—but at the same time, Hawk was the best friend Henry had had in years. The only conversation he'd had in months. Henry desperately wanted to keep talking. To ask a million things. To just enjoy the company of another human being.

But the woodsman stepped swiftly, and Henry couldn't keep up. So he merely watched with disappointment as

Hawk retreated into the woods, making no more sound than a creeping deer.

AT FIRST, HENRY had felt uncomfortable in the cabin alone. He slept on the blanket pile for weeks and refused to disturb the rations in the pantry aside from the dried pemmican. But as the forest around him shook off the slumber of winter, Henry recognized the blooming promise of a new beginning.

A sun shower soaked the mountainside, but Henry was safe and dry indoors. He listened to the raindrops on the roof, and the sound reminded him of popcorn. He remembered there was a jar full of kernels in the pantry, should the craving strike. There was also sugar and spices, sacks of flour, cans of vegetables and beans, coffee, tea, syrup, and chocolate. Sprouts had appeared in the garden. There would soon be carrots, spinach, and potatoes.

It would be a shame for it all to go to waste, Henry thought. Besides, if Ricky hadn't been such a terrible jerk, he'd still be alive. Why did he have to be so mean? Wasn't it really all Ricky's fault? That mean old terrible jerk!

These sorts of thoughts helped soothe Henry's guilt. He shoved his regrets deep down inside and, with great effort, convinced himself he was better off alone. He didn't need any family or friends. He didn't need anyone.

To prove it to himself, he burned the backgammon set in the fireplace. And as the flames consumed the hand-carved wooden pieces, Henry felt his heart freeze over with ice.

He forced himself to forget about the old man. It was his cabin now. He started sleeping in the bed, sitting in the chair, drinking the tea, and eating the oatmeal. He baked himself a loaf of bread, opened a tin of sardines, and made himself a sandwich. He ate chocolate. He read all Ricky's books about homesteading and hunting. He even tried smoking Ricky's pipe, but it almost made him vomit, so he burned that in the fireplace too.

Henry made himself at home. And he planned to stay for a very long time.

The last patches of snow had only just melted from the mountaintop, but Henry knew there was no time to relax. He would have to start preparing if he wanted to survive the next winter. His injuries had left him hunched and walking with a limp, but his paranormal abilities made hard work considerably easier. With proper concentration, Henry found he was able to levitate objects with his mind.

Labor that would have taken several grown men a whole day to complete, Henry could accomplish quickly and easily by himself. He gathered huge logs to use for firewood. He built a stone wall around the edge of the property. He showered himself under floating buckets.

It was the small tasks that took the most time: smoking fish, tending the garden, foraging for plants. But at night, even though he was physically and mentally exhausted, he often found himself unable to sleep.

Sometimes, instead of lying awake and staring at the ceiling of the cabin, he would hobble out to the meadow and lie down under the stars. The distant cosmos made his own problems feel far away. Though he didn't know the name, his favorite star was a bright-white one in the southern part of the sky. A solitary light surrounded by darkness on all sides.

By July, the garden was bountiful, the smokehouse was full of fish, and the woodpile was taller than Henry's head. He found himself with a lot of free time on his hands. He learned how to can berries and make jam. He named all the birds who visited the cabin. He reread all the books he had already finished. He carved himself a new walking stick. But Henry's attempts at distraction didn't change the fact that he was lonely.

In fact, he often fantasized about Hawk returning to check on him before winter set in. Henry would have been thrilled to have a visitor.

Then, one balmy afternoon, he discovered he had several.

THE WOLVES HAD come to investigate the cabin while Henry was out in the meadow on the far side of the ridge, limping through the bushes, collecting blueberries. He heard the leader of the pack howl, and the proximity of the sound made Henry feel nauseous. He was upwind and creeping quietly, so he was able to spot the wolves before they spotted him. But when he crested the ridge, he accidentally spilled his basket of berries and gave himself away.

He turned back to flee, but the wolves were too fast. Before long, they had him surrounded.

Henry spun in a circle, swinging his walking stick wildly, in a futile attempt to keep the wolves at bay. They were twice the size of any dog he'd ever seen.

"Go away!" shouted Henry. "Get out of here!"

He didn't bother calling for help. No one was there to hear his cries. The wolves drew closer and snarled.

One wolf attacked from behind and grabbed Henry's injured leg in its powerful jaws. Henry screamed, and another wolf wrestled the stick from his hand. Another bit his arm, and in a flash he was caught in a frenzy of teeth and claws. The beasts were upon him, and he fell to the ground. The hungry wolves prepared to eat him alive.

But Henry managed to tear one arm free, and he used it to smack the palm of his other hand—*clap*—

KABOOM!

When Henry opened his eyes, his arm and leg were bleeding badly, but all that was left of the wolves were a few tufts of fur floating on the breeze.

He struggled to climb out of the crater he had created, and when he finally did, he found that the trees had been bent over for ten meters in every direction. It was his biggest explosion ever, and he hadn't even had time to focus his concentration.

"Paranormal seismic activity reported in sector 39B, sir!" called Tanya Tremper to Deputy Director Dodson just as he took a sip from his mug.

"PFFFFFWHAAAA?" Dodson spit out his coffee in shock.

Tanya lowered the clipboard she had used to deflect the spray. "A concentrated tremor was just detected by the Canadian Geological Bureau—here." She tapped her pen against the screen. "Remember that red folder that escaped from the junior training facility last year?"

"Boom Boom." Dodson nodded.

"I've been monitoring seismic activity in the region, just in case," Tanya explained. "But if the data is correct, this explosion was more than twice the size of what we assumed he was capable of." Tanya frowned. "If it is him, his power has increased exponentially."

Dodson set down his mug on Tanya's desk and leaned over to get a closer look at her calculations.

"If I'm not mistaken," Tanya continued, "at this rate, his abilities will continue to grow until—"

"He could destroy the whole bleedin' planet," Dodson finished with dread.

"Deputy Director Dodson," called an agent with a phone in his hand, "it's the CIA. They're calling to offer their assistance with the paranormal blast in sector 39B."

"What? How do they . . . ?" Dodson faltered. "Tell those stars-and-stripes know-it-alls that we don't need their help! PLOP is on the case. We'll send out a tactical squad and apprehend the subject ourselves." Dodson rubbed his bald spot and furrowed his brow. "Agent Tremper, connect me with the squadron leader."

"Sir, are you sure you don't want to send in Captain Canada to . . . eliminate the threat?"

"He's still just a kid, Agent Tremper. Maybe we can save him yet."

"Yes, sir."

Dodson looked up at the map on-screen. "He made it through the winter in the bush. He's tougher than I thought. Tell tactical to approach with caution."

HENRY WAS CLEANING his wounds in the cabin when he heard the helicopters approaching. He would sometimes hear seaplanes or forest survey choppers in the distance, but this was different. There were too many. They were flying too fast. Something was wrong. He found Ricky's binoculars and stepped outside to investigate.

When he saw PLOP painted across the sides of the choppers, his heart broke. He imagined leaving all the comforts of his new home behind: the stockpiles of firewood, the vegetable garden, the fresh-baked bread. Somehow they'd found him, and now he'd have to find a new place to hide—if he managed to escape.

Henry scrambled to gather essential supplies and load them into a duffel, but his fresh injuries from the wolf attack made rushing difficult. Plus he underestimated how quickly helicopters can move at top speed. The roar of the choppers grew louder and louder, and by the time he zipped up his bag, they were right on top of him.

Ropes descended, and armed PLOP tactical operatives rappelled to the ground. Henry drew the curtains shut.

"We are not here to hurt you," a gruff voice blared over a megaphone.

Back at PLOP headquarters, Deputy Director Dodson, Tanya, and the rest of the analysts in the command center watched the live feed on the wall of screens.

"Tell him about the Timbits," said Dodson into a microphone.

"We brought doughnuts," said the agent with the megaphone. He opened a box fresh from Tim Hortons.

"Timbits," corrected Dodson. "Better than doughnuts."

Inside the cabin, Henry scoffed. "You brought guns too!" he shouted.

Armed agents moved into position and surrounded the cabin.

"We want to *help* you, Henry," said the voice on the megaphone, but somehow it sounded like a threat.

"Yeah, right," said Henry.

"Listen, kid," said the squad leader, "you're coming with us whether you like it or not." He closed the box of doughnuts. "Move in!"

CRASH!

A tranquilizer bomb flew in through the window and started spewing blue smoke.

Henry dropped his duffel bag and held his breath.

SLAM!

When the PLOP agents kicked in the door, they found the boy sitting cross-legged, hovering in midair. His arms were spread wide.

"Target sighted," grunted an agent into his headset as he stalked forward, Taser aimed at Henry's chest.

"Engage," said the squad leader to his team.

Henry clapped his hands as hard as he could.

KABOOM!

WHEN THE TRANQUILIZER gas wore off, Henry woke up in a pile of rubble. The cabin was obliterated. The helicopters, the agents, the trees, and even the grass were all gone.

The explosion had destroyed half the mountainside.

"Why can't you just leave me alone?!" shouted Henry as he stumbled to his feet.

Twisted visions of his enemies flashed through his mind: his stupid brother, his cowardly parents, the relentless doctor, the meddling guard, the nasty old hermit, the bloodthirsty PLOP agents . . .

"This whole thing is all your fault!"

But no one was left to hear his cries.

He forced himself to climb out of the rubble pit and limp to the edge of the cliff where the top of the mountain had been blown away. At first, he felt a deep sadness over the loss of the cabin, but as he gazed into the ravine and spotted the smoking wreckage of the helicopters below, he was filled with a strange sense of . . . pride. He couldn't help but admire the terrible power of his own abilities.

The wounds from the wolf attack were still fresh, and his old knee injury throbbed with renewed pain. Henry needed time to rest. Time to heal. In his weakened state, he'd be no match for another PLOP tactical squad, and reinforcements were surely already on their way.

Henry took a deep breath and stepped out over the edge of the cliff. The drop was so steep, even a sure-footed mountain goat would have fallen. But Henry had gravity on his side.

He limped across the vertical rock face, feet flat against the cliff, body suspended horizontally over the precipitous drop. Henry had never used his power this way before, but he had no fear of falling.

Slowly but surely, he reached an outcropping of stone. He curled up in the shadows below the rock and hid quietly in a place where not even the most diligent PLOP agent would think to look.

THE TREES NEVER grew back on the mountainside where Ricky's cabin had once stood. It was almost as if the soil had been poisoned. No plants flourished there, and animals tended to avoid the place, even fifteen years later.

Hawk had continued to trap, hunt, and trade in the woods nearby. But his once jet-black hair had faded to silver. He'd only crossed paths with Henry once or twice, and not in many moons, but every time he passed the barren mountaintop where Ricky's cabin had once stood, Hawk's mind wandered to the whereabouts of the kid. He'd heard rumors, reports of sightings, and had a sneaking suspicion he might know where Henry could be found.

The craggy mountain overlooked a river valley that was surrounded by even taller peaks. It was, Hawk had to admit, an excellent place to hide. But as he shuffled up the steep, winding path, his body ached, and he began to regret his decision to come.

Hawk paused for a moment to admire the mighty river that tumbled over the cliff above into the lake below. The waterfall filled the air with a rainbow mist, forcing Hawk to advance carefully. The narrow ledge was slippery, and he was not as strong a climber as he used to be.

Up ahead, the path widened slightly but was blocked by three boulders stacked on top of each other. The stones were far too large for anyone to have carried to that location, and yet they were too perfectly balanced to have accidentally fallen into such a precarious position.

Hawk approached the obstruction cautiously and quickly realized there was no way around. He considered turning back.

Suddenly, he felt an otherworldly vibration in the ground beneath his feet. The swirling mist froze in place. The three enormous stones trembled, levitated into the air, then hovered a few meters away, clearing the path.

Hawk stepped forward and watched in awe as the mighty waterfall was drawn aside, as effortlessly as a beaded curtain, revealing the entrance to a hidden lair.

"Come in," said Henry from the darkness of the cave. His voice had grown deeper, and even cloaked in shadow, Hawk could see that Henry was no longer the same young boy who had run away to the woods all those years ago. He was now a wiry, bearded man.

"Welcome, my friend," said Henry. He sat cross-legged, barefoot—and levitating.

Hawk stopped and blinked his eyes, adjusting to the darkness. Piles of fish bones and empty bags of Hawkins Cheezies littered the cave. The air was thick with the stench of isolation.

"You must leave this place," Hawk said. "Your life is in danger."

For years, the townspeople had told stories of a "shaman" who lived in a cave deep in the mountains. Most people thought it was folklore, or teenagers spreading wild rumors, but after a second deadly encounter with a local hunter, the police had started to take the stories seriously. Detectives determined the matter was paranormal in nature, and it wasn't long before PLOP was called in to investigate.

"You came to warn me." Henry smiled with genuine affection. "Why?"

"To avoid unnecessary destruction," said Hawk.

"You don't have to worry about me, old friend—"

"I don't," Hawk said. "You're not the only living thing who makes their home here. Only the most dangerous."

Henry nodded. "It pleases me to have your respect."

Hawk shook his head. "Fear and respect are not the same."

Henry's smile faded. "I understand."

"I'm not sure that you do." Hawk reached into his bag and dropped a book onto the floor of the cave, a dog-eared copy of *How to Stay Alive in the Woods*. "Life thrives in the forest when it exists in harmony. You learned this lesson long ago."

Henry stared at his old book, thinking many things but saying none out loud.

Hawk turned to leave.

"I just want to be left alone," said Henry.

"Yes," said Hawk. "But how many others must pay the price for your precious solitude?"

The silver-haired woodsman did not wait around to hear the answer. He left the cave, and the waterfall drew shut behind him. The stones stacked back in place once he had passed.

Hawk had hoped his visit might help to avoid further bloodshed, but as he slowly descended from the mountain, he heard menacing laughter erupt from the hidden cave above.

"DEPUTY DIRECTOR, DRONE images indicate that Boom Boom is on the move. He's headed toward a town called Moose Jaw."

The deputy director raised a mug of tea to her lips, took

a sip, and swallowed calmly. "Get me Manoogian," Tanya said.

"Yes, ma'am."

On-screen, drone cameras showed Henry bearded and barefoot, bounding across the landscape as easily as if he were bouncing on a giant trampoline, traveling half a kilometer with each jump.

Dr. Manoogian appeared as a three-dimensional projection. His skin was wrinkled, and he was wearing ocular implants to help him see. "Deputy Director Tremper, how can I help?"

"You said he was dead," Tanya reminded him.

"I hoped that he was." Dr. Manoogian sighed.

"This poor kid's been on his own for almost sixteen years," said Tanya. "What does that kind of isolation do to a person?"

"He's not a kid anymore," said Dr. Manoogian. "There's only one option left."

Tanya nodded. She pressed a button on her command console and leaned over to speak quietly into the microphone. "Call in the Golden Samurai."

SINCE CAPTAIN CANADA'S retirement, the Golden Samurai had become the most famous defender of the Great White North. The beloved captain had officially passed the torch at a ceremony during halftime at the Grey Cup.

Since then, the Golden Samurai had successfully

defended Toronto from a radioactive lake monster, saved Winnipeg from a swarm of mutant bats, and thwarted rogue paranormals from Vancouver Island to Newfoundland.

Even still, Tanya was nervous. Henry grew more powerful each passing year. According to her most recent calculations, he was capable of producing an explosion ten times bigger than a nuclear bomb. A detonation of that size could be enough to throw the planet off its axis. It might be enough to end life on Earth.

A disc of purple light appeared in the middle of the command center. Silver dust sparkled in a vertical column, and the Golden Samurai materialized out of thin air.

Tanya bowed.

The hero was sheathed in glistening golden armor from head to toe. Their helmet was crowned with golden moose antlers.

"Another red folder?" asked the Golden Samurai.

"A level nine."

The Golden Samurai whistled. "I thought I was the only one. This is gonna be fun."

"Don't get cute," Tanya warned the decorated hero. "This will be the most powerful adversary you have ever faced. He's been on his own a long time. He has nothing and no one to lose. Do not underestimate him."

"Don't worry." The Golden Samurai bowed. "I'll be back before your tea gets cold."

As the hero dematerialized, Tanya cupped both hands

around the steaming GO PLOP mug that was a gift from her former boss.

She thought back to the mountainside disaster that had cost him his job and two dozen agents their lives. Tanya stood silent, lost in thought, until a wailing siren jolted her back to the present. She put down her mug and snapped into action.

"Omega alert: Evacuate that town. Get everybody out. Now!"

AFTER DESCENDING FROM his mountain hideaway, Henry entered a town for the first time in years. He was stunned by the cacophony of so many cars and people crammed into one place. He was overwhelmed by the flashing lights and complex aromas.

Henry limped across Main Street, leaning on his ornately carved staff. When he first eased into a seated position in the middle of the four-lane road, impatient motorists honked their horns, thinking he was some sort of disoriented vagrant.

But when the scraggly bearded man started levitating above the pavement, the drivers quickly abandoned their vehicles and fled on foot.

Henry began to meditate. His mind was adrift in an invisible ocean of gravitational energy waves. A force field emanated outward from his body, sliding cars backward and forming an impenetrable bubble. Police launched knockout gas, but the canisters bounced off the pulsating barrier. Snipers fired tranquilizer darts that froze in mid-air, two meters from their intended target.

Henry focused on his breathing, gathering his strength, sharpening his concentration.

Streetlamps and electrical poles bent toward the floating bubble of energy. Sparks rained down from above. Cracks buckled the asphalt below.

A purple disc appeared nearby, and out of the translocation portal stepped the Golden Samurai.

Henry sensed a highly unusual presence. He opened his eyes.

The Golden Samurai was resplendent in shimmering armor.

"Who are you?" asked Henry.

"Who am I?" The Golden Samurai chuckled. "What, have you been living in a cave?"

Henry frowned.

"I am the Golden Samurai," said the Golden Samurai, gesturing to the armor. "Golden armor, golden eyes . . ." Their gleaming irises were famous around the world. "Lightning sword?" They drew the weapon to display the crackling electricity that surged through the white-hot blade.

"Translocation?" The Golden Samurai dropped through a disc of purple light and descended from another a meter away. "The Golden Samurai: Canada's greatest hero . . . You really don't know me, do you?"

"I'm sorry," said Henry.

"Doesn't matter," the Golden Samurai grunted. "I'm here to stop you." They crouched and twirled their lightning sword. "So just give yourself up peacefully, eh? Don't be a chowderhead."

"You don't understand," said Henry.

"Sure I do," said the Golden Samurai. "My parents sent me away too. I was at PLOP not long after you. Almost got red-foldered myself, actually—they said I had emotional issues."

Henry felt a pang of recognition. "They say I'm dangerous."

"Well"—the Golden Samurai shrugged—"*if you don't like the effects, don't produce the cause.* Maybe stop blowing stuff up? Trim the beard? Put on some shoes? It's freezing out here!"

"I just want to be left alone," Henry muttered softly.

"But you've hurt a lot of people," said the Golden Samurai. "You are not the victim here, you're the villain. Can't you see that?"

The Golden Samurai opened a portal and slipped through the force field.

Henry tried to regain focus, but his mind fell into shadow. In the darkness, there were flashes of painful memories. A strange new light made the faces of his enemies look different somehow: his injured brother, his worried parents, the dedicated Dr. Manoogian, the innocent security guard, the lonely old hermit, the PLOP agents who were just trying to do their jobs.

This whole thing was all their fault. Or maybe . . .

Henry's vision blurred with tears. He spread his arms wide.

But then, at the edge of the void, appeared a faint glimmer of hope. The woodsman, Hawk, strong, wise, and beautiful, stepped forward from the darkness. He spread his arms wide, as well.

The next thing Henry knew, he was wrapped in a warm embrace. Something deep within him exploded. Long-standing walls cracked and shattered and the shock wave grew, expanding outward, until Henry's mind was blown wide open and the world around him was never the same again.

— VII. —

THE HUMAN KABOOM

(the one that hasn't been written yet)

Okay, kid, I wrote six stories for you. Now how about you try writing one for me? It's only fair.

Plus, writing stories can be super fun, especially when you get to do whatever you like. Maybe you'll write about some hair-covered cave people who discover fire, or a giant bowling alley where humans are the pins, or an interstellar rocket battle for the future of civilization . . .

Just start with the title "The Human Kaboom" at the top of the page and see where your imagination takes you. If you really get stuck for ideas, you can always write something about farts. (Tell your teacher I said it was okay.)

Look, I know you're very busy with homework and YouTube and practicing the next big TikTok dance craze, so I'll throw in a little extra motivation to encourage you.

?

If you write your own version of "The Human Kaboom," you can mail it to me, and I'll read it with my own personal eyeballs.

Then again, who cares what I think? If you write a story and never show it to anyone at all, I'll still be thrilled that you decided to express your imagination purely for your own amusement. Remember:

YOUR CREATIVE SATISFACTION SHOULD NOT BE BASED ON OTHER PEOPLE'S OPINIONS!

Sorry, that was as much for me as it was for you.

Anyway, I really would love to read whatever you write whenever you write it, and unless an asteroid hits Manhattan, I can always be reached at:

Adam Rubin
c/o Penguin Young Readers
1745 Broadway
New York, NY 10019

Your version of "The Human Kaboom" can be long or short, handwritten or typed out. It can be whimsical, wonderful, wild, or weird. But I do have one piece of advice: Don't send me your first draft. Once you finish writing your story, put it away for a couple of days, then read it as if someone else wrote it. I guarantee you'll find things you'd like to change or improve.

After all, if you're going through the trouble to make up a story and write it down, you might as well make it as good as it can possibly be, right?

?

Speaking of which, if you'd like any help, I put together a series of short videos in which I try to explain my own personal approach to the story-writing process. You can find a link at my website: adamrubinhasawebsite.com.

And as long as you're on the internet, I highly recommend searching for funny videos of river otters. Those little guys are adorable.

Well, the book is pretty much over now, so I should probably go make myself a sandwich and start thinking of what I'm gonna write next . . .

Maybe I've inspired you to give story writing a try for yourself, but if not, I won't be mad. There are lots of other ways to exercise your imagination: sing a song, draw a picture, sew a costume. Heck, read a book like you're doing now. I hope you enjoyed it and you'll join me again next time. Until then, have fun out there.

Your pal,
Adam

CRUNCHY KABOOMS FOR HUMANS TO CONSUME

N ormally, an explosion in the kitchen is a bad thing, but not when you're cooking popcorn. Skip the mystery-goo microwave stuff and use this healthy stove-top recipe instead. Homemade popcorn is a crunchy, delicious snack that's easy and exciting to make.

You'll need:

- 2–3 tablespoons grape-seed or canola oil
- ⅓–½ cup unpopped popcorn kernels (depending how hungry you are)
- A large pot with a lid
- A large bowl
- Salt
- Nutritional yeast (see below)

1. Put the oil and three kernels in the pot over medium heat and cover it tight. If you don't have fire privileges, ask an adult for help with the stove.

2. Wait a minute or two until you hear all three kernels pop. That means the oil is at the perfect popping temperature.

3. Take the pot off the heat and pour in the rest of the kernels. Give the pot a swirl, and the popped kernels will jump on top of the unpopped ones. (That way, they won't get soggy.) Wait thirty seconds or so, cover the pot, and put it back on the heat.

4. When the kernels start to pop, use an oven mitt or folded towel to lift the lid a bit and let the steam out while you jiggle the pot. If a kernel sneaks out through the open crack, consider it good luck. Once the popping slows to once every few seconds, turn off the heat.

5. Carefully pour the popcorn from the pot into a bowl and sprinkle three big pinches of salt over the top. It will get mixed in automatically while you eat.

6. Add a similar amount of nutritional yeast. It's a kind of hippie health powder that my Birkenstock-wearing grandma used to love, and it has a cheesy, savory taste that is perfect on popcorn. You can flavor your fresh-popped crunch bowl with any sort of seasoning combo you like, but please know that if you like your popcorn sweet, we can never be friends.

Popcorn-Popping Problem Solving:

 If you wind up with lots of unpopped kernels at the end, the heat is too low.

 If your popcorn burns, the heat on the stove is too high.

 If you pop every single kernel without burning, congratulations! You've achieved the coveted "perfect pop." Make a wish when you eat the last piece and it just might come true.

ACKNOWLEDGMENTS

——— •◦❖◦• ———

Holy cow, folks, we did it again. I wrote a book and you read the whole thing. Or you just flipped to the back to read the acknowledgments for some strange reason. Either way, thanks for being here.

I wrote *The Ice Cream Machine* while living in Barcelona and basking in the sunshine. I wrote *The Human Kaboom* while locked in a tiny New York City apartment during a global pandemic winter. If you found this collection of stories to be a bit darker than the first one, that's probably why. Thank you for being so perceptive.

Thank you to the illustrators: Dan Salmieri, Rodolfo Montalvo, Marta Altés, Adam de Souza, Gracey Zhang, and Daniel Gray-Barnett. These imaginative artists come from all around the world, and I feel tremendously honored to have such an eclectic collection of talent represented in these pages. An extra thanks to Dan for helping me refine and scan my doodles for the popcorn recipe and wormhole clues. Working through those simple drawings renewed my awe for people who can shoot beautiful art out of their hands at will.

Speaking of which, thanks to John Hendrix for once again conjuring up a cover that makes people want to pick up the book and find out what's inside.

And as far as what's inside, thanks to my wonderful editor, Stephanie Pitts, for guiding me toward the best possible version of each story. I was lucky to have her feedback and encouragement throughout the writing process.

Thanks to my friend Sam Weiner for once again trudging through an early draft to give me notes out of the kindness of his heart. Though he did enjoy a string of solid home-cooked meals in exchange.

Thank you to the whole team at Penguin Young Readers and Putnam for all their hard work and hard-won expertise. Matthew Phipps, Cindy Howle, Elizabeth Johnson, Eileen Savage, Tessa Meischeid, Jen Klonsky, and dozens of others were instrumental in helping to get this book out of my computer and into your hands.

Thanks to my agent, Jennifer Joel, for always seeing the big picture while somehow never missing any of the important details.

Thanks to Alex, Asi, Davide, Denis, Doug, Yorgos, and Vanessa for their help with translation.

Many of the details in this book were inspired by real-life people who will probably never read this. Even still, I feel I should thank Persi Diaconis, Les Stroud, Greg Ovens, Stan Lee & Jack Kirby, George Clinton, Adam Savage, Henri de la Vega, Jean Dodal, Tim Robinson, Sgt. Binkerhoff, Wendy Dewsbury, Pam Thompson, Ethyl, Zuzana, Isa, Cece, Tori/Trish, and Penn & Teller, from whom I stole the idea of an ambiguous doodle (though they used it in a far more brilliant and devious context . . .).

Further sources of inspiration include the X-Men, *The Princess Bride*, *Lucky Grandma*, Agatha Christie, *Rick and*

Morty, the Great Victorina Troupe, Mel Brooks, Tina Fey, the Coen Brothers, *Gardeners' World*, @physicsfun, George Saunders, Donald Barthelme, Jorge Luis Borges, Robin Wall Kimmerer, Kurt Vonnegut, Ted Chiang, Anthony Doerr, Viet Thanh Nguyen, Chuck Jones, Tannen's Magic Shop, Harry Houdini, Ricky Jay, Ivan Moscovich, Tim Rowett, Khruangbin, Johann Sebastian Bach, Chanticleer (a pleasure garden), and the great nation of Canada.

I didn't travel very much while writing these stories, so I'd like to thank the Carroll Gardens neighborhood of Brooklyn for being such a lovely place to pass the time and specifically Hoek, Henry Public, Sahadi's, Lucali, the wine store next to the Key Food, and, of course, Emma Straub and the entire crew at Books Are Magic. Thanks to my 2017 Honda HR-V, the Palisades Parkway, and Harriman State Park.

When I can't get to the actual forest, I spend a lot of time admiring street trees, and it might sound ridiculous, but I'd like to thank the big icing-draped dogwood on Second, the row of school-bus-yellow honey locusts on Union, the bulbous magnolia on the corner of Carroll and Smith, and the magnificent Yoshino cherry in the courtyard behind my apartment. I could go on, but I realize that in an already overindulgent acknowledgments section, thanking a list of comforting trees may be pushing the limit.

Thank you to my friends Enrique, Luis, BJ, Cat, Eric, Josh Foer, Josh Cochran, Kelli, Derek, Vanessa, Jake, Rob, Ben, Mike, Tina, Luke, Jared, Mac, Jacob, Todd, Rafi, Brendan, and Daniel Kibblesmith. Their conversations, suggestions, and laughter fed my spirit and kept me motivated to finish this book even though the first one hadn't even come out yet and I wasn't sure if anyone would like it or not.

Thank you to Bizarre Brooklyn, the most fun and fulfilling pandemic project I could imagine. Thanks to Dr. Hooker and Alex for sparking the idea and to Dan, Hal, and Miltiades for helping to make it happen. Thanks to the Greater Magic Book Club: Gabe, Noah, Ben, Nick, Rob, Adam, and Alex (again). Thanks to Dan & Dave Buck and the wonderfully supportive crew at Art of Play.

Thanks to my family: Mom, Dad, Nana, and also Gisela, Ramón, Nísida, Mike, Kaden, Izzy, Dánae, Abner, Feebs, David, Aldemar, Leandro, Anaeís, Ransés, Lis, Violet, and Ambrose. Thanks to Charlie (and also Bryce). Cooking elaborate meals with my sister was one of the few bright spots of the pandemic.

Thank you to my *wife*, to whom I am now officially married, though we've been officially living together for seven years and I've been officially in love with her since the moment I spotted her across that sushi bar. Thank you, T, for filling my life with laughter, creativity, and adventure.

Wow. You made it through a four-page avalanche of esoteric gratitude. That deserves another thanks. I hope you have a lovely day and get to eat something delicious before you go to bed tonight. Thank you for treasuring stories, for sharing good books with your friends, and for spreading the joy of reading far and wide.

See you next time.

MEET THE ILLUSTRATORS

MARTA ALTÉS is the author and illustrator of many books for children, including the picture books *My Grandpa*, *Little Monkey*, and *Five More Minutes*. She received her MA in children's book illustration at the Cambridge School of Art.

Photo credit: Nuria Rius

You can visit Marta at marta-altes.com or follow her on Twitter and Instagram @martaltes.

DANIEL GRAY-BARNETT is an author and illustrator whose debut picture book, *Grandma Z*, won the Children's Book Council of Australia Award for New Illustrator. He's worked with clients including Disney, Kiehl's, and the *New York Times*.

You can visit Daniel at danielgraybarnett.com or follow him on Twitter and Instagram @dgraybarnett.

RODOLFO MONTALVO's picture book debut is *Bye Land, Bye Sea*, co-authored with René Spencer. He has also illustrated *The Contagious Colors of Mumpley Middle School* by Fowler DeWitt and *Dear Dragon* by Josh Funk, among other books.

You can visit Rodolfo at rodolfomontalvo.com or follow him on Instagram @rodolfomon3.

DANIEL SALMIERI has illustrated many picture books, including the *New York Times* bestsellers *Dragons Love Tacos, Dragons Love Tacos 2: The Sequel, High Five,* and *Robo-Sauce.* He is the author and illustrator of *Before, Now* and *Bear and Wolf.*

Photo credit: Merideth Jenks

You can visit Daniel at danielsalmieri.com or follow him on Instagram @dansalmieri.

ADAM DE SOUZA is an illustrator and cartoonist. His comic strip
Blind Alley received the Cartoonist
Studio Prize for webcomics. He
illustrated *The Sister Who Ate Her
Brothers: And Other Gruesome Tales*
by Jen Campbell.

You can visit Adam at kumerish.com
or follow him on Twitter and Instagram @kumerish.

GRACEY ZHANG is the author
and illustrator of *Lala's Words* and
the illustrator of *The Big Bath House*
by Kyo Maclear, *Nigel and the Moon*
by Antwan Eady, and *The Upside
Down Hat* by Stephen Barr.

You can visit Gracey at graceyzhang.com
or follow her on Instagram @graceyyz.

ABOUT THE AUTHOR

ADAM RUBIN is the author of the middle-grade story collection *The Ice Cream Machine*, which was a #1 *New York Times* bestseller, a #1 Indie bestseller, and called "as delicious as a multilayer sundae" by *Parents* magazine. He has also written a dozen critically acclaimed picture books, which have sold more than five million copies combined. They include *Dragons Love Tacos*, *Dragons Love Tacos 2: The Sequel*, *High Five*, *Gladys the Magic Chicken*, *Secret Pizza Party*, *Robo-Sauce*, the Those Darn Squirrels trilogy, and *El Chupacabras*, which won the Texas Bluebonnet Award.

You can visit Adam at adamrubinhasawebsite.com.

Thank you for reading.

Gracias por leer.

Merci d'avoir lu.

Vielen Dank fürs Lesen.

Спасибо за чтение.

.תודה שקראת

Îți mulțumesc că ai citit.

Ευχαριστούμε για την ανάγνωση.

Hvala na čitanju.